ABOUT THE EDITOR

David Gates is the author of the novels *Jernigan* and *Preston Falls* and the short-story collection *The Wonders of the Invisible World*. He lives in New York City and in a small town in upstate New York.

Also by David Gates

Novels

Jernigan
Preston Falls

Stories

The Wonders of the Invisible World

LABOR DAYS

LABOR DAYS

An Anthology of Fiction
About Work

Selected and
with an Introduction
by David Gates

Random House Trade Paperbacks 🏠 New York

Compilation copyright © 2000 by Random House, Inc.
Introduction copyright © 2004 by David Gates

Owing to limitations of space, permissions acknowledgments begin on page 221.

Library of Congress Cataloging-in-Publication Data
Labor days: an anthology of fiction about work / selected and with an introduction
by David Gates.
p.   cm.
ISBN 0-8129-7161-2 (pbk.)
1. Work—Fiction.   2. American fiction.   3. Labor—Fiction.
I. Gates, David
PS648.W63L33 2004
813.008'03553—dc22   2004042784

Random House website address: www.atrandom.com
Printed in the United States of America
2 4 6 8 9 7 5 3 1
First Edition

Book design by Laurie Jewell

My thanks to Malcolm Jones and Jonathan Lethem for helping me agonize, and for steering me to work I would never have thought of; to Webster Younce and Julia Cheiffetz for their diligence in seeing this project through; and to Tim Farrell for conceiving it and giving me the gig.

This book is for my father, Gene Gates.

CONTENTS

Introduction		xi
Paul Beatty	from *Tuff*	3
William Burroughs	from *Junky*	7
Raymond Carver	Fat	15
John Cheever	Clancy in the Tower of Babel	21
Don DeLillo	from *Libra*	34
Ralph Ellison	from *Invisible Man*	35
William Faulkner	from *As I Lay Dying*	52
Richard Ford	from *Independence Day*	54
Bruce Jay Friedman	from *A Mother's Kisses*	68
Joseph Heller	from *Something Happened*	70
Amy Hempel	Now I Can See the Moon	92
Denis Johnson	Emergency	100
Toni Morrison	from *Beloved*	113
Philip Roth	from *American Pastoral*	125

George Saunders	from "Pastoralia"	141
B. F. Skinner	from *Walden Two*	156
Gertrude Stein	from *Three Lives*	171
Lynne Tillman	from *No Lease on Life*	183
Edith Wharton	from *The House of Mirth*	187
Colson Whitehead	from *John Henry Days*	193
Richard Yates	A Wrestler with Sharks	205
Permissions Acknowledgments		221

INTRODUCTION

David Gates

One moment in Rex Stout's 1949 mystery novel *The Second Confession*—a passage too short to make the cut for this anthology—stopped me dead when I first read it. Stout's narrator, the suave legman Archie Goodwin, is telling about a client who comes to consult Stout's detective (Goodwin's employer), the prickly and sedentary Nero Wolfe. The client gets on Wolfe's good side by saying he likes the office, in Wolfe's own town house on West Thirty-fifth Street, and Archie allows himself "a mild private grin. . . . Wolfe didn't like the office. . . . He didn't like it, he loved it, and it was a good thing he did, because he was spending his life in it." Most of us spend half our waking lives in a workplace of some sort—and people with home offices like Wolfe's, or stay-at-home spouses, are *always* in the workplace. We may prefer not to think much about whether we're making the best use of those hours and days that will never come again. Especially for those of us like the singer in Merle Haggard's "The Way I Am" ("Wish I enjoyed what makes my living / Did what I do with a willing hand"), who daydreams about fishing while working at a job he cares too little about to specify, *only* the unexamined life is worth living.

Writers of fiction may be as unwilling as anybody else to examine their own lives—many of them, too, have to do something they don't enjoy in order to make their living. But since their true occupation is to examine the lives of their characters, it's remarkable how often they prefer not to look at the significant portion of their imaginary people's lives that must also be spent at work. Of course, I don't mean that writers are going about their business in the wrong way: Nearly all of the fiction I most admire looks at the intimate lives of its characters—psychological, sexual, marital, familial—and people typically live this part of life at its most intense outside of business hours. In fact, the novelists in my personal canon, from Jane Austen to Samuel Beckett, tend to write about people who don't work at all: in Austen's case, gentlefolk; in Beckett's, derelicts. And the short stories I consider touchstones—James Joyce's "The Dead," John Cheever's "Goodbye, My Brother," Raymond Carver's "Vitamins"—take place at holiday parties, on family vacations, before and after work.

Still, you have to wonder about the suspicious number of long weekends and subjectively longer evenings at home fictional characters tend to enjoy (if "enjoy" is the word). Many writers don't have much current personal experience of the mainstream workaday world, or much interest in or respect for it: the office, the factory, and the restaurant often represent the world they escaped by rising to the gentility of patching together a living from adjunct-faculty gigs, magazine articles, and the occasional sale of a novel or short story. As a writer gets deeper into the writing life, the temptation becomes more and more intense to make the characters writers too, like Beckett's Molloy or Philip Roth's Nathan Zuckerman, though sometimes disguised as "painters" (Hemingway's Thomas Hudson) or "scholars" (Nabokov's Humbert Humbert) or "journalists" (Richard Ford's Frank Bascombe in *The Sportswriter*). Okay, or "P.R. people" (my own Doug Willis in *Preston Falls*). If some other life interested you more, wouldn't you be living it?

To resist this temptation seems heroic—and sometimes takes some legwork. Frank Bascombe's transformation in Ford's sequel, *Independence Day*, into a real-estate agent (and root-beer-stand entrepreneur) must have put Ford to the trouble of research and observation; so must have Roth's evocation of Swede Levov's glove factory in *American Pastoral*. For writers—that is, people whose idea of how to spend a life is basically to sit in a room, like Nero Wolfe—such trafficking with the world can threaten their romantic self-conception. What if it rubbed off on you? What if you got too interested in this stuff and ended up like Tom Clancy, with a bestselling fixation on military hardware? Equally disgraceful, what if you just don't know enough to make it convincing? I remember my father, a master auto mechanic, souring *The Grapes of Wrath* for me by demonstrating that Steinbeck is faking it when he has a character repair a broken-down car. On the other hand, if you get the nuts and bolts *too* ostentatiously right, don't you run the risk of a sort of reverse preciosity, ostentatiously reveling in the trade names of pneumatic wrenches?

So I'm not making the philistine argument, advanced by the likes of Tom Wolfe, that what's wrong with contemporary fiction is a self-referential estrangement from the common life. For one thing, there *is* nothing wrong with contemporary fiction except that it's not all good—and when was that *not* the case? For another, self-referential estrangement from the common life is a perfectly legitimate stance for fiction—who doesn't feel it? The mass-marketers of pop music, fashion, even automobiles, base their campaigns on the premise that self-referential estrangement *is* the common life these days. Rock and hip-hop stars affect an obligatory alienation—misunderstood me against the world. Unshaven young men and sullen young women strike glowering attitudes in clothing ads; armored-looking SUVs off-road it by their lonesomes through desert landscapes—literally lighting out for the territories. And who's to say that broadening the focus of fiction to take in characters' social and cultural dealings necessarily yields a truer or more accurate, or even more useful, imitation of human life than attentive navel-gazing? Would you rather read a bad novel about a factory worker, or a bad novel about a writer? The only answer is neither. The best argument for moving characters out of the drawing room, the bedroom, or the writer's own head isn't moral but aesthetic. It opens possibilities, introduces complications, gets characters into revelatory conflict, expands the canvas, colors up the palette, cuts down the chances of boring the reader. (Maybe.) Any other justification amounts, at bottom, to propaganda.

So I've chosen these short stories and excerpts from novels as much because they please me as to present a range of American workplaces and modes of American writing. I've approached this the way I'd approach putting together a mix CD for friends, shooting for a maximum of variety, juxtaposing the canonical with the surprising and the neglected, hoping that what pleases me will please others. I've defined work broadly, from corporate politicking to rolling drunks and guarding drug dens; the workers range from America's archetypal steel-drivin' man to its most famous schoolbook depository employee. I haven't limited workplaces to those in the real—that is, the journalizable—world: by alphabetical happenstance, a selection from George Saunders's dystopian story "Pastoralia" sits next to a surprisingly witty chapter from B. F. Skinner's utopian *Walden Two*. And the same workplace may be different for different characters: in Richard Yates's "A Wrestler with Sharks," the narrator sees his small-time labor newspaper as a grubby and degraded enterprise, while a new reporter sees it as a promising forum for his autodidactic grandiosity.

These pieces vary in genre, manner, and style: from the classic well-made short story (Cheever's "Clancy in the Tower of Babel") to the amateur novel of ideas (*Walden Two*) to the voice-music of Gertrude Stein. I've tried not to favor a single literary mode any more than a single conception of work: in both cases, it's a big world out there. At the same time, I've had to narrow the selections painfully. The decision to include only work written after 1900, for instance, knocked out the story that inspired this anthology in the first place: Melville's forever-startling "Bartleby the Scrivener," the ur-text about office life, which puts a character out of Kafka or Beckett into a Dickensian counting house. (But its tricksy spirit hovers over the whole project: I see somebody sneaked Bartleby's catchphrase "prefer not to" into two different paragraphs.) There's nothing here about war—work at its most extreme—no firefighters, musicians, bankers, athletes, politicians, computer jockeys, or panhandlers. Or lawyers. Sue me.

What most of these pieces have in common is a knowledgeable specificity about how work gets done: the techniques, the terminology. Amy Hempel lets us in on how you tell a guide dog to relieve itself; Ford's realtor talks of thirty-year notes, bathroom louvers, and mature plantings. Skinner and Saunders do something even more remarkable: they make convincing workplaces that exist nowhere but in their imaginations. How do you parcel out the duties in an egalitarian behaviorist commune, or impersonate a cave-dweller in a theme park? Somehow, we come to believe they know all about it. But there are significant and deliberate exceptions. The selections from Bruce Jay Friedman's *A Mother's Kisses* and Joseph Heller's *Something Happened* revel in their very vagueness. We learn nothing (and are meant to learn nothing) about "cutting couches" or exactly what Bob Slocum's company actually *does*: in Friedman's case, because his main character, Joseph, doesn't understand or care; in Heller's case, because it absolutely doesn't matter.

And, ultimately, *none* of this work really matters in itself. Accuracy of detail and terminology helps us trust the author and suspend our disbelief, and we take touristic pleasure in watching characters do what we couldn't or wouldn't do ourselves (building a coffin, rolling a drunk) or witnessing familiar transactions (eating in a restaurant, riding in an apartment-house elevator) from the other side. But we can get better information from journalists, documentarians, anthropologists, or the writers of instruction manuals. These pieces aren't about work, but about people at work. The work these people choose (though some of them may think it's been chosen for them) and the way they choose to do it reveal who they are—which is the whole point—as surely as whom they choose to marry and how they choose to spend their weekends. Such characters as Saunders's faux cave-people and Lynne Tillman's proofreader work in an atmosphere of claustrophobic, unfriendly intimacy. For Roth's glove manufacturer, the workplace is a repository of cherished, dying values; for Heller's Bob Slocum or Ford's Frank Bascombe, it's a corrupt stage on which to act out their self-hatred.

For fiction writers, the world of work is ultimately like any other world: a place for them to get people, feelings, and ideas in motion and in conflict and to see what happens. In some ways, it's an even more useful world, from a writer's viewpoint, than that of domestic life. The workplace is the everyday equivalent of Homer's battlefield and Shakespeare's court—which are now, for better or worse, mostly the province of pop fiction—where power can be won and lost, used and abused, where character can be tested. And it has at its center an endlessly useful contradiction: that people are expected to leave personality behind. They never do, never can: even the coffin-maker in Faulkner's "As I Lay Dying," who lists and numbers the reasons that putting seams and joints "on the bevel" will make "a neater job," reveals his dread and his compassion in the process of so rigorously excluding those emotions from his work. The workplace is a playground for all the Seven Deadlies, from Gluttony (Raymond Carver's "Fat") to Lust (ubiquitous); the latter's official exclusion from the work world naturally gives it all the more power. The virtues emerge, too, when push comes to shove. Colson Whitehead's John Henry shows a stubborn, becoming dignity when his competence—that is, the ultimate value of what he does and who he is—comes into question, while Cheever's elevator man comes to a compassionate understanding of the character with whom he least wants to sympathize. And, ultimately, the workplace can be society in miniature: a laboratory in which writers conduct experiments on the effects of race (Ralph Ellison, Toni Morrison), class (Edith Wharton), and gender (both in Heller's grown-up boys' club and in Stein's female-centered household) on the individual soul. Even the most housebound fiction writer can't just do this stuff at home and phone it in. If you're a reader—or a writer—to whom the world of work has seemed less promising, less juicy and abundant, than the worlds of love, marriage, family, or the boundless self, these pieces might change your mind.

LABOR DAYS

from **TUFF**

Paul Beatty

Now on this, the last cool night of spring, Brooklyn was short three more niggers for Winston to hate. Although he addressed all black men as "God," Chilly Most, apparently less than divine, was unable to resurrect himself. Zoltan Yarborough, who was always running off at the mouth about his proud Brooklyn roots, "Brownsville, never ran, never will," had become the rigid embodiment of his slogan. He had one leg over the windowsill, and a bullet hole in him that, like everything his mother ever told him, went in one ear and out the other. Demetrius Broadnax from "Do-or-die Bed-Stuy" was shirtless on the floor with a column of bullet holes from sternum to belly button in his muddy brown torso. Winston gloated over Demetrius's body, looking into his ex-boss's glassy eyes, tempted to say "I quit" and ask for his severance pay. Instead he walked to the aquarium, pressed his nose against the glass, and wondered who was going to feed the goldfish.

Like most of the jobs Winston had taken since graduating high school, this one also ended prematurely, after a job interview only two weeks ago where the look on his face was his résumé and two sentences from his best friend, Fariq Cole, were his references. "This fat nigger ain't no joke. Yo—known uptown for straight

KO'ing niggers." There was no "So, Mr. Foshay, how do your personal career goals mesh with our corporate mission? Would you consider yourself to be a self-starter? What was the last book you read?" Demetrius simply handed Winston the inner-city union card, a small black .22 Raven automatic pistol, which Winston coolly, but immediately, handed back.

"What, your ass don't need a burner?"

"Naw."

"Look, fool, maybe you can body-slam niggers out on the street, but in this business, people don't walk in the door shaking their fists in your face. You ain't shook, are you? You don't seem the scary type."

"Never back down. Once a nigger back down, he stay down, know what I'm saying? Just don't like guns."

"Well, when some niggers do come in blasting, your big ass be in the way and shit, two, three motherfuckers can hide behind you. Be here tomorrow afternoon at four."

When Winston started work, he was "in the way and shit," but not in the manner Demetrius had hoped. Winston's job description was simple: four to ten, five days a week, answer the door, look mean and yell, "Pay this motherfucker, now!" at the balky customers. But the trip into Brooklyn made Winston edgy. His childhood traumas kicked in, undoing his cool. Instead of suavely sauntering around counting his money every five minutes, Winston fumbled about the drug den, stepping on people's toes, toppling everything he touched, and talking nonstop. He tried to lighten the somber felonious atmosphere by telling embarrassingly bad jokes. ("You hear the one about why Scots wear kilts?") After the flat punch lines ("Because sheep can hear a zipper open from one hundred meters away") there would be a barely audible metallic click, the sound of Demetrius switching the gun's safety to the off position.

Winston had trouble keeping track of the Brooklyn drug mores. Which colored caps went with what size plastic vials? Were portable televisions an acceptable form of payment? He

was unable to distinguish one crew's secret whistle from another's. How often had Demetrius yelled at him, "You moron,
don't flush the drugs! That's the mating call of the ruby-crowned
kinglet!" Then Chilly Most and the others would join in with their
snide castigations: "As opposed to our secret signal—"

"The flight song of the skylark."

"A gentle *woo-dukkadukka-woo.*"

"Good ol' *Alauda arvenis,* indigenous to Eurasia, but common
in the Northwest Territories of Canada, if I'm not mistaken."

"You are not, you nigger ornithologist, you."

The last time Winston heard the cherished secret whistle, he
answered the door and two niggers he'd never seen before, bran-
dishing firearms, rushed past him and, before they could be prop-
erly announced, introduced themselves with a bullet in Chilly
Most's newly shorn bald head. Winston did what his coworkers
always said he'd do if he'd ever found himself face-to-face with a
gun: he fainted "like a bitch."

Three minutes had passed since Winston regained consciousness, and he couldn't leave the apartment. It was as if he were
spacewalking, tethered to some mother ship treading Brooklyn
ether. He would clamber for the door and a muffled sound in the
hallway or a distant siren would drive him back into the living
room. He began to mumble: "This like that flick, the bugged-out
Spanish one where the rich people couldn't leave the house. Luis
Bustelo or some shit. What is it . . . surrealism? Well, I got the
surrealisms."

A creak in the floor behind him stopped Winston's babbling.
He quickly about-faced, balling his shaky hands into fists.

"Who dat?"

"Who dat?" came the response. Winston relaxed. He smiled,
"Nigger," unclenched his fists, and plopped down on the sofa.

Fariq Cole hobbled into the living room, his crutches splayed
out to the side, propelling him forward. Fariq's friends called him
Smush because his nose, lips, and forehead shared the same Eu-
clidean plane, giving him a profile that had all the contours of

a cardboard box. Each herky-jerky step undulated Fariq's body toward Winston like a Slinky, alternately coiling and uncoiling. A solid gold dollar-sign pendant and a diamond-inlaid ankh whipped about his neck in an elliptical orbit like a jewel-encrusted satellite. Fariq stopped next to the doorjamb, tilted his head to the side, and cut his friend a dubious look.

"Who was you talking to?"

"Nobody. Just trying figure out why I was still here."

"You still here because you couldn't leave without me, your so-called boy."

"You is. But it wasn't you—I barely got to work ten minutes ago, I didn't even know you was here. Naw, it's something else."

Fariq was the coolest of the many cool handicapped Harlem-ites. His appearance was inner-city dapper, functional and physically fit assimilationist. Despite the soft spot in his head where his skull had never fused, it'd been a long time since he'd worn a cyclist's helmet. The bill of his fiberglass-reinforced Yankee baseball cap hung over his left eye, shadowing the surgical scars. The baggy corduroys covered up his leg braces. His clubfeet were squeezed into a pair of expensive sneakers, though he'd never run a step in his life. Fariq ran his tongue over his precious-metal-filled mouth, the front four incisors, top and bottom, capped in a gold-and-silver checkerboard pattern. Etched on his two front teeth were small black king and queen chess pieces, christened "Fariq" and "Nadine" in microscopic handwriting.

"Now look at these no-money motherfuckers—who going to take care of their families?" Fariq said, a rubber-tipped crutch sweeping across the carnage. "That's why a prudent motherfucker like me has an IRA account, some short-term T-bills, a grip invested in long-term corporate bonds and high-risk foreign stock. Shit, the twenty-first-century nigger gots to have a diversified portfolio—never know when you gon' have a rainy day. And look like it was thunderin' and lightnin' in this motherfucker."

from **JUNKY**

William Burroughs

The H caps cost three dollars each and you need at least three per day to get by. I was short, so I began "working the hole" with Roy. We would ride along, each looking out one side of the subway car until one of us spotted a "flop" sleeping on a bench. Then we would get off the train. I stood in front of the bench with a newspaper and covered Roy while he went through the lush's pockets. Roy would whisper instructions to me—"a little left, too far, a little back, there, hold it there"—and I would move to keep him covered. Often, we were late and the lush would be lying there with his pockets turned inside out.

We also worked on the cars. I would sit down next to the lush and open a newspaper. Roy would reach across my back and go through the lush's pockets. If the lush woke up, he could see that I had both hands on the paper. We averaged about ten dollars per night.

An average night went more or less like this. We started work about eleven o'clock, getting on the uptown IRT at Times Square. At 149th Street, I spotted a flop and we got off. 149th Street is a station with several levels and dangerous for lush-workers because there are so many spots where cops can hide, and it is not possible to cover from every angle. On the lower level the only way out is by the elevator.

We approached the flop casually, as though we did not see him. He was middle-aged, sprawled against the wall, breathing loudly. Roy sat down beside him and I stationed myself in front of them with an open newspaper. Roy said, "A little to the right, too far, back a little, there, that's good."

Suddenly the heavy breathing stopped. I thought of the scene in the movies where the breathing stops during the operation. I could feel Roy's tense immobility behind me. The drunk muttered something and shifted his position. Slowly the breathing started again. Roy got up. "Okay," he said, and walked rapidly to the other end of the platform. He took a crumpled mass of bills from his pocket and counted out eight dollars. He handed me four. "Had it in his pants pocket. I couldn't find a poke. I thought for a minute he was going to come up on us."

We started back downtown. At 116th we spotted one and got off, but the flop got up and walked away before we could get near him. A shabby man with a wide, loose mouth accosted Roy and started talking. He was another lush-worker.

"The Fag scored again," he said. "Two notes and a wristwatch down at 96th Street." Roy muttered something and looked at his paper. The man went on talking in a loud voice. "I had one come up on me. 'What are you doing with your hand in my pocket?' he says."

"For Chris' sake, don't talk like that!" Roy said and walked away from him. "Fucking wrong bastard," he muttered. "There aren't many lush-workers around now. Only the Fag, the Beagle, and that tramp. They all envy the Fag because he makes good scores. If a sucker comes up on him he pretends to feel his leg like he was a fag. Those tramps at 103rd Street go around saying 'Goddam Fag' because they can't score. He's no more a fag than I am." Roy paused reflectively. "Not as much, in fact."

We rode to the end of the line in Brooklyn without spotting a single flop. On the way back there was a drunk asleep in a car. I sat down beside him and opened my paper. I could feel Roy's arm across my back. Once, the drunk woke up and looked at me sharply. But both my hands were clearly visible on the paper. Roy pretended to be reading the paper with me. The drunk went back to sleep.

"Here's where we get off," Roy said. "We better go out on the street for a bit. Doesn't pay to ride too long."

We had a cup of coffee at the 34th Street automat and split the last take. It was three dollars.

"When you take a lush on the car," Roy was explaining, "you got to gauge yourself to the movement of the car. If you get the right rhythm you can work it out even if the mooch is awake. I went a little too fast on that one. That's why he woke up. He felt something was wrong, but he didn't know what it was."

At Times Square we ran into Subway Mike. He nodded but did not stop. Mike always worked alone.

"Let's take a run out to Queens Plaza," Roy said. "That's on the Independent. The Independent has special cops hired by the company, but they don't carry guns. Only saps. So if one grabs you, run if you can break loose."

Queens Plaza is another dangerous station where it is impossible to cover yourself from every angle. You just have to take a chance. There was a drunk sleeping full length on a bench, but we couldn't risk taking him because too many people were around.

"We'll wait a bit," Roy said. "Remember, though, never pass more than three trains. If you don't get a clear chance by then, forget it no matter how good it looks."

Two young punks got off a train carrying a lush between them. They dropped him on a bench, then looked at Roy and me.

"Let's take him over to the other side," said one of the punks.

"Why not take him right here?" Roy asked.

The punks pretended not to understand. "Take him? I don't get it. What does our queer friend mean?" They picked up their lush and carried him to the other side of the platform.

Roy walked over to our mark and pulled a wallet out of his pocket. "No time for finesse," he remarked. The wallet was empty. Roy dropped it on the bench.

One of the punks shouted across the tracks, "Take your hands out of his pockets." And they both laughed.

"Fucking punks," said Roy. "If I catch one of them on the West Side line I'll push the little bastard onto the tracks."

One of the punks came over and asked Roy for a cut.

"I tell you he didn't have nothing," said Roy.

"We saw you take out his wallet."

"There wasn't nothing in it."

A train stopped and we got on, leaving the punk there undecided whether or not to get tough.

"Fucking punks think it's a joke," Roy said. "They won't last long. They won't think it's so funny when they get out on the Island doing five-twenty-nine." We were in a run of bad luck. Roy said, "Well, that's the way it goes. Some nights you make a hundred dollars. Some nights you don't make anything."

One night, we got on the subway at Times Square. A flashily dressed man, weaving slightly, was walking ahead of us. Roy looked him over and said, "That's a good fucking mooch. Let's see where he goes."

The mooch got on the IRT headed for Brooklyn. We waited standing up in the space between cars until the mooch appeared to be sleeping. Then we walked into the car, and I sat down beside the mooch, opening *The New York Times*. The *Times* was Roy's idea. He said it made me look like a businessman. The car was almost empty, and there we were wedged up against the mooch with twenty feet of empty seats available. Roy began working over my back. The mooch kept stirring and once he woke up and looked at me with bleary annoyance. A Negro sitting opposite us smiled.

"The shine is wise," said Roy in my ear. "He's O.K."

Roy was having trouble finding the poke. The situation was getting dangerous. I could feel sweat running down my arms.

"Let's get off," I said.

"No. This is a good mooch. He's sitting on his overcoat and I can't get into his pocket. When I tell you, fall up against him, and I'll move the coat at the same time. . . . *Now!* . . . For Chris' sake! That wasn't near hard enough."

"Let's get off," I said again. I could feel the fear stirring in my stomach. "He's going to wake up."

"No. Let's go again . . . *Now!* . . . What in hell is wrong with you? Just let yourself flop against him hard."

"Roy," I said. "For Chris' sake let's get off! He's going to wake up."

I started to get up, but Roy held me down. Suddenly he gave me a sharp push, and I fell heavily against the mooch.

"Got it that time," Roy said.

"The poke?"

"No, I got the coat out of the way."

We were out of the underground now and on the elevated. I was nauseated with fear, every muscle rigid with the effort of control. The mooch was only half asleep. I expected him to jump up and yell at any minute.

Finally I heard Roy say, "I got it."

"Let's go then."

"No, what I got is a loose roll. He's got a poke somewhere and I'm going to find it. He's got to have a poke."

"I'm getting off."

"No. Wait." I could feel him fumbling across my back so openly it seemed incredible that the man could go on sleeping.

It was the end of the line. Roy stood up. "Cover me," he said. I stood in front of him with the paper shielding him as much as possible from the other passengers. There were only three left, but they were in different ends of the car. Roy went through the man's pockets openly and crudely. "Let's go outside," he said. We went out onto the platform.

The mooch woke up and put his hand in his pocket. Then he came out onto the platform and walked up to Roy.

"All right, Jack," he said. "Give me my money."

Roy shrugged and turned his hands out, palm up. "What money? What are you talking about?"

"You know Goddamned well what I'm talking about! You had your hand in my pocket."

Roy held his hands out again in a gesture of puzzlement and deprecation. "Aw, what are you talking about? I don't know anything about your money."

"I've seen you on this line every night. This is your regular route." He turned and pointed to me. "And there's your partner right there. Now, are you going to give me my dough?"

"What dough?"

"Okay. Just stay put. We're taking a ride back to town and this had better be good." Suddenly, the man put both hands in Roy's coat pockets. "You sonofabitch!" he yelled. "Give me my dough!"

Roy hit him in the face and knocked him down. "Why you—" said Roy, dropping abruptly his conciliatory and puzzled manner. "Keep your hands off me!"

The conductor, seeing a fight in progress, was holding up the train so that no one would fall on the tracks.

"Let's cut," I said. We started down the platform. The man got up and ran after us. He threw his arms around Roy, holding on stubbornly. Roy couldn't break loose. He was pretty well winded.

"Get this mooch off me!" Roy yelled.

I hit the man twice in the face. His grip loosened and he fell to his knees.

"Kick his head off," said Roy.

I kicked the man in the side and felt a rib snap. The man put his hand to his side. "Help!" he shouted. He did not try to get up.

"Let's cut," I said. At the far end of the platform, I heard a police whistle. The man was still lying there on the platform holding his side and yelling "Help!" at regular intervals.

There was a slight drizzle of rain falling. When I hit the street,

I slipped and skidded on the wet sidewalk. We were standing by a closed filling station, looking back at the elevated.

"Let's go," I said.

"They'll see us."

"We can't stay here."

We started to walk. I noticed that my mouth was bone dry. Roy took two goof balls from his shirt pocket.

"Mouth's too dry," he said. "I can't swallow them."

We went on walking.

"There's sure to be an alarm out for us," Roy said. "Keep a lookout for cars. We'll duck in the bushes if any come along. They'll be figuring us to get back on the subway, so the best thing we can do is keep walking."

The drizzle continued. Dogs barked at us as we walked.

"Remember our story if we get nailed," Roy said. "We fell asleep and woke up at the end of the line. This guy accused us of taking his money. We were scared, so we knocked him down and ran. They'll beat the shit out of us. You have to expect that."

"Here comes a car," I said. "Yellow lights, too."

We crawled into the bushes at the side of the road and crouched down behind a signboard. The car drove slowly by. We started walking again. I was getting sick and wondered if I would get home to the M.S. I had stashed in my apartment.

"When we get closer in we better split up," Roy said. "Out here we might be able to do each other some good. If we run into a cop on the beat we'll tell him we've been with some girls and were looking for the subway. This rain is a break. The cops will all be in some all-night joint drinking coffee. For Chris' sake!" he rasped irritably. "Don't round like that!"

I had turned around and looked over my shoulder. "It's natural to turn around," I said.

"Natural for thieves!"

We finally ran into the BMT line and rode back to Manhattan.

Roy said, "I don't think I'm just speaking for myself when I say I was scared. Oh. Here's your cut."

He handed me three dollars.

Next day I told him I was through as a lush-worker.

"I don't blame you," he said. "But you got a wrong impression. You're bound to get some good breaks if you stick around long enough."

FAT

Raymond Carver

I am sitting over coffee and cigarettes at my friend Rita's and I am telling her about it.

Here is what I tell her.

It is late of a slow Wednesday when Herb seats the fat man at my station.

This fat man is the fattest person I have ever seen, though he is neat-appearing and well dressed enough. Everything about him is big. But it is the fingers I remember best. When I stop at the table near his to see to the old couple, I first notice the fingers. They look three times the size of a normal person's fingers—long, thick, creamy fingers.

I see to my other tables, a party of four businessmen, very demanding, another party of four, three men and a woman, and this old couple. Leander has poured the fat man's water, and I give the fat man plenty of time to make up his mind before going over.

Good evening, I say. May I serve you? I say.

Rita, he was big, I mean big.

Good evening, he says. Hello. Yes, he says. I think we're ready to order now, he says.

He has this way of speaking—strange, don't you know. And he makes a little puffing sound every so often.

I think we will begin with a Caesar salad, he says. And then a bowl of soup with some extra bread and butter, if you please. The lamb chops, I believe, he says. And baked potato with sour cream. We'll see about dessert later. Thank you very much, he says, and hands me the menu.

God, Rita, but those were fingers.

I hurry away to the kitchen and turn in the order to Rudy, who takes it with a face. You know Rudy. Rudy is that way when he works.

As I come out of the kitchen, Margo—I've told you about Margo? The one who chases Rudy? Margo says to me, Who's your fat friend? He's really a fatty.

Now that's part of it. I think that is really part of it.

I make the Caesar salad there at his table, him watching my every move, meanwhile buttering pieces of bread and laying them off to one side, all the time making this puffing noise. Anyway, I am so keyed up or something, I knock over his glass of water.

I'm so sorry, I say. It always happens when you get into a hurry. I'm very sorry, I say. Are you all right? I'll get the boy to clean up right away, I say.

It's nothing, he says. It's all right, he says, and he puffs. Don't worry about it, we don't mind, he says. He smiles and waves as I go off to get Leander, and when I come back to serve the salad, I see the fat man has eaten all his bread and butter.

A little later, when I bring him more bread, he has finished his salad. You know the size of those Caesar salads?

You're very kind, he says. This bread is marvelous, he says.

Thank you, I say.

Well, it is very good, he says, and we mean that. We don't often enjoy bread like this, he says.

Where are you from? I ask him. I don't believe I've seen you before, I say.

He's not the kind of person you'd forget, Rita puts in with a snicker.

Denver, he says.

I don't say anything more on the subject, though I am curious.

Your soup will be along in a few minutes, sir, I say, and I go off to put the finishing touches to my party of four businessmen, very demanding.

When I serve his soup, I see the bread has disappeared again. He is just putting the last piece of bread into his mouth.

Believe me, he says, we don't eat like this all the time, he says. And puffs. You'll have to excuse us, he says.

Don't think a thing about it, please, I say. I like to see a man eat and enjoy himself, I say.

I don't know, he says. I guess that's what you'd call it. And puffs. He arranges the napkin. Then he picks up his spoon.

God, he's fat! says Leander.

He can't help it, I say, so shut up.

I put down another basket of bread and more butter. How was the soup? I say.

Thank you. Good, he says. Very good, he says. He wipes his lips and dabs his chin. Do you think it's warm in here, or is it just me? he says.

No, it is warm in here, I say.

Maybe we'll take off our coat, he says.

Go right ahead, I say. A person has to be comfortable, I say.

That's true, he says, that is very, very true, he says.

But I see a little later that he is still wearing his coat.

My large parties are gone now and also the old couple. The place is emptying out. By the time I serve the fat man his chops and baked potato, along with more bread and butter, he is the only one left.

I drop lots of sour cream onto his potato. I sprinkle bacon and chives over his sour cream. I bring him more bread and butter.

Is everything all right? I say.

Fine, he says, and he puffs. Excellent, thank you, he says, and puffs again.

Enjoy your dinner, I say. I raise the lid of his sugar bowl and look in. He nods and keeps looking at me until I move away.

I know now I was after something. But I don't know what.

How is old tub-of-guts doing? He's going to run your legs off, says Harriet. You know Harriet.

For dessert, I say to the fat man, there is the Green Lantern Special, which is a pudding cake with sauce, or there is cheesecake or vanilla ice cream or pineapple sherbet.

We're not making you late, are we? he says, puffing and looking concerned.

Not at all, I say. Of course not, I say. Take your time, I say. I'll bring you more coffee while you make up your mind.

We'll be honest with you, he says. And he moves in the seat. We would like the Special, but we may have a dish of vanilla ice cream as well. With just a drop of chocolate syrup, if you please. We told you we were hungry, he says.

I go off to the kitchen to see after his dessert myself, and Rudy says, Harriet says you got a fat man from the circus out there. That true?

Rudy has his apron and hat off now, if you see what I mean.

Rudy, he is fat, I say, but that is not the whole story.

Rudy just laughs.

Sounds to me like she's sweet on fat-stuff, he says.

Better watch out, Rudy, says Joanne, who just that minute comes into the kitchen.

I'm getting jealous, Rudy says to Joanne.

I put the Special in front of the fat man and a big bowl of vanilla ice cream with chocolate syrup to the side.

Thank you, he says.

You are very welcome, I say—and a feeling comes over me.

Believe it or not, he says, we have not always eaten like this.

Me, I eat and I eat and I can't gain, I say. I'd like to gain, I say. No, he says. If we had our choice, no. But there is no choice. Then he picks up his spoon and eats.

What else? Rita says, lighting one of my cigarettes and pulling her chair closer to the table. This story's getting interesting now, Rita says.

That's it. Nothing else. He eats his desserts, and then he leaves and then we go home, Rudy and me.

Some fatty, Rudy says, stretching like he does when he's tired. Then he just laughs and goes back to watching the TV.

I put the water on to boil for tea and take a shower. I put my hand on my middle and wonder what would happen if I had children and one of them turned out to look like that, so fat.

I pour the water in the pot, arrange the cups, the sugar bowl, carton of half and half, and take the tray in to Rudy. As if he's been thinking about it, Rudy says, I knew a fat guy once, a couple of fat guys, really fat guys, when I was a kid. They were tubbies, my God. I don't remember their names. Fat, that's the only name this one kid had. We called him Fat, the kid who lived next door to me. He was a neighbor. The other kid came along later. His name was Wobbly. Everybody called him Wobbly except the teachers. Wobbly and Fat. Wish I had their pictures, Rudy says.

I can't think of anything to say, so we drink our tea and pretty soon I get up to go to bed. Rudy gets up too, turns off the TV, locks the front door, and begins his unbuttoning.

I get into bed and move clear over to the edge and lie there on my stomach. But right away, as soon as he turns off the light and gets into bed, Rudy begins. I turn on my back and relax some, though it is against my will. But here is the thing. When he gets on me, I suddenly feel I am fat. I feel I am terrifically fat, so fat that Rudy is a tiny thing and hardly there at all.

That's a funny story, Rita says, but I can see she doesn't know what to make of it.

I feel depressed. But I won't go into it with her. I've already told her too much.

She sits there waiting, her dainty fingers poking her hair.

Waiting for what? I'd like to know.

It is August.

My life is going to change. I feel it.

CLANCY IN THE TOWER OF BABEL

John Cheever

James and Nora Clancy came from farms near the little town
of Newcastle. Newcastle is near Limerick. They had been poor in
Ireland and they were not much better off in the new country, but
they were cleanly and decent people. Their home farms had been
orderly places, long inhabited by the same families, and the Clan-
cys enjoyed the grace of a tradition. Their simple country ways
were so deeply ingrained that twenty years in the New World had
had little effect on them. Nora went to market with a straw basket under her arm, like a woman going out to a kitchen garden,
and Clancy's pleasant face reflected a simple life. They had only
one child, a son named John, and they had been able to pass on
to him their peaceable and contented views. They were people
who centered their lives in half a city block, got down on their
knees on the floor to say "Hail Mary, full of grace," and took turns
in the bathtub in the kitchen on Saturday night.

When Clancy was still a strong man in his forties, he fell down
some stairs in the factory and broke his hip. He was out of work
for nearly a year, and while he got compensation for this time, it
was not as much as his wages had been and he and his family suffered the pain of indebtedness and need. When Clancy recov-
ered, he was left with a limp and it took him a long time to find

another job. He went to church every day, and in the end it was the intercession of a priest that got work for him, running an elevator in one of the big apartment houses on the East Side. Clancy's good manners and his clean and pleasant face pleased the tenants, and with his salary and the tips they gave him he made enough to pay his debts and support his wife and son.

The apartment house was not far from the slum tenement where James and Nora had lived since their marriage, but financially and morally it was another creation, and Clancy at first looked at the tenants as if they were made out of sugar. The ladies wore coats and jewels that cost more than Clancy would make in a lifetime of hard work, and when he came home in the evenings, he would, like a returned traveler, tell Nora what he had seen. The poodles, the cocktail parties, the children and their nursemaids interested him, and he told Nora that it was like the Tower of Babel.

It took Clancy a while to memorize the floor numbers to which his tenants belonged, to pair the husbands and wives, to join the children to their parents, and the servants (who rode on the back elevators) to these families, but he managed at last and was pleased to have everything straight. Among his traits was a passionate sense of loyalty, and he often spoke of the Building as if it were a school or a guild, the product of a community of sentiment and aspiration. "Oh, I wouldn't do anything to harm the Building," he often said. His manner was respectful but he was not humorless, and when 11-A sent his tailcoat out to the dry cleaner's, Clancy put it on and paraded up and down the back hall. Most of the tenants were regarded by Clancy with an indiscriminate benevolence, but there were a few exceptions. There was a drunken wife-beater. He was a bulky, duck-footed lunk head, in Clancy's eyes, and he did not belong in the Building. Then there was a pretty girl in 11-B who went out in the evenings with a man who was a weak character—Clancy could tell because he had a cleft chin. Clancy warned the girl, but she did not act on his advice. But the tenant about whom he felt most concerned was Mr. Rowantree.

Mr. Rowantree, who was a bachelor, lived in 4-A. He had been in Europe when Clancy first went to work, and he had not returned to New York until winter. When Mr. Rowantree appeared, he seemed to Clancy to be a well-favored man with graying hair who was tired from his long voyage. Clancy waited for him to reestablish himself in the city, for friends and relatives to start telephoning and writing, and for Mr. Rowantree to begin the give-and-take of parties in which most of the tenants were involved.

Clancy had discovered by then that his passengers were not made of sugar. All of them were secured to the world intricately by friends and lovers, dogs and songbirds, debts, inheritances, trusts, and jobs, and he waited for Mr. Rowantree to put out his lines. Nothing happened. Mr. Rowantree went to work at ten in the morning and returned home at six; no visitors appeared. A month passed in which he did not have a single guest. He sometimes went out in the evening, but he always returned alone, and for all Clancy knew he might have continued his friendless state in the movies around the corner. The man's lack of friends amazed and then began to aggravate and trouble Clancy. One night when he was on the evening shift and Mr. Rowantree came down alone, Clancy stopped the car between floors.

"Are you going out for dinner, Mr. Rowantree?" he asked.

"Yes," the man said.

"Well, when you're eating in this neighborhood, Mr. Rowantree," Clancy said, "you'll find that Bill's Clam Bar is the only restaurant worth speaking of. I've been living around here for twenty years and I've seen them come and go. The others have fancy lighting and fancy prices, but you won't get anything to eat that's worth sticking to your ribs excepting at Bill's Clam Bar."

"Thank you, Clancy," Mr. Rowantree said. "I'll keep that in mind."

"Now, Mr. Rowantree," Clancy said, "I don't want to sound inquisitive, but would you mind telling me what kind of a business you're in?"

"I have a store on Third Avenue," Mr. Rowantree said. "Come over and see it someday."

"I'd like to do that," Clancy said. "But now, Mr. Rowantree, I should think you'd want to have dinner with your friends and not be alone all the time." Clancy knew that he was interfering with the man's privacy, but he was led on by the thought that this soul might need help. "A good-looking man like you must have friends," he said, "and I'd think you'd have your supper with them."

"I'm going to have supper with a friend, Clancy," Mr. Rowantree said.

This reply made Clancy feel easier, and he put the man out of his mind for a while. The Building gave him the day off on St. Patrick's, so that he could march in the parade, and when the parade had disbanded and he was walking home, he decided to look for the store. Mr. Rowantree had told him which block it was in. It was easy to find. Clancy was pleased to see that it was a big store. There were two doors to go in by, separated by a large glass window. Clancy looked through the window to see if Mr. Rowantree was busy with a customer, but there was no one there. Before he went in, he looked at the things in the window. He was disappointed to see that it was not a clothing store or a delicatessen. It looked more like a museum. There were glasses and candlesticks, chairs and tables, all of them old. He opened the door. A bell attached to the door rang and Clancy looked up to see the old-fashioned bell on its string. Mr. Rowantree came out from behind a screen and greeted him cordially.

Clancy did not like the place. He felt that Mr. Rowantree was wasting his time. It troubled him to think of the energy in a man's day being spent in this place. A narrow trail, past tables and desks, urns and statues, led into the store and then branched off in several directions. Clancy had never seen so much junk. Since he couldn't imagine it all being manufactured in any one country, he guessed that it had been brought there from the four corners of the world. It seemed to Clancy a misuse of time to have gathered all these things into a dark store on Third Avenue. But it was more than the confusion and the waste that troubled him; it was the feeling that he was surrounded by the symbols of frustration and that all the china youths and maidens in their attitudes of love were the company of bitterness. It may have been because he had spent his happy life in bare rooms that he associated goodness with ugliness.

He was careful not to say anything that would offend Mr. Rowantree. "Do you have any clerks to help you?" he asked.

"Oh, yes," Mr. Rowantree said. "Miss James is here most of the time. We're partners."

That was it, Clancy thought. Miss James. That was where he went in the evenings. But why, then, wouldn't Miss James marry him? Was it because he was already married? Perhaps he had suffered some terrible human misfortune, like having his wife go crazy or having his children taken away from him.

"Have you a snapshot of Miss James?" Clancy asked.

"No," Mr. Rowantree said.

"Well, I'm glad to have seen your store and thank you very much," Clancy said. The trip had been worth his while, because he took away from the dark store a clear image of Miss James. It was a good name, an Irish name, and now in the evenings when Mr. Rowantree went out, Clancy would ask him how Miss James was.

Clancy's son, John, was a senior in high school. He was captain of the basketball team and a figure in school government, and that spring he entered an essay he had written on democracy in a contest sponsored by a manufacturer in Chicago. There were millions of entries, but John won honorable mention, which entitled him to a trip to Chicago in an airplane and a week's visit there with all expenses paid. The boy was naturally excited by this bonanza and so was his mother, but Clancy was the one who seemed to have won the prize. He told all the tenants in the

Building about it and asked them what kind of city Chicago was and if traveling in airplanes was safe. He would get up in the middle of the night and go into John's room to look at the wonderful boy while he slept. The boy's head was crammed with knowledge, Clancy thought. His heart was kind and strong. It was sinful, Clancy knew, to confuse the immortality of the Holy Spirit and earthly love, but when he realized that John was his flesh and blood, that the young man's face was *his* face improved with mobility and thought, and that when he, Clancy, was dead, some habit or taste of his would live on in the young man, he felt that there was no pain in death.

John's plane left for Chicago late one Saturday afternoon. He went to confession and then walked over to the Building to say goodbye to his father. Clancy kept the boy in the lobby as long as he could and introduced him to the tenants who came through. Then it was time for the boy to go. The doorman took the elevator, and Clancy walked John up to the corner. It was a clear, sunny afternoon in Lent. There wasn't a cloud in the sky. The boy had on his best suit and he looked like a million dollars. They shook hands at the corner, and Clancy limped back to the Building. Traffic was slow on the elevator, and he stood at the front door, watching the people on the sidewalk. Most of them were dressed in their best clothes and they were off to enjoy themselves. Clancy's best wishes followed them all. At the far end of the street he saw Mr. Rowantree's head and shoulders and saw that he was with a young man. Clancy waited and opened the door for them.

"Hello, Clancy," Mr. Rowantree said. "I'd like to have you meet my friend Bobbie. He's going to live here now."

Clancy grunted. The young man was not a young man. His hair was cut short and he wore a canary-yellow sweater and a padded coat but he was as old as Mr. Rowantree, he was nearly as old as Clancy. All the qualities and airs of youth, which a good man puts aside gladly when the time comes, had been preserved obscenely in him. He had dope in his eyes to make them shine and he smelled of perfume, and Mr. Rowantree took his arm to help him through the door, as if he were a pretty girl. As soon as Clancy saw what he had to deal with, he took a stand. He stayed at the door. Mr. Rowantree and his friend went through the lobby and got into the elevator. They reached out and rang the bell.

"I'm not taking you up in my car!" Clancy shouted down the lobby.

"Come here, Clancy," Mr. Rowantree said.

"I'm not taking that up in my car," Clancy said.

"I'll have you fired for this," Mr. Rowantree said.

"That's no skin off my nose," Clancy said. "I'm not taking you up in my car."

"Come here, Clancy," Mr. Rowantree said. Clancy didn't answer. Mr. Rowantree put his finger on the bell and held it there. Clancy didn't move. He heard Mr. Rowantree and his friend talking. A moment later, he heard them climb the stairs. All the solicitude he had felt for Mr. Rowantree, the times he had imagined him walking in the Park with Miss James, seemed like money lost in a terrible fraud. He was hurt and bitter. The idea of Bobbie's being in the Building was a painful one for him to take, and he felt as if it contested his own simple view of life. He was curt with everyone for the rest of the day. He even spoke sharply to the children. When he went to the basement to take off his uniform, Mr. Coolidge, the superintendent, called him into his office.

"Rowantree's been trying to get you fired for the last hour, Jim," he said. "He said you wouldn't take him up in your car. I'm not going to fire you, because you're a good, steady man, but I'm warning you now. He knows a lot of rich and influential people, and if you don't mind your own business, it won't be hard for him to get you kicked out." Mr. Coolidge was surrounded by all the treasures he had extricated from the rubbish baskets in the back halls—broken lamps, broken vases, a perambulator with three wheels.

"But he—" Clancy began.

"It's none of your business, Jim," Mr. Coolidge said. "He's been very quiet since he come back from Europe. You're a good, steady man, Clancy, and I don't want to fire you, but you got to remember that you aren't the boss around here."

The next day was Palm Sunday, and, by the grace of God, Clancy did not see Mr. Rowantree. On Monday, Clancy joined his bitterness at having to live in Sodom to the deep and general grief he always felt at the commencement of those events that would end on Golgotha. It was a gloomy day. Clouds and darkness were over the city. Now and then it rained. Clancy took Mr. Rowantree down at ten. He didn't say anything, but he gave the man a scornful look. The ladies began going off for lunch around noon. Mr. Rowantree's friend Bobbie went out then.

About half past two, one of the ladies came back from lunch, smelling of gin. She did a funny thing. When she got into the elevator, she stood with her face to the wall of the car, so that Clancy couldn't see it. He was not a man to look into somebody's face if they wanted to hide it, and this made him angry. He stopped the car. "Turn around," he said. "Turn around. I'm ashamed of you, a woman with three grown children, standing with your face to the wall like a crybaby." She turned around. She was crying about something. Clancy put the car into motion again. "You ought to fast," he mumbled. "You ought to go without cigarettes or meat during Lent. It would give you something to think about." She left the car, and he answered a ring from the first floor. It was Mr. Rowantree. He took him up. Then he took Mrs. DePaul up to 9. She was a nice woman, and he told her about John's trip to Chicago. On the way down, he smelled gas.

For a man who has lived his life in a tenement, gas is the odor of winter, sickness, need, and death. Clancy went up to Mr. Rowantree's floor. That was it. He had the master key and he opened the door and stepped into that hellish breath. It was dark. He could hear the petcocks hissing in the kitchen. He put a rug against the door to keep it open and threw up a window in the hall. He stuck his head out for some air. Then, in terror of being blown into hell himself, and swearing and praying and half closing his eyes as if the poisonous air might blind him, he started for the kitchen and gave himself a cruel bang against the doorframe that made him cold all over with pain. He stumbled into the kitchen and turned off the gas and opened the doors and windows. Mr. Rowantree was on his knees with his head in the oven. He sat up. He was crying. "Bobbie's gone, Clancy," he said. "Bobbie's gone."

Clancy's stomach turned over, his gorge opened and filled up with bitter spit. "Dear Jesus!" he shouted. "Dear Jesus!" He stumbled out of the apartment. He was shaking all over. He took the car down and shouted for the doorman and told him what had happened.

The doorman took the elevator, and Clancy went into the locker room and sat down. He didn't know how long he had been there when the doorman came in and said that he smelled more gas. Clancy went up to Mr. Rowantree's apartment again. The door was shut. He opened it and stood in the hall and heard the petcocks. "Take your God-damned fool head out of that oven, Mr. Rowantree!" he shouted. He went into the kitchen and turned off the gas. Mr. Rowantree was sitting on the floor. "I won't do it again, Clancy," he said. "I promise, I promise."

Clancy went down and got Mr. Coolidge, and they went into the basement together and turned off Mr. Rowantree's gas. He went up again. The door was shut. When he opened it, he heard the hissing of the gas. He yanked the man's head out of the oven. "You're wasting your time, Mr. Rowantree!" he shouted. "We've turned off your gas! You're wasting your time!" Mr. Rowantree scrambled to his feet and ran out of the kitchen. Clancy heard him running through the apartment, slamming doors. He followed him and found him in the bathroom, shaking pills out of a bottle into his mouth. Clancy knocked the pill bottle out of his hand and knocked the man down. Then he called the precinct station on Mr. Rowantree's phone. He waited there until a policeman, a doctor, and a priest came.

Clancy walked home at five. The sky was black. It was raining soot and ashes. Sodom, he thought, the city undeserving of clemency, the unredeemable place, and, raising his eyes to watch the rain and the ashes fall through the air, he felt a great despair for his kind. They had lost the warrants for mercy, there was no movement in the city around him but toward self-destruction and sin. He longed for the simple life of Ireland and the City of God, but he felt that he had been contaminated by the stink of gas.

He told Nora what had happened, and she tried to comfort him. There was no letter or card from John. In the evening, Mr. Coolidge telephoned. He said it was about Mr. Rowantree.

"Is he in the insane asylum?" Clancy asked.

"No," Mr. Coolidge said. "His friend came back and they went out together. But he's been threatening to get you fired again. As soon as he felt all right again, he said he was going to get you fired. I don't want to fire you, but you got to be careful, you got to be careful." This was the twist that Clancy couldn't follow, and he felt sick. He asked Mr. Coolidge to get a man from the union to take his place for a day or so, and he went to bed.

Clancy stayed in bed the next morning. He got worse. He was cold. Nora lighted a fire in the range, but he shivered as if his heart and his bones were frozen. He doubled his knees up to his chest and snagged the blankets around him, but he couldn't keep warm. Nora finally called the doctor, a man from Limerick. It was after ten before he got there. He said that Clancy should go to the hospital. The doctor left to make the arrangements, and Nora got Clancy's best clothes together and helped him into them. There was still a price tag on his long underwear and there were pins in his shirt. In the end, nobody saw the new underwear and the clean shirt. At the hospital, they drew a curtain around his bed and handed the finery out to Nora. Then he stretched out in bed, and Nora gave him a kiss and went away.

He groaned, he moaned for a while, but he had a fever and this put him to sleep. He did not know or care where he was for the next few days. He slept most of the time. When John came back from Chicago, the boy's company and his story of the trip picked Clancy's spirits up a little. Nora visited him every day, and one day, a couple of weeks after Clancy entered the hospital, she brought Frank Quinn, the doorman, with her. Frank gave Clancy a narrow manila envelope, and when Clancy opened it, asking crossly what it was, he saw that it was full of currency.

"That's from the tenants, Clancy," Frank said.

"Now, why did they do this?" Clancy said. He was smitten. His eyes watered and he couldn't count the money. "Why did they do this?" he asked weakly. "Why did they go to this trouble? I'm nothing but an elevator man."

"It's nearly two hundred dollars," Frank said.

"Who took up the collection?" Clancy said. "Was it you, Frank?"

"It was one of the tenants," Frank said.

"It was Mrs. DePaul," Clancy said. "I'll bet it was that Mrs. DePaul."

"One of the tenants," Frank said.

"It was you, Frank," Clancy said warmly. "You was the one who took up the collection."

"It was Mr. Rowantree," Frank said sadly. He bent his head.

"You're not going to give the money back, Jim?" Nora asked.

"I'm not a God-damned fool!" Clancy shouted. "When I pick up a dollar off the street, I'm not the man to go running down to the lost-and-found department with it!"

"Nobody else could have gotten so much, Jim," Frank said. "He went from floor to floor. They say he was crying."

Clancy had a vision. He saw the church from the open lid of his coffin, before the altar. The sacristan had lighted only a few of the Vaseline-colored lamps, for the only mourners were those few people, all of them poor and old, who had come from Limerick with Clancy on the boat. He heard the priest's youthful voice mingling with the thin music of the bells. Then in the back of the church he saw Mr. Rowantree and Bobbie. They were crying and crying. They were crying harder than Nora. He could see their shoulders rise and fall, and hear their sighs.

"Does he think I'm dying, Frank?" Clancy asked.

"Yes, Jim. He does."

"He thinks I'm dying," Clancy said angrily. "He's got one of them soft heads. Well, I ain't dying. I'm not taking any of his grief. I'm getting out of here." He climbed out of bed. Nora and Frank tried unsuccessfully to push him back. Frank ran out to get a nurse. The nurse pointed a finger at Clancy and commanded him to get back into bed, but he had put on his pants and was tying his shoelaces. She went out and got another nurse, and the two young women tried to hold him down, but he shook them off easily. The first nurse went to get a doctor. The doctor who returned with her was a young man, much smaller than Clancy. He said that Clancy could go home. Frank and Nora took him back in a taxi, and as soon as he got into the tenement, he telephoned Mr. Coolidge and said that he was coming back to work in the morning. He felt a lot better, surrounded by the smells and lights of his own place. Nora cooked him a nice supper and he ate it in the kitchen.

After supper, he sat by the window in his shirtsleeves. He thought about going back to work, about the man with the cleft chin, the wife-beater, Mr. Rowantree and Bobbie. Why should a man fall in love with a monster? Why should a man try to kill himself? Why should a man try to get a man fired and then collect money for him with tears in his eyes, and then perhaps, a week later, try to get him fired again? He would not return the money, he would not thank Mr. Rowantree, but he wondered what kind of judgment he should pass on the pervert. He began to pick the words he would say to Mr. Rowantree when they met. "It's my suggestion, Mr. Rowantree," he would say, "that the next time you want to kill yourself, you get a rope or a gun. It's my suggestion, Mr. Rowantree," he would say, "that you go to a good doctor and get your head examined."

The spring wind, the south wind that in the city smells of

drains, was blowing. Clancy's window looked onto an expanse of clotheslines and ailanthus trees, yards that were used as dumps, and the naked backs of tenements, with their lighted and un-lighted windows. The symmetry, the reality of the scene heart-ened Clancy, as if it conformed to something good in himself. Men with common minds like his had built these houses. Nora brought him a glass of beer and sat near the window. He put an arm around her waist. She was in her slip, because of the heat. Her hair was held down with pins. She appeared to Clancy to be one of the glorious beauties of his day, but a stranger, he guessed, might notice the tear in her slip and that her body was bent and heavy. A picture of John hung on the wall. Clancy was struck with the strength and intelligence of his son's face, but he guessed that a stranger might notice the boy's glasses and his bad complexion. And then, thinking of Nora and John and that this half blindness was all that he knew himself of mortal love, he decided not to say anything to Mr. Rowantree. They would pass in silence.

from **LIBRA**

Don DeLillo

It was a seven-story brick building with a Hertz sign on the roof. Lee was an order-filler. He picked up orders from the chute on the first floor and fixed them to his clipboard. Then he went up to six, usually, to find the books. Most of the order-fillers were Negroes. They had elevator races in the afternoon. Gates slamming, voices echoing down the shaft, laughter, name-calling. He took the books down to the girls on one, to the wrapping bench, where the merchandise was checked and shipped.

All these books. Books stacked ten cartons high. Cartons stamped Books. Stamped Ten Rolling Readers. Stacked higher than the tall windows. The cartons are a size you have to wrestle. When you open a fresh carton you get the fragrance of paper, of book pages and binding. It floods you with memories of school.

He liked carrying a clipboard. The clipboard made him feel this was a half-decent way to earn a dollar. He didn't have to listen to crazy-ass machines. There was no dirt or grease on the job. Just dust rising when the men ran to the elevators in the afternoon, three or four men pounding across the old wood floors to begin the race down—sunny dust forming among the books.

from **INVISIBLE MAN**

Ralph Ellison

I looked around me. It was not just an engine room; I knew, for I had been in several, the last at college. It was something more. For one thing, the furnaces were made differently and the flames that flared through the cracks of the fire chambers were too intense and too blue. And there were the odors. No, he was *making* something down here, something that had to do with paint, and probably something too filthy and dangerous for white men to be willing to do even for money. It was not paint because I had been told that the paint was made on the floors above, where, passing through, I had seen men in splattered aprons working over large vats filled with whirling pigment. One thing was certain: I had to be careful with this crazy Brockway; he didn't like my being here . . . And there he was, entering the room now from the stairs.

"How's it going?" he asked.

"All right," I said. "Only it seems to have gotten louder."

"Oh, it gets pretty loud down here, all right; this here's the uproar department and I'm in charge . . . Did she go over the mark?"

"No, it's holding steady," I said.

"That's good. I been having plenty trouble with it lately. Haveta bust it down and give it a good going over soon as I can get the tank clear."

Perhaps he *is* the engineer, I thought, watching him inspect the gauges and go to another part of the room to adjust a series of valves. Then he went and said a few words into a wall phone and called me, pointing to the valves.

"I'm fixing to shoot it to 'em upstairs," he said gravely. "When I give you the signal I want you to turn 'em wide open. 'N when I give you the second signal I want you to close 'em up again. Start with this here red one and work right straight across . . ."

I took my position and waited, as he took a stand near the gauge.

"Let her go," he called. I opened the valves, hearing the sound of liquids rushing through the huge pipes. At the sound of a buzzer I looked up . . .

"Start closing," he yelled. "What you looking at? Close them valves!"

"What's wrong with you?" he asked when the last valve was closed.

"I expected you to call."

"I said I'd *signal* you. Caint you tell the difference between a signal and a call? Hell, I buzzed you. You don't want to do that no more. When I buzz you I want you to do something and do it quick!"

"You're the boss," I said sarcastically.

"You mighty right, I'm the boss, and don't forgit it. Now come on back here, we got work to do."

We came to a strange-looking machine consisting of a huge set of gears connecting a series of drum-like rollers. Brockway took a shovel and scooped up a load of brown crystals from a pile on the floor, pitching them skillfully into a receptacle on top of the machine.

"Grab a scoop and let's git going," he ordered briskly. "You ever done this before?" he asked as I scooped into the pile.

"It's been a long time," I said. "What is this material?"

He stopped shoveling and gave me a long, black stare, then returned to the pile, his scoop ringing on the floor. You'll have to remember not to ask this suspicious old bastard any questions, I thought, scooping into the brown pile.

Soon I was perspiring freely. My hands were sore and I began to tire. Brockway watched me out of the corner of his eye, snickering noiselessly.

"You don't want to overwork yourself, young feller," he said blandly.

"I'll get used to it," I said, scooping up a heavy load.

"Oh, sho, sho," he said. "Sho. But you better take a rest when you git tired."

I didn't stop. I piled on the material until he said, "That there's the scoop we been trying to find. That's what we want. You better stand back a little, 'cause I'm fixing to start her up."

I backed away, watching him go over and push a switch. Shuddering into motion, the machine gave a sudden scream like a circular saw, and sent a tattoo of sharp crystals against my face. I moved clumsily away, seeing Brockway grin like a dried prune. Then with the dying hum of the furiously whirling drums, I heard the grains sifting lazily in the sudden stillness, sliding sand-like down the chute into the pot underneath.

I watched him go over and open a valve. A sharp new smell of oil arose.

"Now she's all set to cook down; all we got to do is put the fire to her," he said, pressing a button on something that looked like the burner of an oil furnace. There was an angry hum, followed by a slight explosion that caused something to rattle, and I could hear a low roaring begin.

"Know what that's going to be when it's cooked?"

"No, sir," I said.

"Well that's going to be the guts, what they call the *vee*hicle of the paint. Least it will be by time I git through putting other stuff with it."

"But I thought the paint was made uptairs . . ."

"Naw, they just mixes in the color, make it look pretty. Right down here is where the real paint is made. Without what I do they couldn't do nothing, they be making bricks without straw. An' not only do I make up the base, I fixes the varnishes and lots of the oils too . . ."

"So that's it," I said. "I was wondering what you did down here."

"A whole lots of folks wonders about that without gitting anywhere. But as I was saying, caint a single doggone drop of paint move out of the factory lessen it comes through Lucius Brockway's hands."

"How long have you been doing this?"

"Long enough to know what I'm doing," he said. "And I learned it without all that education that them what's been sent down here is suppose to have. I learned it by doing it. Them personnel fellows don't want to face the facts, but Liberty Paints wouldn't be worth a plugged nickel if they didn't have me here to see that it got a good strong base. Old Man Sparland know it though. I caint stop laughing over the time when I was down with a touch of pneumonia and they put one of them so-called engineers to pooting around down here. Why, they started to having so much paint go bad they didn't know what to do. Paint was bleeding and wrinkling, wouldn't cover or nothing—you know, a man could make hisself all kinds of money if he found out what makes paint bleed. Anyway, everything was going bad. Then word got to me that they done put that fellow in my place and when I got well I wouldn't come back. Here I been with 'em so long and loyal and everything. Shucks, I just sent 'em word that Lucius Brockway was retiring!

"Next thing you know here come the Old Man. He so old hisself his chauffeur has to help him up them steep stairs at my place. Come in a-puffing and a-blowing, says, 'Lucius, what's this I hear 'bout you retiring?'

"'Well, sir, Mr. Sparland, sir,' I says, 'I been pretty sick, as you well know, and I'm gitting kinder along in my years, as you well know, and I hear that this here Italian fellow you got in my place is doing so good I thought I'd might as well take it easy round the house.'

"Why, you'd a thought I'd done cursed him or something. 'What kind of talk is that from you, Lucius Brockway,' he said, 'taking it easy round the house when we need you out to the plant? Don't you know the quickest way to die is to retire? Why, that fellow out at the plant don't know a thing about those furnaces. I'm so worried about what he's going to do, that he's liable to blow up the plant or something that I took out some extra insurance. He can't do your job,' he said. 'He don't have the touch. We haven't put out a first-class batch of paint since you been gone.' Now that was the Old Man hisself!" Lucius Brockway said.

"So what happened?" I said.

"What you mean, what happened?" he said, looking as though it were the most unreasonable question in the world. "Shucks, a few days later the Old Man had me back down here in full control. That engineer got so mad when he found out he had to take orders from me he quit the next day."

He spat on the floor and laughed. "Heh, heh, heh, he was a fool, that's what. A fool! He wanted to boss *me* and I know more about this basement than anybody, boilers and everything. I helped lay the pipes and everything, and what I mean is I knows the location of each and every pipe and switch and cable and wire and everything else—both in the floors and in the walls *and* out in the yard. Yes, sir! And what's more, I got it in my head so good I can trace it out on paper down to the last nut and bolt; and ain't never been to nobody's engineering school neither, ain't even passed by one, as far as I know. Now what you think about that?"

"I think it's remarkable," I said, thinking, I don't like this old man.

"Oh, I wouldn't call it that," he said. "It's just that I been round here so long. I been studying this machinery for over twenty-five years. Sho, and that fellow thinking 'cause he been to some school and learned how to read a blueprint and how to fire a boiler he knows more 'bout this plant than Lucius Brockway. That fool couldn't make no engineer 'cause he can't see what's staring him straight in the face . . . Say, you forgittin' to watch them gauges."

I hurried over, finding all the needles steady.

"They're okay," I called.

"All right, but I'm warning you to keep an eye on 'em. You caint forgit down here, 'cause if you do, you liable to blow up something. They got all this machinery, but that ain't everything; *we the machines inside the machine.*

"You know the best selling paint we got, the one that *made* this here business?" he asked as I helped him fill a vat with a smelly substance.

"No, I don't."

"Our white, Optic White."

"Why the white rather than the others?"

"'Cause we started stressing it from the first. We make the best white paint in the world, I don't give a damn what nobody says. Our white is so white you can paint a chunka coal and you'd have to crack it open with a sledge hammer to prove it wasn't white clear through!"

His eyes glinted with humorless conviction and I had to drop my head to hide my grin.

"You notice that sign on top of the building?"

"Oh, you can't miss that," I said.

"You read the slogan?"

"I don't remember, I was in such a hurry."

"Well, you might not believe it, but I helped the Old Man make up that slogan. 'If It's Optic White, It's the Right White,' " he quoted with an upraised finger, like a preacher quoting holy writ. "I got me a three-hundred-dollar bonus for helping to think that up. These newfangled advertising folks is been tryin' to work up something about the other colors, talking about rainbows or something, but hell, *they* caint get nowhere."

" 'If It's Optic White, It's the Right White,' " I repeated and suddenly had to repress a laugh as a childhood jingle rang through my mind:

" 'If you're white, you're right,' " I said.

"That's it," he said. "And that's another reason why the Old Man ain't goin' to let nobody come down here messing with me. *He* knows what a lot of them new fellers don't; *he* knows that the reason our paint is so good is because of the way Lucius Brockway puts the pressure on them oils and resins before they even leaves the tanks." He laughed maliciously. "They thinks 'cause everything down here is done by machinery, that's all there is to it. They crazy! Ain't a continental thing that happens down here that ain't as iffen I done put my black hands into it! Them machines just do the cooking, these here hands right here do the sweeting. Yes, sir! Lucius Brockway hit it square on the head! I dips my finger in and sweets it! Come on, let's eat . . ."

"But what about the gauges?" I said, seeing him go over and take a thermos bottle from a shelf near one of the furnaces.

"Oh, we'll be here close enough to keep an eye on 'em. Don't you worry 'bout that."

"But I left my lunch in the locker room over at Building No. 1."

"Go on and git it and come back here and eat. Down here we have to always be on the job. A man don't need no more'n fifteen minutes to eat no-how; then I say let him git on back on the job."

Upon opening the door I thought I had made a mistake. Men dressed in splattered painters' caps and overalls sat about on benches, listening to a thin tubercular-looking man who was addressing them in a nasal voice. Everyone looked at me and I was starting out when the thin man called, "There's plenty of seats for late comers. Come in, brother . . ."

Brother? Even after my weeks in the North this was surprising. "I was looking for the locker room," I spluttered.

"You're in it, brother. Weren't you told about the meeting?"

"Meeting? Why, no, sir, I wasn't."

The chairman frowned. "You see, the bosses are not cooperating," he said to the others. "Brother, who's your foreman?"

"Mr. Brockway, sir," I said.

Suddenly the men began scraping their feet and cursing. I looked about me. What was wrong? Were they objecting to my referring to Brockway as *Mister*?

"Quiet, brothers," the chairman said, leaning across his table, his hand cupped to his ear. "Now what was that, brother; who is your foreman?"

"Lucius Brockway, sir," I said, dropping the *Mister*.

But this seemed only to make them more hostile. "Get him the hell out of here," they shouted. I turned. A group on the far side of the room kicked over a bench, yelling, "Throw him out! Throw him out!"

I inched backwards, hearing the little man bang on the table for order. "Men, brothers! Give the brother a chance . . ."

"He looks like a dirty fink to me. A first-class enameled fink!"

The hoarsely voiced word grated my ears like "nigger" in an angry southern mouth . . .

"Brothers, *please!*" The chairman was waving his hands as I reached out behind me for the door and touched an arm, feeling it snatch violently away. I dropped my hand.

"Who sent this fink into the meeting, brother chairman? Ask him that!" a man demanded.

"No, wait," the chairman said. "Don't ride that word too hard . . ."

"Ask him, brother chairman!" another man said.

"Okay, but don't label a man a fink until you know for sure." The chairman turned to me. "How'd you happen in here, brother?"

The men quieted, listening.

"I left my lunch in my locker," I said, my mouth dry.

"You weren't *sent* into the meeting?"

"No, sir, I didn't know about any meeting."

"The hell he says. None of these finks ever knows!"

"Throw the lousy bastard out!"

"Now, wait," I said.

They became louder, threatening.

"Respect the chair!" the chairman shouted. "We're a democratic union here, following democratic—"

"Never mind, git rid of the fink!"

". . . procedures. It's our task to make friends with all the workers. And I mean *all*. That's how we build the union strong. Now let's hear what the brother's got to say. No more of that beefing and interrupting!"

I broke into a cold sweat, my eyes seeming to have become extremely sharp, causing each face to stand out vivid in its hostility.

I heard, "When were you hired, friend?"

"This morning," I said.

"See, brothers, he's a new man. We don't want to make the mistake of judging the worker by his foreman. Some of you also work for sonsabitches, remember?"

Suddenly the men began to laugh and curse. "Here's one right here," one of them yelled.

"Mine wants to marry the boss's daughter—a frigging eight-day wonder!"

This sudden change made me puzzled and angry, as though they were making me the butt of a joke.

"Order, brothers! Perhaps the brother would like to join the union. How about it, brother?"

"Sir . . . ?" I didn't know what to say. I knew very little about unions—but most of these men seemed hostile . . . And before I could answer a fat man with shaggy gray hair leaped to his feet, shouting angrily.

"I'm against it! Brothers, this fellow could be a fink, even if he was hired right this minute! Not that I aim to be unfair to anybody, either. Maybe he ain't a fink," he cried passionately, "but brothers, I want to remind you that nobody knows it; and it seems to me that anybody that would work under that sonofabitching, double-crossing Brockway for more than fifteen minutes is just as apt as not to be *naturally* fink-minded! Please, brothers!" he cried, waving his arms for quiet. "As some of you brothers have learned, to the sorrow of your wives and babies, a fink don't have to know about trade unionism to be a fink! Finkism? Hell, I've made a study of finkism! Finkism is *born* into some guys. It's born into some guys, just like a good eye for color is born into other guys. That's right, that's the honest, scientific truth! A fink don't even have to have heard of a union before," he cried in a frenzy of words. "All you have to do is bring him around the neighborhood of a union and next thing you know, why, zip! he's finking his finking ass off!"

He was drowned out by shouts of approval. Men turned violently to look at me. I felt choked. I wanted to drop my head but faced them as though facing them was itself a denial of his statements. Another voice ripped out of the shouts of approval, spilling with great urgency from the lips of a little fellow with glasses who spoke with the index finger of one hand upraised and the thumb of the other crooked in the suspender of his overalls.

"I want to put this brother's remarks in the form of a motion: I move that we determine through a thorough investigation whether the new worker is a fink or no; and if he is a fink, let us discover who he's finking for! And this, brother members, would give the worker time, if he *ain't* a fink, to become acquainted with the work of the union and its aims. After all, brothers, we don't want to forget that workers like him aren't so highly developed as some of us who've been in the labor movement for a long time. So *I* says, let's give him time to see what we've done to improve the condition of the workers, and then, if he *ain't* a fink, we can decide in a democratic way whether we want to accept this brother into the union. Brother union members, I thank you!" He sat down with a bump.

The room roared. Biting anger grew inside me. So I was not so highly developed as they! What did he mean? Were they all Ph.D.'s? I couldn't move; too much was happening to me. It was as though by entering the room I had automatically applied for membership—even though I had no idea that a union existed, and had come up simply to get a cold pork chop sandwich. I stood trembling, afraid that they would ask me to join but angry that so many rejected me on sight. And worst of all, I knew they were forcing me to accept things on their own terms, and I was unable to leave.

"All right, brothers. We'll take a vote," the chairman shouted. "All in favor of the motion, signify by saying 'Aye' . . ."

The ayes drowned him out.

"The ayes carried it," the chairman announced as several men turned to stare at me. At last I could move. I started out, forgetting why I had come.

"Come in, brother," the chairman called. "You can get your lunch now. Let him through, you brothers around the door!"

My face stung as though it had been slapped. They had made their decision without giving me a chance to speak for myself. I felt that every man present looked upon me with hostility; and though I had lived with hostility all my life, now for the first time it seemed to reach me, as though I had expected more of these men than of others—even though I had not known of their existence. Here in this room my defenses were negated, stripped away, checked at the door as the weapons, the knives and razors and owlhead pistols of the country boys were checked on Saturday night at the Golden Day. I kept my eyes lowered, mumbling "Pardon me, pardon me," all the way to the drab green locker, where I removed the sandwich, for which I no longer had an appetite, and stood fumbling with the bag, dreading to face the men on my way out. Then still hating myself for the apologies made coming over, I brushed past silently as I went back.

When I reached the door the chairman called, "Just a minute, brother, we want you to understand that this is nothing against you personally. What you see here is the results of certain conditions here at the plant. We want you to know that we are only trying to protect ourselves. Some day we hope to have you as a member in good standing."

From here and there came a half-hearted applause that quickly died. I swallowed and stared unseeing, the words spurting to me from a red, misty distance.

"Okay, brothers," the voice said, "let him pass."

I stumbled through the bright sunlight of the yard, past the office workers chatting on the grass, back to Building No. 2, to the basement. I stood on the stairs, feeling as though my bowels had been flooded with acid. Why hadn't I simply left, I thought with anguish. And since I had remained, why hadn't I *said* something, defended myself? Suddenly I snatched the wrapper off a sandwich and tore it violently with my teeth, hardly tasting the dry lumps that squeezed past my constricted throat when I swallowed. Dropping the remainder back into the bag, I held on to the handrail, my legs shaking as though I had just escaped a great danger. Finally, it went away and I pushed open the metal door.

"What kept you so long?" Brockway snapped from where he sat on a wheelbarrow. He had been drinking from a white mug now cupped in his grimy hands.

I looked at him abstractedly, seeing how the light caught on his wrinkled forehead, his snowy hair.

"I said, what kept you so long!"

What had he to do with it, I thought, looking at him through a kind of mist, knowing that I disliked him and that I was very tired.

"I say . . . " he began, and I heard my voice come quiet from my tensed throat as I noticed by the clock that I had been gone only twenty minutes.

"I ran into a union meeting—"

"Union!" I heard his white cup shatter against the floor as he uncrossed his legs, rising. "I knowed you belonged to that bunch of troublemaking foreigners! I knowed it! Git out!" he screamed. "Git out of my basement!"

He started toward me as in a dream, trembling like the needle of one of the gauges as he pointed toward the stairs, his voice shrieking. I stared; something seemed to have gone wrong, my reflexes were jammed.

"But what's the matter?" I stammered, my voice low and my

mind understanding and yet failing exactly to understand. "What's wrong?"

"You heard me. Git out!"

"But I don't understand . . ."

"Shut up and git!"

"But, Mr. Brockway," I cried, fighting to hold something that was giving way.

"You two-bit, trouble-making union louse!"

"Look, man," I cried, urgently now, "I don't belong to any union."

"If you don't git outta here, you low-down skunk," he said, looking wildly about the floor, "I'm liable to kill you. The Lord being my witness, I'LL KILL YOU!"

It was incredible, things were speeding up. "You'll do what?" I stammered.

"I'LL KILL YOU, THAT'S WHAT!"

He had said it again and something fell away from me, and I seemed to be telling myself in a rush: *You were trained to accept the foolishness of such old men as this, even when you thought them clowns and fools; you were trained to pretend that you respected them and acknowledged in them the same quality of authority and power in your world as the whites before whom they bowed and scraped and feared and loved and imitated, and you were even trained to accept it when, angered or spiteful, or drunk with power, they came at you with a stick or strap or cane and you made no effort to strike back, but only to escape unmarked.* But this was too much . . . he was not grandfather or uncle or father, nor preacher or teacher. Something uncoiled in my stomach and I was moving toward him, shouting, more at a black blur that irritated my eyes than at a clearly defined human face, "YOU'LL KILL WHO?"

"*YOU*, THAT'S WHO!"

"Listen here, you old fool, don't talk about killing me! Give me a chance to explain. I don't belong to anything—Go on, pick it up! Go on!" I yelled, seeing his eyes fasten upon a twisted iron bar. "You're old enough to be my grandfather, but if you touch that bar, I swear I'll make you eat it!"

"I done tole you, GIT OUTTA MY BASEMENT! *You impudent son'bitch,*" he screamed.

I moved forward, seeing him stoop and reach aside for the bar; and I was throwing myself forward, feeling him go over with a grunt, hard against the floor, rolling beneath the force of my lunge. It was as though I had landed upon a wiry rat. He scrambled beneath me, making angry sounds and striking my face as he tried to use the bar. I twisted it from his grasp, feeling a sharp pain stab through my shoulder. He's using a knife, flashed through my mind and I slashed out with my elbow, sharp against his face, feeling it land solid and seeing his head fly backwards and up and back again as I struck again, hearing something fly free and skitter across the floor, thinking, It's gone, the knife is gone . . . and struck again as he tried to choke me, jabbing at his bobbing head, feeling the bar come free and bringing it down at his head, missing, the metal clinking against the floor, and bringing it up for a second try and him yelling, "No, no! You the best, you the best!"

"I'm going to beat your brains out!" I said, my throat dry, "stabbing me . . ."

"No," he panted. "I got enough. Ain't you heard me say I got enough?"

"So when you can't win you want to stop! Damn you, if you've cut me bad, I'll tear your head off!"

Watching him warily, I got to my feet. I dropped the bar, as a flash of heat swept over me: His face was caved in.

"What's wrong with you, old man?" I yelled nervously. "Don't you know better than to attack a man a third your age?"

He blanched at being called old, and I repeated it, adding insults I'd heard my grandfather use. "Why, you old-fashioned, slavery-time, mammy-made, handkerchief-headed bastard, you should know better! What made you think you could threaten *my* life? You meant nothing to me, I came down here because I was sent. I didn't know anything about you or the union either. Why'd you start riding me the minute I came in? Are you people crazy? Does this paint go to your head? Are you drinking it?"

He glared, panting tiredly. Great tucks showed in his overalls where the folds were stuck together by the goo with which he was covered, and I thought, Tar Baby, and wanted to blot him out of my sight. But now my anger was flowing fast from action to words.

"I go to get my lunch and they ask me who I work for and when I tell them, they call me a fink. *A fink!* You people must be out of your minds. No sooner do I get back down here than *you* start yelling that you're going to kill me! What's going on? What have you got against me? What did I do?"

He glowered at me silently, then pointed to the floor.

"Reach and draw back a nub," I warned.

"Caint a man even git his teeth?" he mumbled, his voice strange.

"TEETH?"

With a shamed frown, he opened his mouth. I saw a blue flash of shrunken gums. The thing that had skittered across the floor was not a knife, but a plate of false teeth. For a fraction of a second I was desperate, feeling some of my justification for wanting to kill him slipping away. My fingers leaped to my shoulder, finding wet cloth but no blood. The old fool had *bitten* me. A wild flash of laughter struggled to rise from beneath my anger. He had bitten me! I looked on the floor, seeing the smashed mug and the teeth glinting dully across the room.

"Get them," I said, growing ashamed. Without his teeth, some of the hatefulness seemed to have gone out of him. But I stayed close as he got his teeth and went over to the tap and held them beneath a stream of water. A tooth fell away beneath the pressure of his thumb, and I heard him grumbling as he placed the plate in his mouth. Then, wiggling his chin, he became himself again.

"You was really trying to kill me," he said. He seemed unable to believe it.

"You started the killing. I don't go around fighting," I said. "Why didn't you let me explain? Is it against the law to belong to the union?"

"That damn union," he cried, almost in tears. "That *damn* union! They after my job! I know they after my job! For one of us to join one of them damn unions is like we was to bite the hand of the man who teached us to bathe in a bathtub! I hates it, and I mean to keep on doing all I can to chase it outta the plant. They after my job, the chickenshit bastards!"

Spittle formed at the corners of his mouth; he seemed to boil with hatred.

"But what have I to do with that?" I said, feeling suddenly the older.

"'Cause them young colored fellers up in the lab is trying to join that outfit, that's what! Here the white man done give 'em jobs," he wheezed as though pleading a case. "He done give 'em *good* jobs too, and they so ungrateful they goes and joins up with that backbiting union! I never seen such a no-good ungrateful bunch. All they doing is making things bad for the rest of us!"

"Well, I'm sorry," I said, "I didn't know about all that. I came here to take a temporary job and I certainly didn't intend to get mixed up in any quarrels. But as for us, I'm ready to forget our disagreement—if you are . . . " I held out my hand, causing my shoulder to pain.

He gave me a gruff look. "You ought to have more self-respect than to fight an old man," he said. "I got grown boys older than you."

"I thought you were trying to kill me," I said, my hand still extended. "I thought you had stabbed me."

"Well, I don't like a lot of bickering and confusion myself," he said, avoiding my eyes. And it was as though the closing of his sticky hand over mine was a signal. I heard a shrill hissing from the boilers behind me and turned, hearing Brockway yell, "I tole you to watch them gauges. Git over to the big valves, quick!"

I dashed for where a series of valve wheels projected from the wall near the crusher, seeing Brockway scrambling away in the other direction, thinking, Where's he going? as I reached the valves, and hearing him yell, "Turn it! Turn it!"

"Which?" I yelled, reaching.

"The white one, fool, the white one!"

I jumped, catching it and pulling down with all my weight, feeling it give. But this only increased the noise and I seemed to hear Brockway laugh as I looked around to see him scrambling for the stairs, his hands clasping the back of his head, and his neck pulled in close, like a small boy who has thrown a brick into the air.

"Hey you! Hey you!" I yelled. "Hey!" But it was too late. All my movements seemed too slow, ran together. I felt the wheel resisting and tried vainly to reverse it and tried to let go, and it sticking to my palms and my fingers stiff and sticky, and I turned, running now, seeing the needle on one of the gauges swinging madly, like a beacon gone out of control, and trying to think clearly, my eyes darting here and there through the room of tanks and machines and up the stairs so far away and hearing the clear new note arising while I seemed to run swiftly up an incline and shot forward with sudden acceleration into a wet blast of black emptiness that was somehow a bath of whiteness.

It was a fall into space that seemed not a fall but a suspension. Then a great weight landed upon me and I seemed to sprawl in an interval of clarity beneath a pile of broken machinery, my head pressed back against a huge wheel, my body splattered with a stinking goo. Somewhere an engine ground in furious futility, grating loudly until a pain shot around the curve of my head and bounced me off into blackness for a distance, only to strike another pain that lobbed me back. And in that clear instant of consciousness I opened my eyes to a blinding flash.

Holding on grimly, I could hear the sound of someone wading, sloshing, nearby, and an old man's garrulous voice saying, "I tole 'em these here young Nineteen-Hundred boys ain't no good for the job. They ain't got the nerves. Naw, sir, they just ain't got the nerves."

I tried to speak, to answer, but something heavy moved again, and I was understanding something fully and trying again to answer but seemed to sink to the center of a lake of heavy water and pause, transfixed and numb with the sense that I had lost irrevocably an important victory.

from **AS I LAY DYING**

William Faulkner

Cash

I made it on the bevel.

1. There is more surface for the nails to grip.
2. There is twice the gripping-surface to each seam.
3. The water will have to seep into it on a slant. Water moves easiest up and down or straight across.
4. In a house people are upright two thirds of the time. So the seams and joints are made up-and-down. Because the stress is up-and-down.
5. In a bed where people lie down all the time, the joints and seams are made sideways, because the stress is sideways.
6. Except.
7. A body is not square like a crosstie.
8. Animal magnetism.
9. The animal magnetism of a dead body makes the stress come slanting, so the seams and joints of a coffin are made on the bevel.

10. You can see by an old grave that the earth sinks down on the bevel.
11. While in a natural hole it sinks by the center, the stress being up-and-down.
12. So I made it on the bevel.
13. It makes a neater job.

from **INDEPENDENCE DAY**

Richard Ford

A tangy metallic fruitiness filters through the Jersey ozone—the scent of overheated motors and truck brakes on Route 1—reaching clear back to the rolly back road where I am now passing by an opulent new pharmaceutical world headquarters abutting a healthy wheat field managed by the soil-research people up at Rutgers. Just beyond this is Mallards Landing (two ducks coasting in on a colonial-looking sign made to resemble wood), its houses-to-be as yet only studded in on skimpy slabs, their bald, red-dirt yards awaiting sod. Orange and green pennants fly along the roadside: "Models Open." "Pleasure You Can Afford!" "New Jersey's Best-Kept Secret." But there are still long ragged heaps of bulldozed timber and stumps piled up and smoldering two hundred yards to one side, more or less where the community center will be. And a quarter mile back and beyond the far wall of third-growth hardwoods where no animal is native, a big oil-storage depot lumps up and into what's becoming thickened and stormy air, the beacons on its two great canisters blinking a red and silver *steer clear, steer clear* to the circling gulls and the jumbo jets on Newark approach.

When I make the final right into the Sleepy Hollow, two cars are nosed into the potholed lot, though only one has the tiresome green Vermont plate—a rusted-out, lighter-green Nova, borrowed from the Markhams' Slave Lake friends, and with a muddy bumper sticker that says ANESTHETISTS ARE NOMADS. A cagier realtor would've already phoned up with some manufactured "good news" about an unexpected price reduction in a previously out-of-reach house, and left this message at the desk last night as a form of torture and enticement. But the truth is I've become a little sick of the Markhams—given our long campaign—and have fallen into a not especially hospitable mood, so that I simply stop midway in the lot, hoping some emanations of my arrival will penetrate the flimsy motel walls and expel them both out the door in grateful, apologetic humors, fully ready to slam down their earnest money the instant they set eyes on this house in Penns Neck that, of course, I have yet to tell them about.

A thin curtain does indeed part in the little square window of room #7. Joe Markham's round, rueful face—which looks changed (though I can't say how)—floats in a small sea of blackness. The face turns, its lips move. I make a little wave, then the curtain closes, followed in five seconds by the banged-up pink door opening, and Phyllis Markham, in the uncomfortable gait of a woman not accustomed to getting fat, strides out into the mid-morning heat. Phyllis, I see from the driver's seat, has somehow amplified her red hair's coppery color to make it both brighter and darker, and has also bobbed it dramatically into a puffy, mushroomy bowl favored by sexless older moms in better-than-average suburbs, and which in Phyllis's case exposes her tiny ears and makes her neck look shorter. She's dressed in baggy khaki culottes, sandals and a thick damask Mexican pullover to hide her extra girth. Like me, she is in her forties, though unclear where, and she carries herself as if there were a new burden of true woe on the earth and only she knows about it.

"All set?" I say, my window down now, cracking a smile into the new pre-storm breeze. I think about Paul's horse joke and consider telling it, as I said I would.

"He says he's not going," Phyllis says, her bottom lip slightly enlarged and dark, making me wonder if Joe has given her a stiff smack this morning. Though Phyllis's lips are her best feature and it's more likely Joe has gifted himself with a manly morning's woogling to take his mind off his realty woes.

I'm still smiling. "What's the problem?" I say. Paper trash and parking lot grit are kicking around on the hot breeze now, and when I peek in the rearview there's a dark-purple thunderhead closing fast from the west, toiling the skies and torquing up winds, making ready to dump a big bucket of rain on us. Not a good augury for a home sale.

"We had an argument on the way down." Phyllis lowers her eyes, then casts an unhappy look back at the pink door, as if she expects Joe to come bursting through it in camo gear, screaming expletives and commands and locking and loading an M-16. She takes a self-protective look at the teeming sky. "I wonder if you'd mind just talking to him." She says this in a clipped, back-of-the-mouth voice, then elevates her small nose and stiffens her lips as two tears teeter inside her eyelids. (I've forgotten how much Joe's gooby western PA accent has rubbed off on her.)

Most Americans will eventually transact at least some portion of their important lives in the presence of realtors or as a result of something a realtor has done or said. And yet my view is, people should get their domestic rhubarbs, verbal fisticuffs and emotional jugular-snatching completely out of the way *before* they show up for a house tour. I'm more or less at ease with steely silences, bitter cryptic asides, eyes rolled to heaven and dagger stares passed between prospective home buyers, signaling but not actually putting on display more dramatic after-midnight wrist-twistings, shoutings and real rock-'em, sock-'em discord. But the client's code of conduct ought to say: Suppress all important horseshit by appointment time so I can get on with my job of lifting sagging spirits, opening fresh, unexpected choices, and offering much-needed assistance toward life's betterment. (I haven't said so, but the Markhams are on the brink of being written off, and I in fact feel a strong temptation just to run up my window, hit reverse, shoot back into the traffic and head for the Shore.)

But instead I simply say, "What would you like me to say?"

"Just tell him there's a great house," she says in a tiny, defeated voice.

"Where's Sonja?" I'm wondering if she's inside, alone with her dad.

"We had to leave her home." Phyllis shakes her head sadly. "She was showing signs of stress. She's lost weight, and she wet the bed night before last. This has been pretty tough for all of us, I guess." (She has yet to torch any animals, apparently.)

I reluctantly push open my door. Occupying the lot beside the Sleepy Hollow, inside a little fenced and razor-wire enclosure, is a shabby hubcap emporium, its shiny silvery wares nailed and hung up everywhere, all of it clanking and stuttering and shimmering in the breeze. Two old white men stand inside the compound in front of a little clatter-board shack that's completely armored with shiny hub-caps. One of them is laughing about something, his arms crossed over his big belly, swaying side to side. The other seems not to hear, just stares at Phyllis and me as if some different kind of transaction were going on.

"That's exactly what I was going to tell him anyway," I say, and try to smile again. Phyllis and Joe are obviously nearing a realty meltdown, and the threat is they may just dribble off elsewhere, feeling the need for an unattainable fresh start, and end up buying the first shitty split-level they see with another agent.

Phyllis says nothing, as if she hasn't heard me, and just looks morose and steps out of the way, hugging her arms as I head for the pink door, feeling oddly jaunty with the breeze at my back.

I half tap, half push on the door, which is ajar. It's dark and warm inside and smells like roach dope and Phyllis's coconut shampoo. "Howzit goin' in here?" I say into the gloom, my voice, if not full of confidence, at least half full of false confidence. The door to a lighted bathroom is open; a suitcase and some strewn clothes are on top of an unmade bed. I have the feeling Joe might be on the crapper and I may have to conduct a serious conversation about housing possibilities with him there.

Though I make him out then. He's sitting in a big plastic-covered recliner chair back in a shadowed corner between the bed and the curtained window where I saw his face before. He's wearing—I can make out—turquoise flip-flops, tight silver Mylar-looking stretch shorts and some sort of singlet muscle shirt. His short, meaty arms are on the recliner's arms, his feet on the elevated footrest and his head firmly back on the cushion, so that he looks like an astronaut waiting for the first big G thrust to drive him into oblivion.

"*Sooou,*" Joe says meanly in his Aliquippa accent. "You got a house you want to sell me? Some dump?"

"Well, I do think I've got something you ought to see, Joe, I really do." I am just addressing the room, not specifically Joe. I would sell a house to anyone who happened to be here.

"Like what?" Joe is unmoving in his spaceship chair.

"Well. Like pre-war," I say, trying to bring back to memory what Joe wants in a house. "A yard on the side and in back and in front too. Mature plantings. Inside, I think you'll like it." I've never been inside, of course. My info comes from the rap sheet. Though I may have driven past with an agents' cavalcade, in which case you can pretty well guess about the inside.

"It's just your shitty job to say that, Bascombe." Joe has never called me "Bascombe" before, and I don't like it. Joe, I notice, has the beginnings of an aggressive little goatee encircling his small red mouth, which makes it seem both smaller and redder, as though it served some different function. Joe's muscle shirt, I also see, has *Potters Do It With Their Fingers* stenciled on the front. It's clear he and Phyllis are suffering some pronounced personality and appearance alterations—not that unusual in advanced stages of house hunting.

I'm self-conscious peeking in the dark doorway with the warm, blustery storm breeze whipping at my backside. I wish Joe would just get the hell on with what we're all here for.

"D'you know what *I* want?" Joe's begun to fiddle for something on the table beside him—a package of generic cigarettes. As far as I know, Joe hasn't been a smoker until this morning. He lights up now though, using a cheap little plastic lighter, and blows a huge cloud of smoke into the dark. I'm certain Joe considers himself a ladies' man in this outfit.

"I thought you came down here to buy a house," I say.

"What I want is for reality to set in," Joe says in a smug voice, setting his lighter down. "I've been kidding myself about all this bullshit down here. The whole goddamn mess. I feel like my whole goddamn life has been in behalf of bullshit. I figured it out this morning while I was taking a dump. You don't get it, do you?"

"What's that?" Holding this conversation with Joe is like consulting a cut-rate oracle (something I in fact once did).

"You think your life's leading someplace, Bascombe. You *do* think that way. But I saw myself this morning. I closed the door to the head and there I was in the mirror, looking straight at myself in my most human moment in this bottom-feeder motel I wouldn't have taken a whore to when I was in college, just about to go look at some house I would never have wanted to live in in a hundred years. Plus, I'm taking a fucked-up job just to be able to afford it. That's something, isn't it? There's a sweet scenario."

"You haven't seen the house yet." I glance back and see that Phyllis has climbed into the back seat of my car before the rain starts but is staring at me through the windshield. She's worried Joe's scotching their last chance at a good house, which he may be.

Big, noisy splats of warm rain all at once begin thumping the car roof. The wind gusts up dirty. It is truly a bad day for a showing, since ordinary people don't buy houses in a rainstorm.

Joe takes a big, theatrical drag on his generic and funnels smoke expertly out his nostrils. "Is it a Haddam address?" he asks (ever a prime consideration).

I'm briefly bemused by Joe's belief that I'm a man who believes life's leading someplace. I *have* thought that way other times in life, but one of the fundamental easements of the Existence Period is not letting whether it is or whether it isn't worry you—as loony as that might be. "No," I say, recollecting myself. "It's not. It's in Penns Neck."

"I see." Joe's stupid half-bearded red mouth rises and lowers in the dark. "Penns Neck. I live in Penns Neck, New Jersey. What does that mean?"

"I don't know," I say. "Nothing, I guess, if you don't want it to." (Or better yet if the bank doesn't want you to, or if you've got a mean Chapter 7 lurking in your portfolio, or a felony conviction, or too many late payments on your Trinitron, or happen to enjoy the services of a heart valve. In that case it's back to Vermont.) "I've shown you a lot of houses, Joe," I say, "and you haven't liked any of them. But I don't think you'd say I tried to force you into any of them."

"You don't offer advice, is that it?" Joe is still cemented to his lounge chair, where he obviously feels in a powerful command modality.

"Well. Shop around for a mortgage," I say. "Get a foundation inspection. Don't budget more than you can pay. Buy low, sell high. The rest isn't really my business."

"Right," Joe says, and smirks. "I know who pays your salary."

"You can always offer six percent less than asking. That's up to you. I'll still get paid, though."

Joe takes another drastic slag-down on his weed. "You know, I like to have a view of things from above," he says, absolutely mysteriously.

"Great," I say. Behind me, air is changing rapidly with the rain, cooling my back and neck as the front passes by. A sweet rain aroma envelops me. Thunder is rumbling over Route 1.

"You remember what I said when you first came in here?"

"You said something about reality setting in. That's all I remember." I'm staring at him impatiently through the murk, in his flip-flops and Mylar shorts. Not your customary house-hunting attire. I take a surreptitious look at my watch. Nine-thirty.

"I've completely quit becoming," Joe says, and actually smiles. "I'm not out on the margins where new discoveries take place anymore."

"I think that's probably too severe, Joe. You're not doing plasma research, you're just trying to buy a house. You know, it's my experience that it's when you don't think you're making progress that you're probably making plenty." This is a faith I in fact hold—the Existence Period notwithstanding—and one I plan to pass on to my son if I can ever get where he is, which at the moment seems out of the question.

"When I got divorced, Frank, and started trying to make pots up in East Burke, Vermont"—Joe crosses his short legs and cozies down authoritatively in his lounger—"I didn't have the foggiest idea about what I was doing. Okay? I was out of control, actually. But things just worked out. Same when Phyllis and I got together—just slammed into each other one day. But I'm not out of control anymore."

"Maybe you are more than you think, Joe."

"Nope. I'm *in* control way too much. That's the problem."

"I think you're confusing things you're already sure about, Joe. All this has been pretty stressful on you."

"But I'm on the verge of something here, I think. That's the important part."

"Of what?" I say. "I think you're going to find this Houlihan house pretty interesting." Houlihan is the owner of the Penns Neck property.

"I don't mean *that*." He pops both his chunky little fists on the plastic armrests. Joe may be verging on a major disorientation here—a legitimate rent in the cloth. This actually appears in textbooks: Client abruptly begins to see the world in some entirely new way he feels certain, had he only seen it earlier, would've directed him down a path of vastly greater happiness—only (and this, of course, is the insane part) he inexplicably senses that way's still open to him; that the past, just this once, doesn't operate the way it usually operates. Which is to say, irrevocably. Oddly enough, only home buyers in the low to middle range have these delusions, and for the most part all they bring about is trouble.

Joe suddenly bucks up out of his chair and goes slappety-slap through the dark little room, taking big puffs on his cigarette, looking into the bathroom, then crossing and peeping out between the curtains to where Phyllis waits in my car. He then turns like an undersized gorilla in a cage and stalks past the TV to the bathroom door, his back to me, and stares out the frosted, louvered window that reveals the dingy motel rear alley, where there's a blue garbage lugger, full to brimming with white PVC piping, which I sense Joe finds significant. Our talk now has the flavor of a hostage situation.

"What do you think you mean, Joe?" I say, because I detect that what he's looking for, like anybody on the skewers of dilemma, is *sanction:* agreement from beyond himself. A nice house he could both afford and fall in love with the instant he sees it could be a perfect sanction, a sign some community recognizes him in the only way communities ever recognize anything: financially (tactfully expressed as a matter of compatibility).

"What I mean, Bascombe," Joe says, leaning against the doorjamb and staring pseudo-casually through the bathroom at the blue load lugger (the mirror where he's caught himself on the can must be just behind the door), "is that the reason we haven't bought a house in four months is that I don't *want* to goddamned buy one. And the reason for that is I don't want to get trapped in some shitty life I'll never get out of except by dying." Joe swivels toward me—a small, round man with hirsute butcher's arms and a little sorcerer's beard, who's come to the sudden precipice of what's left of life a little quicker than he knows how to cope with. It's not what I was hoping for, but anyone could appreciate his predicament.

"It *is* a big decision, Joe," I say, wanting to sound sympathetic. "If you buy a house, you own it. That's for sure."

"So are you giving up on me? Is that it?" Joe says this with a mean sneer, as if he's observed now what a shabby piece of realty dreck I am, only interested in the ones that sell themselves. He is probably indulging in the idyll of what it'd be like to be a realtor himself, and what superior genius strategies he'd choose to get his point across to a crafty, interesting, hard-nut-to-crack guy like Joe Markham. This is another well-documented sign, but a good one: when your client begins to see things as a realtor, half the battle's won.

My wish of course is that after today Joe will spend a sizable portion if not every minute of his twilight years in Penns Neck, NJ, and it's even possible he believes it'll happen, himself. My job, therefore, is to keep him on the rails—to supply sanction *pro tempore,* until I get him into a buy-sell agreement and cinch the rest of his life around him like a saddle on a bucking horse. Only it's not that simple, since Joe at the moment is feeling isolated and scared through no fault of anyone but him. So that what I'm counting on is the phenomenon by which most people will feel they're not being strong-armed if they're simply allowed to advocate (as stupidly as they please) the position opposite the one they're really taking. This is just another way we create the fiction that we're in control of anything.

"I'm not giving up on you, Joe," I say, feeling a less pleasant dampness on my back now and inching forward into the room. Traffic noise is being softened by the rain. "I just go about selling houses the way I'd want one sold to me. And if I bust my ass showing you property, setting up appointments, checking out this and that till I'm purple in the face, then you suddenly back out, I'll be ready to say you made the right decision if I believe it."

"Do you believe it this time?" Joe is still sneering, but not quite as much. He senses we're getting to the brassier tacks now, where I take off my realtor's hat and let him know what's right and what's wrong in the larger sphere, which he can then ignore.

"I sense your reluctance pretty plainly, Joe."

"Right," Joe says adamantly. "If you feel like you're tossing your life in the ter-let, why go through with it, right?"

"You'll have plenty more opportunities before you're finished."

"Yup," Joe says. I hazard another look toward Phyllis, whose mushroom head is in motionless silhouette inside my car. The glass has already fogged up from her heavy body exhalations. "These things aren't easy," he says, and tosses his stubby cigarette directly into the toilet he was no doubt referring to.

"If we're not going to do this, we better get Phyllis out of the car before she suffocates in there," I say. "I've got some other things to do today. I'm going away with my son for the holiday."

"I didn't know you had a son," Joe says. He, of course, has never asked me one question about me in four months, which is fine, since it's not his business.

"And a daughter. They live in Connecticut with their mother." I smile a friendly, not-your-business smile.

"Oh yeah."

"Let me get Phyllis," I say. "She'll need a little talking to by you, I think."

"Okay, but let me just ask one thing." Joe crosses his short arms and leans against the doorjamb, feigning even greater casualness. (Now that he's off the hook, he has the luxury of getting back on it of his own free and misunderstood will.)

"Shoot."

"What do you think's going to happen to the realty market?"

"Short term? Long term?" I'm acting ready to go.

"Let's say short."

"Short? More of the same's my guess. Prices are soft. Lenders are pretty retrenched. I expect it to last the summer, then rates'll probably bump up around ten-nine or so after Labor Day. Course, if one high-priced house sells way under market, the whole structure'll adjust overnight and we'll all have a field day. It's pretty much a matter of perception out there."

Joe stares at me, trying to act as though he's mulling this over and fitting his own vital data into some new mosaic. Though if he's smart he's also thinking about the cannibalistic financial forces gnashing and churning the world he's claiming he's about to march back into—instead of buying a house, fixing his costs onto a thirty-year note and situating his small brood behind its solid wall. "I see," he says sagely, nodding his fuzzy little chin. "And what about the long term?"

I take another stagy peek at Phyllis, though I can't see her now. Possibly she's started hitchhiking down Route 1 to Baltimore.

"The long term's less good. For you, that is. Prices'll jump after the first of the year. That's for sure. Rates'll spurt up. Property really doesn't go down in the Haddam area as a whole. All boats pretty much rise on a rising whatever." I smile at him blandly. In realty, all boats most certainly *do* rise on a rising whatever. But it's still being right that makes you rich.

Joe, I'm sure, has been brooding all over again this morning about his whopper miscues—miscues about marriage, divorce, remarriage, letting Dot marry a Hell's Commando, whether he should've quit teaching trig in Aliquippa, whether he should've joined the Marines and right now be getting out with a fat pension and qualifying for a VA loan. All this is a natural part of the aging process, in which you find yourself with less to do and more opportunities to eat your guts out regretting everything you *have* done. But Joe doesn't want to make another whopper, since one more big one might just send him to the bottom.

Except he doesn't know bread from butter beans about which is the fatal miscue and which is the smartest idea he ever had.

"Frank, I've just been standing here thinking," he says, and peers back out the dirty bathroom louvers as if he'd heard someone call his name. Joe may at this moment be close to deciding what he actually thinks. "Maybe I need a new way to look at things."

"Maybe you ought to try looking at things across a flat plain, Joe," I say. "I've always thought that looking at things from above, like you said, forced you to see all things as the same height and made decisions a lot harder. Some things are just bigger than others. Or smaller. And I think another thing too."

"What's that?" Joe's brows give the appearance of knitting together. He is vigorously trying to fit my "viewpoint" metaphor into his own current predicament of homelessness.

"It really won't hurt you to take a quick run over to this Penns Neck house. You're already down here. Phyllis is in the car, scared to death you're not going to look at it."

"Frank, what do you think about me?" Joe says. At some point of dislocatedness, this is what all clients start longing to know. Though it's almost always insincere and finally meaningless, since once their business is over they go right back to thinking you're either a crook or a moron. Realty is not a friendly business. It only seems to be.

"Joe, I may just queer my whole deal here," I say, "but what I think is you've done your best to find a house, you've stuck to your principles, you've put up with anxiety as long as you know how. You've acted responsibly, in other words. And if this Penns Neck house is anywhere close to what you like, I think you ought to take the plunge. Quit hanging onto the side of the pool."

"Yeah, but you're paid to think that, though," Joe says, sulky again in the bathroom door. "Right?"

But I'm ready for him. "Right. And if I can get you to spend a hundred and fifty on this house, then I can quit working and move to Kitzbühel, and you can thank me by sending me a bottle of good gin at Christmas because you're not freezing your nuts off in a barn while Sonja gets further behind in school and Phyllis files fucking divorce papers on you because you can't make up your mind."

"Point taken," Joe says, moodily.

"I really don't want to go into it any further," I say. There's no place further to go, of course, realty being not a very complex matter. "I'm going to take Phyllis on up to Penns Neck, Joe. And if she likes it we'll come get you and you can make up your mind. If she doesn't I'll bring her back anyway. It's a win-win proposition. In the meantime you can stay here and look at things from above."

Joe stares at me guiltily. "Okay, I'll just come along." He virtually blurts this out, having apparently blundered into the sanction he was looking for: the win-win, the sanction not to be an idiot. "I've come all this fucking way."

With my damp right arm I give a quick thumbs-up wave out to Phyllis, who I hope is still in the car.

Joe begins picking up change off the dresser top, stuffing a fat wallet into the tight waistband of his shorts. "I should let you and Phyllis figure this whole goddamn thing out and follow along like a goddamn pooch."

"You're still looking at things from above." I smile at Joe across the dark room.

"You just see everything from the fucking middle, that's all," Joe says, scratching his bristly, balding head and looking around the room as though he'd forgotten something. I have no idea what he means by this and am fairly sure he couldn't explain it either. "If I died right now, you'd go on about your business."

"What else should I do?" I say. "I'd be sorry I hadn't sold you a house, though. I promise you that. Because you at least could've died at home instead of in the Sleepy Hollow."

"Tell it to my widow out there," Joe Markham says, and stalks by me and out the door, leaving me to pull it shut and to get out to my car before I'm soaked to my toes. All this for the sake of what? A sale.

from **A MOTHER'S KISSES**

Bruce Jay Friedman

"**G**et close to your father," Joseph's mother said to him. "This is a good time for it."

The father was a quiet man who worked on sectional couches. One morning Joseph awakened early to accompany him to his plant, crusty-eyed, dressing glumly in the dusk, feeling he was going to a hospital. His father stopped at the corner to buy a newspaper and said, "I buy a paper here." In the subway car he said, "I usually stand at this end and hold on to a strap."

He took Joseph up to a great gray loft full of couch skeletons, steering him directly over to a machine. "This cuts couches," he said to Joseph. He flipped it on, letting it slice a piece of couch in half.

"It's plenty sharp, isn't it? I use that machine a lot. If you go over and fool around with it, I'll smack you."

When they had taken off their coats, Joseph's father went right to work, spreading a large piece of paper on a table and writing on it. "I draw up my couch on this and then I do the couch right next to the table here."

His father's boss came over then and put his hand on Joseph's shoulder, his eyes at the ceiling.

"What do you want to be when you're ready?" he asked, looking past Joseph to the end of the loft.

"I don't think I want to be in couch work," said Joseph.

The boss seemed greatly relieved. He began to dart about excitedly, finally picking up a piece of leather and handing it to Joseph. "Here, kid," he said. "Keep it. Take it home with you." Then he said to Joseph's father, "You got a nice son there. Smart boy."

Joseph's father worked a while on his paper, then said, "The fellow I'm going to bring over now, I'm the boss of him."

A terribly round-shouldered Greek man approached. "This is Freddy," Joseph's father said. "He works for me."

The man gave Joseph a wringing-wet hand. "Hi, kid. I work for your dad."

When the man walked away, Joseph's father whispered, "He only makes ninety-eight a week. Imagine that."

At lunchtime, Joseph and his father had a sandwich at a crowded counter nearby. The older man tossed down his last few bites, then began to walk briskly back toward his office, finally breaking into a trot. "I only take a fast bite," he said to Joseph, who was trotting by his side. When he got back to the loft, the father flung off his coat, looking warily about him, then buried his head in his planning paper. At the end of the day, closing up the loft, Joseph's father locked the front door and said, "I've been in the couch game for twenty-seven years." Then on the subway, he said to Joseph, "Now is when I read my paper."

from **SOMETHING HAPPENED**

Joseph Heller

And where would I be if that happened?

Andy Kagle, as head of our Sales Department, has a very powerful position with the company and is now afraid of losing it.

He may be right. His name is all wrong. (Half wrong. Andrew is all right, but Kagle?) So are his clothes. He shows poor judgment in colors and styles, as well as in fabrics, and his suits and coats and shirts do not fit him well enough. He moves to madras and paisley months after others have gone to linen or hopsack or returned to worsted and seersucker. He wears terrible brown shoes with *fleur-de-lis* perforations. He wears anklets (and I want to scream or kick him when I see his shin). Kagle is a stocky man of less than middle height and was born with a malformation of the hip and leg (which also doesn't help his image much); he walks with a slight limp.

Kagle has ability and experience, but they don't count anymore. What does count is that he has no tone. His manners are not good. He lacks wit (his wisecracks are bad, and so are the jokes he tells) and did not go to college, and he does not mix smoothly enough with people who did go to college. He knows he is awkward. He is not a hearty extrovert; he is a nervous extrovert, the worst kind (especially to other nervous extroverts), and so he may be doomed.

Kagle is one of those poor fellows who started at the bottom and worked his way up, and it shows. He is a self-made man and unable to hide it. He knows he doesn't fit, but he doesn't know when he doesn't or why, or how to alter himself so that he will fit in as well as he should. Gauche is what he is, and gauche is what he knows he is (although he is so gauche he doesn't even know what the word *gauche* means, but Green does, and so do I). He has a good record as head of sales, but that hardly matters. (Nothing damages us much any more.) He thinks it counts. He really thinks that what he does is more important than what he is, but I know he's wrong and that the beautiful Countess Consuelo Crespi (if there is such a thing) will always matter more than Albert Einstein, Madame Curie, Thomas Alva Edison, Andy Kagle, and me.

Kagle is a church-going Lutheran with a strong anti-Catholic bias that he confides to me in smirking, bitter undertones when we are alone. He begins small meetings at which Catholic salesmen are present with joking references to the Pope in an effort to radiate an attitude of camaraderie. The jokes are bad, and nobody laughs. I have advised him to stop. He says he will. He doesn't. He seems compelled.

Kagle is not comfortable with people on his own level or higher. He tends to sweat on his forehead and upper lip, and to bubble in the corners of his mouth. He feels he doesn't belong with them. He is not much at ease with people who work for him. He tries to pass himself off as one of them. This is a gross (and gauche) mistake, for his salesmen and branch managers don't want him to identify with them. To them, he is management; and they know that they are nearly wholly at his mercy, with the exception of the several salesmen below him from very good families above him who do mingle smoothly with higher executives in the company who have *him* at *their* mercy, making him feel trapped and squeezed in between.

Kagle relies on Johnny Brown, whom he fears and distrusts, to keep the salesmen in line (to be the bad guy for him). And Brown does this job efficiently and with great relish. (Brown is related to Black, by his marriage to Black's niece.) Brown's success in scaring the salesmen merely strengthens Kagle's insecurity and weakens his sense of control. Kagle is convinced that Brown is after his job, but he lacks the courage to confront Brown, transfer him, or fire him. Kagle (wisely) avoids a showdown with Brown, who is blunt and belligerent with almost everybody, especially in the afternoon if he's been drinking at lunch. Kagle would rather go out of town on an unnecessary business trip than have a showdown here with anybody about anything, and he usually manufactures excuses for travel whenever his problems here or at home with his wife and children build toward a crisis he wants other people to settle. He hopes they'll be over by the time he returns, and they usually are.

With the exception of Brown (whom Kagle hates, fears, and distrusts, and can do nothing about), Kagle tries to like everyone who works for him and to have everyone like him. He is reluctant to discipline his salesmen or reprimand them, even when he (or Brown) catches them cheating on their expense accounts or lying about their sales calls or business trips. (Kagle lies about his own business trips and, like the rest of us, probably cheats at least a little on his expense accounts.) He is unwilling to get rid of people, even those who turn drunkard, like Red Parker, or useless in other ways. This is one of the criticisms heard about him frequently. (It is occasionally made against him by the same people other people want him to get rid of.) He won't, for example, retire Ed Phelps, who wants to hang on. ("I'd throw half those lying sons of bitches right out on their ass," Brown enjoys bragging out loud to me and Kagle about Kagle's sales force, as though challenging Kagle to do the same. "And I'd put the other half of those lazy bastards on notice.")

Kagle wants desperately to be popular with all the "lying sons of bitches" and "lazy bastards" who work for him, even the clerks, receptionists, and typists, and goes out of his way to make conversation with them; as a result, they despise him. The more they despise him, the better he tries to be to them; the better he is to them, the more they despise him. There are days when his despair is so heavy that he seems almost incapable of stirring from his office or allowing anyone (but me) in to see him. He keeps his door shut for long periods of time, skips lunch entirely rather than allow even his secretary to deliver it, and does everything he can by telephone.

Kagle is comfortable with me (even on his very bad days), and I am comfortable with him. Sometimes he sends for me just to have me confirm or deny rumors he has heard (or made up) and help dispel his anxieties and shame. I do not test or threaten him; I pose no problem; on the contrary, he knows I aid him (or try to) in handling the problems created by others. Kagle trusts me and knows he is safe with me. Kagle doesn't scare me any longer. (In fact, I feel that I could scare him whenever I chose to, that he is weak in relation to me and that I am strong in relation to him, and I have this hideous urge every now and then while he is confiding in me to shock him suddenly and send him reeling forever with some brutal, unexpected insult, or to kick his crippled leg. It's a weird mixture of injured rage and cruel loathing that starts to rise within me and has to be suppressed, and I don't know where it comes from or how long I will be able to master it.) Kagle has lost faith in himself; this could be damaging, for people here, like people everywhere, have little pity for failures, and no affection.

I have pity for Kagle (as though I have already delivered my insult or kicked him in his deformed leg viciously—I know it will happen sooner or later, the wish is sometimes so strong), as I have pity for myself. I am sorry for him because he is basically a decent person, if not especially dazzling or admirable. I do worry and sympathize with him often, because he has been good to me from the day I came to work here for Green, and is good to me still. He makes my job easier. He relies on my judgment, takes my word, and backs me up in disputes I have with his salesmen. Many of his salesmen, particularly the new ones, hold me in some kind of awe because they sense I operate under his protection. (A number of the old ones who are not doing well hold me to blame, I'm sure, for having helped bring them to ruin.) Invariably in these disagreements with his salesmen, I am right and they are wrong. I am patient, practical, rational, while they are emotional and insistent. It is easy for me to be practical and rational in these situations because I am not the least bit endangered by the business problems that threaten *them*.

Kagle often comments jokingly to Arthur Baron and other important people, sometimes even in my presence, that I would be much better in Green's job than Green is; Kagle does this with a gleam of mischief if I am there, because I have begged him not to. I am not certain if Kagle really believes I would be better than Green or is merely making an amiable gesture that he thinks will honor me and get back to Green to irritate and concern him. Because Andy Kagle is good to me and doesn't scare me any longer, I despise him a little bit too.

I try my best to conceal it (although I am often surprised to discover a harder edge to my sarcasms and admonitions than I intended. There is something cankered and terrifying inside me that wishes to burst out and demolish him, lame and imperfect as he is). I try my best to help and protect him in just about every way I can. I am the one who even offers regularly to carry censures and instructions from him to Johnny Brown that he shrinks from delivering himself, although I will never risk anything with Brown after lunch if I can possibly avoid it. Along with everyone else who knows Brown, I endeavor to steer clear of him after lunch (unless I need him on my side in an argument with someone else), when he is apt to be red-eyed and irritable with drink and in a contrary, bellicose mood. Brown in a bad temper with whiskey working inside him always gives the clear impression that he is eager for a fist fight. And there is no doubt that with his deep chest, sturdy shoulders, and thick, powerful hands, he can handle himself in one. And there is also no doubt that Brown is usually right.

The current (and recurrent) antagonism between Kagle and Brown is over call reports again. The salesmen are reluctant to fill out these small printed pink, blue, and white forms (pink for prospects, blue for active, and white for formerly active; that is, accounts that have lapsed and are therefore prospects again, though not necessarily lively ones) describing with some hope and detail the sales calls they have made (or allege they have made). The salesmen are reluctant to come to grips with any kind of paperwork more elaborate than writing out order forms; they especially hate to fill out their expense account reports and fall weeks, sometimes months, behind. The salesmen know beforehand that most of the information they will have to supply in their call reports will be false. Brown maintains that call reports are a waste of everybody's time, and he is reluctant to compel the salesmen to fill them out. Kagle is afraid of Brown, and he is reluctant to compel Brown to compel the salesmen to fill them out.

But Arthur Baron wants the call reports. Arthur Baron has no other way of keeping familiar with what the salesmen are up to (or say they are) and a no more reliable source of knowledge on which to base his own decisions and reports, even though he is certainly aware that most of the knowledge on which he bases his decisions and prepares his own reports is composed of lies.

I try to keep out of it and expel an air of innocence and sympathetic understanding to all concerned. I would rather sit here in my office writing, doodling, flirting on the telephone with Jane, or talking to a good girl named Penny I've known a long time, or classifying people in the company and constructing my Happiness Charts, than get mixed up in this one. I don't care about the call reports and don't have to. The matter is trivial; yet, it seems to be one of those trivial matters that might destroy a person or two, and I don't see how I can gain favor with one person in this situation without losing favor with another. So, prudently, I contrive to keep as far away from it as I can, although I *will* manage to mention every now and then to a salesman I happen to be with on some other business that Kagle, Brown, or Arthur Baron has been asking about his call reports and that it is extremely urgent they be handed in as soon as possible for prompt study and evaluation. (I don't manage to mention—and never would—that I think they're a waste of everybody's time but mine.)

In this and other small ways I do what I can to be of help to Kagle (and Brown) (and Arthur Baron). I give him advice and I bring him gossip and news and portents from other parts of the company that I think will be of value or concern to him.

"What do you hear?" he wants to know.

"About what?"

"You know."

"What do you mean?"

"Jesus Christ," he complains, "you used to be truthful with me. Now I can't even trust you, either."

"What are you talking about?"

"I hear that I'm out and Brown's in, and that you probably know all about it. I was tipped off in Denver."

"You're full of shit."

"I like your honesty."

"I like yours."

Kagle grins mechanically, sardonically, and moves with his slight limp across the carpet of his office to close the door. I smile back at him and settle smugly into his brown leather armchair. I always feel very secure and very superior when I'm sitting inside someone's office with the door closed and other people, perhaps Kagle or Green or Brown, are doing all the worrying on the outside about what's going on inside. Kagle has a large, lush corner office in which he seems out of place. He looks nervous and tries to smile as he comes back and sits down behind his desk.

"Seriously, you hear everything," he says to me. "Haven't you heard anything?"

"About what?"

"About me."

"No."

"The grapevine says I'm finished. They're going to listen to Green and Horace White and get rid of me. Brown's got the job."

"Who told you that?"

"I can't name names. But I was tipped off by people in Denver who passed it along to me in strictest confidence. It's true. You can take my word for it."

"You're full of shit again."

"No, I'm not."

"There's nobody in our Denver office who would know something like that or tip you off about it if they did."

"Only about the Denver part. The rest is true."

"You tell terrible lies," I say. "You tell the worst lies of anybody in the whole business. I don't see how you ever made it as a salesman."

Kagle grins for an instant to acknowledge my humor and then turns glum again.

"Brown tells you things," he says. "Hasn't he given any hints?"

"No." I shake my head. (Everybody seems to think I know everything. "You know everything," Brown said to me. "What's going on?" "I didn't even know there was anything going on," I answered. Jane asked: "What's going on? Are they really getting rid of the whole Art Department?" "I wouldn't *let* them get rid of you, honey," I answered. "Even if I had to pay your salary myself.")

I shake my head again. "And it's probably not true. They'd never put Brown in. He fights with everybody."

"Then you *have* heard something," Kagle exclaims.

"No, I haven't."

"Who would they put in?"

"Nobody. Andy, why don't you stop all this horseshit and buckle down to your job if you're so really worried? If you're really so worried, why don't you start doing the things you're supposed to do?"

"What am I supposed to do?"

"The things you're supposed to do. Stop trying to be such a

good guy to all the people who work for you. You ain't succeeding, and nobody wants you to be. You're a member of management now. Your sales force is your enemy, not your buddy, and you're supposed to be theirs and drive them like slaves. Brown is right."

"I don't like Brown."

"He knows his business. Make Ed Phelps retire."

"No."

"That's what Horace White wants you to do."

"Phelps is an old man now. He wants to stay."

"That's why you have to force him out."

"His son was divorced last year. His daughter-in-law just took his granddaughter away to Seattle. He might never see the little girl again."

"That's all very sad."

"How much does it cost the company to keep him on, even if he doesn't do anything?"

"Very little."

"Then why should I make him retire?"

(Kagle is right, here, and I like him enormously for his determination to let Phelps stay. Phelps is old and will soon be dead, anyway, or too sick to continue.)

"Because he's past the official retirement age. And Horace White wants you to."

"I don't like Horace White," Kagle observes softly, irrelevantly. "And he doesn't like me."

"He knows his business also," I point out.

"How can I tell it to Ed Phelps?" Kagle wants to know. "What could I say to him? Will you do it for me? It's not so easy, is it?"

"Get Brown to do it," I suggest.

"No."

"It's part of *your* job, not mine."

"But it's not so easy, is it?"

"That's why they pay you so much."

"I don't get so much," he disgresses almost automatically, "what with taxes and all."

"Yes, you do. And stop traveling all the time. Nobody likes that. What the hell were you doing in Denver all this week when there's nothing going on there and you're supposed to be here organizing the next convention and working on your sales projections?"

"I've got Ed Phelps working on the convention."

"A lot he'll do."

"And my sales projections are always wrong."

"So what? At least they're done."

"What else?"

"Play more golf. Talk to Red Parker and buy a blue blazer. Buy better suits. Wear a jacket in the office and keep your shirt collar buttoned and your necktie up tight around your neck where it belongs. Jesus, look at you right now. You're supposed to be a distinguished white-collar executive."

"Don't take the name of the Lord in vain," he jokes.

"Don't you."

"I've got a good sales record," he argues.

"Have you got a good sports jacket?" I demand.

"Jesus Christ, what does a good sports jacket matter?"

"More than your good sales record. Nobody wears jackets with round leather patches on the elbows to the office, unless it's on a weekend. Get black shoes for your blue and gray suits. And stop driving into the city in your station wagon."

"Okay," he gives in with a gloomy, chastised smile and exhales a long, low whistle of mock surprise and resignation. "You win." He gets up slowly and moves toward the coat rack in the corner of his office for his jacket. "I promise. I'll get a blue blazer."

It will be too big—I can see it in advance—and hang over his shoulders and sag sloppily around his chest, and he will probably get his worsted blue blazer just about the time the rest of us have switched to mohair or shantung or back to madras, plaids, and seersucker. It is already too late for him, I suspect; I suspect it is no longer in his power (if it ever was in his power) to change himself to everyone's satisfaction. For the moment, though (while I am still with him), he makes an effort: he buttons his shirt collar, and slides tight to his neck the knot of his tie, and puts on his jacket. It is a terrible jacket of coarse, imitation tweed, with oval suede patches at the elbows.

"Better?" he wants to know.

"Not much."

"I'll throw out these brown shoes."

"That will help."

"How's Green treating you these days?" he asks casually.

"Pretty good," I reply. "Why?"

"If you were in my department," he offers with a cagey, more confident air, and the beginnings of a mischievous smile, "I would let you make as many speeches as you want to at the next convention. The salesmen are always very interested in the work you're doing for them and what you have to say."

"So long," I answer. "I'll see you around."

We both laugh, because we each know what the other wants and where the fears and sore spots are. Kagle knows I want to keep my job and be allowed to make a speech at the next company convention. (God dammit—it would be an honor and an act of recognition, even if it is only three minutes, and I've earned it and I want it, and that's all!) And I know that Kagle wants my help in defending himself against Green (and Brown) (and Black) (and White) (and Arthur Baron, as well).

"You'll let me know if you do hear anything, won't you?" he asks, as we walk to the door.

"Of course I will," I assure him.

"But don't ask questions," he cautions with a dark, moody snicker. "You might give them the idea."

We laugh.

And we are both still chuckling when Kagel opens the door of his office and we find my secretary outside talking to his secretary.

"Oh, Mr. Slocum," she sings out cheerily, because that is her way, and I wish I were rid of her. "Mr. Baron wants to see you right away."

Kagle pulls me to the side. "What does he want?" he asks with alarm.

"How should I know?"

"Go see him."

"What did you think I was going to do?"

"And come and tell me if he says anything about getting rid of me."

"Sure."

"You will, won't you?"

"Of course I will. For Christ sakes, Andy, can't you trust me?"

"Where are *you* going?" Green wants to know, as I pass him in the corridor on my way to Arthur Baron's office.

"Arthur Baron wants to see me."

Green skids to a stop with a horrified glare; and it's all I can do not to laugh in his face.

"What does he want with *you?*" Green wants to know.

"I haven't any idea."

"You'd better go see him."

"I thought of doing that."

"Don't be so God-damned sarcastic," Green snaps back at me angrily, and I lower my eyes, abashed and humbled by his vehemence. "I'm not even sure I trust *you,* either."

"I'm sorry, Jack," I mumble. "I didn't intend that to sound rude."

"You come see me as soon as you've finished talking to him," he orders. "I want to know what he says. I want to know if I'm being fired or not."

"What was Kagle talking to you about?" Brown asks when I bump into him.

"He wanted to know what you were up to while he was away in Denver."

"I was correcting his mistakes and protecting his God-damned job, that was what I was up to," Brown retorts.

"That's just what I told him."

"You're a liar," Brown tells me pleasantly.

"Johnny, that's what they pay me for."

"But everybody knows it . . ."

"So?"

" . . . so I guess it doesn't matter."

"A diplomat, Johnny. Not a liar."

"Yeah, a diplomat," Brown agrees with a gruff and hearty laugh. "You lying son of a bitch."

"I was just coming to see you," Jane says to me. "I want to show you this layout."

I stare brazenly at her tits. "I can see your layout." She starts to giggle and blush deliciously, but I turn serious. "Not now, Jane. I have to go see Arthur Baron."

"Oh, hello, Mr. Slocum," Arthur Baron's secretary says to me. "How are you?"

"You look fine today."

The door to Arthur Baron's office is closed, and I don't know how to cope with it, whether to turn the knob and go right in or knock diffidently and wait to be asked. But Arthur Baron's twenty-eight-year-old secretary, who is fond of me and having trouble with her husband (he's probably queer), nods encouragingly and motions me to go right through. I turn the knob gingerly and open the door. Arthur Baron sits alone at his desk and greets me with a smile. He rises and comes forward slowly to shake my hand. He is always very cordial to me (and everyone) and always very gentle and considerate. Yet I am always afraid of him. He's got the whammy on me, I guess (just as everyone I've ever worked for in my whole life has had the whammy on me), and I guess he always will.

"Hello, Bob," he says.

"Hi, Art."

"Come in." He closes the door noiselessly.

"Sure."

"How are you, Bob?"

"Fine, Art. You?"

"I want you to begin preparing yourself," he tells me, "to re-place Andy Kagle."

"Kagle?" I ask.

"Yes."

"Not Green?"

"No." Arthur Baron smiles, knowledgeable and reassuring. "We don't really think you're ready for Green's job yet."

There is polite irony here, for we both know that Kagle's job is bigger and more important than Green's, and that Green would be subordinate to Kagle if Kagle were of stronger character. The proposition stuns me, and for a few bewildered seconds I have absolutely no idea what to say or do or what expression to keep on my face. Arthur Baron watches me steadily and waits.

"I've never done any real selling," I say finally, very meekly.

"We won't want you to do any," he replies. "We want you to manage. You're loyal and intelligent and you've got good character and good work habits. You seem to have a good understanding of policy and strategy, and you get along well with all kinds of people. You're diplomatic. You're perceptive and sensitive, and you seem to be a good administrator. Is that enough to encourage you?"

"Kagle's a good man, Art," I say.

"He's a good salesman, Bob," Arthur Baron replies, emphasizing the distinction. "And you'll probably be allowed to keep him on as a salesman if we decide to make the change and you decide you want to."

"I know I'd want to."

"We'll probably let you keep him as an assistant even, or as a consultant on special projects with people he'd be good with. But he hasn't been a good manager, and we don't think he's going to be able to get better. Kagle doesn't go along with the rest of us on too many things, and that's very important in his job. He lies a lot.

Horace White wants me to get rid of him just because he does tell lies to us. He still travels too much, although I've told him I want him to spend more time here. He dresses terribly. He still wears brown shoes. That shouldn't count, I know, but it does count, and he ought to know that by now. He doesn't send in my call reports."

"Most of the stuff on the call reports isn't true."

"I know that. But I have to have them anyway for my own work."

"Brown is in charge of that," I have to point out.

"He doesn't control Brown."

"That isn't easy."

"He's afraid of him."

"So am I," I admit.

"And so am I," he admits. "But I would control him or get rid of him if he worked for me. Would you?"

"Brown is married to Black's niece."

"I wouldn't let that matter. We wouldn't let Black interfere if it came to doing something about Brown."

"Would you let me fire him?"

"If you decided you really wanted to, although we'd prefer to transfer him. Kagle could have had him fired, but by now Brown has a better grasp of specifics than he has. Kagle never wants to fire anybody, even the ones who are drunks or dishonest or useless in other ways. He won't fire Parker or retire Phelps, and he doesn't cooperate with Green. And he still discriminates in the people he hires, although he's been warned about that, too."

"It's a very big job," I say.

"We think you might be able to handle it."

"If I couldn't?"

"Let's not think about that now."

"I have to," I say with a grin.

He grins back sympathetically. "We'd find another good job for you somewhere else in the company if you found you wanted to stay here, unless you did something disgraceful or dishonest, and

I'm sure that wouldn't happen. You don't have to decide now. This is just an idea of mine, and it's anything but definite, so please keep it secret. But we are trying to look ahead, and we'd like to know what we're going to do by convention time. So give it some serious thought; will you, and let me know if you would take it if we did decide to move Kagle out and give it to you. You don't have to take it if you don't want to—I promise you that—and you won't be penalized if you don't." He smiles again as he stands up and continues in a lighter tone. "You'll still get your raise this year and a good cash bonus. But we think you should. And you might just as well begin preparing yourself while you make up your mind."

"What should I do?"

"Keep close to Kagle and the salesmen and try to find out even more about everything that's happening. Decide what realistic goals to establish and what changes you would have to make to achieve them if we did put you in charge."

"I like Andy Kagle."

"So do I."

"He's been very good to me."

"It isn't your fault. We'd move him out anyway. He'll probably be happier working for you on special projects. Will you think about it?"

"Of course."

"Good. You'll keep this quiet, won't you?"

"Sure."

"Thank you, Bob."

"Thank you, Art."

"What did Arthur Baron want?" Green demands, the instant I'm out in the corridor.

"Nothing," I answer.

"Did he say anything?"

"No."

"Anything about me, I mean."

"No."

"Well, what did he say? He must have wanted to see you about something."

"He wants me to put some jokes in a speech his son has to make at school."

"Is that all?" Green snorts with contempt, satisfied. "I could do that," he sneers. "Better than you."

Up yours, I think in reply, because I know I could squash him to the ground and make him crawl like a caterpillar if I ever do find myself in Kagle's job. But he does believe me, doesn't he?

"What did Arthur Baron want?" Johnny Brown asks.

"He wants me to put some jokes in a speech his son has to make at school."

"You're still a liar."

"A diplomat, Johnny."

"But I'll find out."

"Should I start looking for another job?" asks Jane.

"I've got a job you can do, right here at hand."

"You're terrible, Mr. Slocum," she laughs, her color rising with embarrassment and pleasure. She is aglow, tempting. "You're worse than a boy."

"I'm better than a boy. Come into my office now and I'll show you. What boy that you go with has an office with a couch like mine and pills in the file cabinet?"

"I'd like to," she says (and for a second I am in terror that she will). "But Mr. Kagle is waiting for you there."

"What did Arthur Baron want?" Kagle asks as soon as I step inside my office and find him lurking anxiously in a corner there.

I close the door before I turn to look at him. He is shabby again, and I am dismayed and angry. The collar of his shirt is unbuttoned, and the knot of his tie is inches down. (For a moment, I have an impulse to seize his shirt front furiously in both fists and begin shaking some sense into him; and at exactly the same time, I have another impulse to kick him as hard as I can in the ankle or shin of his crippled leg.) His forehead is wet with beads of perspiration, and his mouth is glossy with a suggestion of spittle, and dry with the powdered white smudge of what was probably an antacid tablet.

"Nothing," I tell him.

"Didn't he say anything?"

"No. Nothing important."

"About me?"

"Not a word."

"You mean that?"

"I swear."

"Well, I'll be damned," Kagle marvels with relief. "What did he talk about? Tell me. He must have wanted to see you about something."

"He wants me to put some jokes in a speech his son has to make at school."

"Really?"

"Yeah."

"And he didn't say anything about me, anything at all?"

"No."

"Or the call reports or the trip to Denver?"

"No."

"Ha! In that case, I may be safe, you know. I might even make vice-president this year. What did he talk about?"

"Just his son. And the speech. And the jokes."

"I'm probably imagining the whole thing," he exclaims exultantly. "You know, maybe I can use those same jokes someday if one of *my* kids is ever asked to make a speech at school." He frowns, his face clouding suddenly with a distant distress. "Both my kids are no good," he reminds himself aloud abstractedly. "Especially the boy."

Kagle trusts me also. And I'm not so sure I want him to.

"Andy," I call out to him suddenly. "Why don't you play it safe? Why don't you behave? Why don't you start doing everything everybody wants you to do?"

He is startled. "Why?" he cries. "What's the matter?"

"To keep your job, that's why, if it's not too late. Why don't you start trying to go along? Stop telling lies to Horace White. Don't travel so much. Transfer Parker to another office if you can't get him to stop drinking and retire Ed Phelps."

"Did somebody say something?"

"No."

"Then how do you know all that?" he demands. "Who told you?"

"You did," I bark back at him with exasperation and disgust. "You've been telling me about all those things over and over again for months. So why don't you start doing something about them instead of worrying about them all the time and taking chances? Settle down, will you? Control Brown and cooperate with Green, and why don't you hire a Negro and a Jew?"

Kagle scowls grimly and broods in heavy silence for several seconds. I wait, wondering how much is sinking in.

"What would I do with a coon?" he asks finally, as though thinking aloud, his mind wandering.

"I don't know."

"I could use a Jew."

"Don't be too sure."

"We sell to Jews."

"They might not like it."

"But what would I do with a coon?"

"You would begin," I advise, "by finding something else to call him."

"Like what?"

"A Black. Call him a Black."

"That's funny."

"Yeah."

"I've always called them coons," Kagle says. "I was brought up to call niggers coons."

"I was brought up to call Negroes coons."

"What should I do?" he asks. "Tell me what to do."

"Grow up, Andy," I tell him earnestly, trying with all my heart now to help him. "You're a middle-aged man with two kids and a big job in a pretty big company. There's a lot that's expected of you. It's time to mature. It's time to take it seriously and start doing all the things you should be doing. You know what they are. You keep telling me what they are."

Kagle nods pensively. His brow furrows as he ponders my advice without any hint of levity. I am getting through to him. I watch him tensely as I wait for his reply. Kagle, you bastard, I want to scream at him desperately as he meditates solemnly, I am trying to help you. Say something wise. For once in your mixed-up life, come to an intelligent conclusion. It's almost as though he hears me, for he makes up his mind finally and his face brightens. He stares up at me with a slight smile and then, while I hang on his words hopefully, says:

"Let's go get laid."

The company has a policy about getting laid. It's okay.

And everybody seems to know that (although it's not spelled out in any of the personnel manuals). Talking about getting laid is even more okay than doing it, but doing it is okay too, although talking about getting laid with your own wife is never okay. (Imagine: "Boy, what a crazy bang I got from my wife last night!" That wouldn't be nice, not with gentlemen you associate with in business who might know her.) But getting laid with somebody else's wife is very okay, and so is talking about it, provided the husband is not with the company or somebody anybody knows and likes. The company is in favor of getting laid if it is done with a dash of élan, humor, vulgarity, and skill, without emotion, with girls who are young and pretty or women who are older and foreign or glamorous in some other way, without too much noise and with at least some token gesture toward discretion, and without scandal, notoriety, or any of the other serious complications of romance.

Falling in love, for example, is *not* usually okay, although marrying someone else right after a divorce is, and neither is "having an affair," at least not for a man.

Getting laid (or talking about getting laid) is an important component of each of the company conventions and a decisive consideration in the selection of a convention site; and the salesmen who succeed in getting laid there soonest are likely to turn out to be the social heroes of the convention, though not necessarily the envy. (That will depend on the quality of whom they find to get laid with.) Getting laid at conventions is usually done in groups of three or four (two decide to go out and try and take along one or two others). Just about everybody in the company gets laid (or seems to), or at least talks as though he does (or did). In fact, it has become virtually *comme il faut* at company conventions for even the very top and very old, impotent men in the company—in fact, *especially* those—to allude slyly and boastfully to their own and each other's sexual misconduct in their welcoming addresses, acknowledgments, introductions, and informal preambles to speeches on graver subjects. Getting laid is a joking matter on all levels of the company, even with people like Green and Horace White. But it's not a matter for Andy Kagle to joke about now.

"Andy, I'm serious," I say.

"So," he says, "am I."

I close the door of my office after Kagle leaves, sealing myself inside and shutting everybody else out, and try to decide what to do about my conversation with Arthur Baron. I cancel my lunch appointment and put my feet up on my desk.

I've got bad feet. I've got a jawbone that's deteriorating and someday soon I'm going to have to have all my teeth pulled. It will hurt. I've got an unhappy wife to support and two unhappy children to take care of. (I've got that other child with irremediable brain damage who is neither happy nor unhappy, and I don't know what will happen to him after we're dead.) I've got eight unhappy people working for me who have problems and unhappy dependents of their own. I've got anxiety; I suppress hysteria. I've got politics on my mind, summer race riots, drugs, violence, and teen-age sex. There are perverts and deviates everywhere who might corrupt or strangle any one of my children. I've got crime in my streets. I've got old age to face. My boy, though only nine, is already worried because he does not know what he wants to be when he grows up. My daughter tells lies. I've got the decline of American civilization and the guilt and ineptitude of the whole government of the United States to carry around on these poor shoulders of mine.

And I find I am being groomed for a better job.

And I find—God help me—that I want it.

NOW I CAN SEE THE MOON

Amy Hempel

On the last night of the marriage, my husband and I went to the ballet. We sat behind a blind man; his guide dog, in harness, lay beside him in the aisle of the theater. I could not keep my attention on the performance; instead, I watched the guide dog watch the performance. Throughout the evening, the dog's head moved, following the dancers across the stage. Every so often the dog would whimper slightly. "Because he can hear high notes we can't?" my husband said. "No," I said, "because he was disappointed in the choreography!"

I work with these dogs every day, and their capability, their decency, shames me.

I am trying not to take things personally. This on advice from the evaluator at the school for the blind where I train dogs. She had overheard me ask a Labrador retriever, "Are you *trying* to ruin my day?"

I suppose there are many things one should try not to take personally. An absence of convenient parking, inclement weather, a husband who finds that he loves someone else.

When I get low, I take a retired guide to the local hospital. Any time is good, but around the holidays is best. I will dress a handsome shepherd in a Santa suit and visit the Catholic hospital and bust in on the morning spiritual counseling. Once I heard a nun ask a patient if he was nervous about the test that was scheduled for him that afternoon, and the patient, a young man, told the nun he hadn't known there *was* a test scheduled, but now that he did, he could truthfully say that, yes, he was nervous. Then he saw "Santa" in the hallway outside his door and called, "My God! Get that dog in here!" And so we perform a service.

At work, what I technically do is *pre*-train. I do basic obedience and then some. If I am successful, and the dog has the desired temperament, a more skilled trainer will work for months to turn the dog into a guide for a blind partner. I don't know any blind people. I'm in it for the dogs. Although I remember the job interview I had before this job. I thought I might want to work in the music business, but my husband urged me in the direction of my first love, dogs. The man who would have been my employer at the record company asked me why I wanted to work there. I said, "Because I love music," and he said, "Maybe the love affair is best carried on outside the office."

"Are guide dogs happy?" asked my husband at the start. I considered this, and cited the expert who believes that an animal's happiness derives from doing his job. So in that respect, yes, I said, I would think that guide dogs are happy. "Then why do they all look like Eleanor Roosevelt?" he said.

I told him about the way they get to know you. Not the way people do, the way people flatter you by wanting to know every last thing about you, only it isn't a compliment, it is just efficient, a person getting more quickly to the end of you. Correction—dogs *do* want to know every last thing about you. They take in the smell of you, they know from the next room, asleep, when a mood settles over you. The difference is there's not an end to it.

I could tell my husband now about Goodman in the garden. I raised Goodman myself—solid black Lab—and, after a year, I gave him up, the way you do, for further training and a life with Alice Banks. Alice was a gardener. She and her husband relaxed on weekends tending beds of annuals and several kinds of tomatoes. When Alice and Goodman graduated from the program, Alice said I was welcome to stay in touch. It is always the blind person's call. We exchanged letters for several months, and in the spring, I sent her a package of things for the yard. Then I got a letter from Alice's husband, Paul. He said they had been weeding in the garden, Goodman off-duty and retrieving a tossed ball. When Goodman found himself in the tomato patch, Paul wrote, he picked something up in his mouth and began yipping with excitement, tossing the thing into the air and running in circles to retrieve it. Paul told me that Goodman had found one of the sachets I had made to keep away deer; it was a packet of cheesecloth stuffed with my own hair.

It was something I learned from my husband, who trusted natural ways to keep predators away.

Today I am known as the Unusual Person. This is a test wherein I pull my windbreaker up over my head from behind and stagger around the corner and lurch menacingly down the walkway toward the dog-in-training. A volunteer will have the dog on a lead and attempt to walk the dog past me. We will see if the dog startles or balks or demonstrates curiosity; if the dog does startle, we'll see if he recovers quickly and continues on his way.

Before lunch I test half a dozen dogs. The first one walks by without more than a glance—he is being raised in New York City. The suburban dogs are skittish when they pass, but only one barks, and on the second approach, she, too, is quiet and passes. I am not a threat.

I eat quickly and head over across the quad to the best part of this place, the Whelping Center. The broods are brought here a couple of days before their due dates and are settled in quiet kennels where there will be a quilt on the floor and a handful of biscuits waiting. Chicken soup for dinner. The women who work here are unflappable and funny and intuitive and have substantial personalities though they are, some of them, elfin—if only *I* had been raised here, is what I'm saying.

I contrive excuses to bring myself often to the Whelping Center. Sometimes I scoot into a kennel and warm my hands under the heat lamp trained over the newborns sleeping inside a plastic kiddie pool lined with towels, their eyes not yet open, their ears leathery tabs. I feel, here, optimistic, yet hopeful. Jubilant, yet happy. This is the way I thought and spoke for an irritating year as a girl, annoying the teachers at the girls' school I attended. In school I was diligent, yet hard-working. The headmistress, I felt, was judicious, yet fair.

Jeanette will find me like this—sitting in the pen, eyes closed, puppies "nursing" on my fingertips—and say, "Don't just sit there, get busy." Ha ha, Jeanette. It's the command—"get busy" is—for a guide dog to eliminate.

I often time my visits to when the older puppies are fed. A Labrador eating looks like time-lapse photography. After the pups have been weaned and are on to softened kibble, their food is set down for them in bowls like Bundt cake pans, a kind of circular trough. They crowd in around it and the pan begins to turn. It spins faster as they eat and push, until the pups are like propeller blades. Then they'll move in the opposite direction, and the bowl spins the other way, as though they are in the southern hemisphere. One of the staff put a cartoon on the wall: "Why dogs never survive shipwrecks." It's the captain dog standing up in a lifeboat addressing the other dogs: "Those in favor of eating all the food now, say 'Aye.' "

A beauty came in yesterday—Savoy, out of Barnstormer Billy and one-eyed Tara. Savoy will have an "A" litter (we name the litters alphabetically), so in the time I have left I write down the names in a tiny three-ring binder: Avalon, Ardor, Able, Axel. Jeanette looks over my shoulder and says, "Like Axl Rose? You don't look like a headbanger."

Acre. I was looking in the dictionary, and after "acre" it said, "From the Latin *agere*: to lead."

In the afternoon: stairs—closed and open, up and down, on a short lead.

It is astonishing to find out how quickly the wrong things come into your head. I don't mean the vain thoughts that are unseemly and irrelevant in surroundings such as these. I mean that I can pause outside a kennel to dip my shoes in bleach and be visited by the memory of shattering glass, the way the etched glass of the heirloom globe exploded. I had lit a candle in the old lamp but had not fitted it carefully; as it burned, it tilted until it touched the handblown glass, handily prefiguring the news, over dessert, that my husband was going to get on with it because how long *was* a person supposed to give the other person to come back.

Last night, Savoy delivered early. Nine healthy puppies, and one—the smallest, a female—with a cleft palate. She died within minutes. Fran, the staffer present at the whelp, entered it in her log, her notation including the name she gave this pup: Angel. There are those of us who seek Fran out in the hope that something of her rubs off. Fran helped Savoy deliver over a period of seven hours. At midnight, when there had been three quiet hours, Fran helped Savoy to her feet and ran the ultrasound scanner over the dog's belly. Nothing showed on the monitor, so Fran left the kennel to get some sleep. Yet in the morning when she checked in on the mother, there were ten healthy puppies nursing. During the night, Savoy had given birth to one more, a female, as though to replace the one who had died. I said why didn't we name her "After," or put a little French on it—"Après"—but Fran said no, she wanted to name her for Angel. Sentimental? I am not the one to say; before I gave up Goodman, I made a tape recording of his snores.

Maybe it was fatigue, or the sadness of losing the runt, but Fran snapped at me when I showed up for work. She asked a perfunctory question. I should have said I was fine. But instead I observed that this was the day my husband left for Paris with his new girlfriend.

"Like you have a right to complain," Fran said, incredulous. "Let's think back one short year, babe."

I was stung, and flushed, and fumbled at the sink. Did I expect sympathy? Browbeaten, yet subdued. Subdued, yet humbled. I left the room before she could say I didn't have a leg to stand on, or the shoe was on the other foot.

Back in the lounge, I wiped at the antibacterial wash I had splashed on my jeans. What gets on my clothes here—if it came from a person I'd be sick. Last week I was in the infirmary when a Lab was brought in with the tip of his tail cut off by a car door. Yet he was so happy to see the veterinarian that he wagged his tail madly and sprayed us all with blood, back and forth, in wide arcs. The walls and cabinets too.

There is much to learn from these dogs. And we must learn these things over and over!

In the way that we know things before we know them, I dreamed that I swam across Lake Michigan, then pulled myself up on a raft near shore; just then the light changed in such a way that everything underwater was visible in silhouette, and giant hammerheads shadowed by. This was the night before my husband told me about Paris, and even in the dream I remember thinking: If I had known what was in the lake, I never would have gone in.

It's a warmish day for December, so I take one of the broods for a walk on the grounds. It's a lovely old neighborhood. Down the road from the school is one of those classic mansions you admire until you notice it's a funeral home. Every day I drive past it to get here, and an image undoes me, though I can't say quite why: a pair of white gloves folded over the wheel of an old Ford Fairlane outside a funeral home in Georgia in June. The sight of geese has this effect on me too. The dogs scare them up from the pond. When my best friend and I were in the first grade, her father acquired a dozen German Embdens. He let them roam freely about the yard. Every evening when he came home from work, he would turn a hose on the droppings they left in the drive; the grass along both sides of blacktop was a stripe of vivid green. He was a little eccentric, and the first of my friends' parents to die.

Buddha, Baxter, Bailey, Baywatch. I throw in that last for Jeanette. Working a litter ahead. We don't name the pups until they are four weeks old and get their ears tattooed, but still, it's good to be ready.

Back in the lounge there are letters from a sister school in Canada that has taken several of our dogs who failed the qualifying exam—except we don't say "failed," we say the dog was *reassigned,* or *released* for adoption as a pet. Canada will take a "soft" dog, one who maybe startles or is a bit less independent. Maybe it is like William Faulkner not making it into the U.S. Army air force and then going to fly for Canada. What's *with* Canada?

Trying to smooth things over, I guess, Fran asks for a hand in putting together the invitation for the Christmas party. I make James Thurber look like da Vinci, but I stay late—it's the night of the six-months-and-under class, the babies—and work up a festive border. The party is a high point for the volunteers who raise the puppies. They bring them to the high school gymnasium we borrow, and dress them up in Santa hats or felt reindeer antlers with chin straps, and there are cookies for everyone, and in the center of the gym floor there is a large cardboard box filled with wrapped gifts. On the command, the volunteers walk their dogs, one at a time, up to the box, where the dog is allowed to reach in and select a present, then return in a mannerly way to his spot. They get excited, of course, and invariably there will be a dog, like Ivan last year, who will get to the box and jump in.

Everyone wants to know how you do it, how you raise a puppy and train it for a year and a half and then give it up. Because you don't just love the dogs, you *fall* in love with them. A love affair begins with a fantasy. For instance, that the beloved will always be there. But *these* love affairs begin with yearning, for a future that won't be shared. Good training. There is a Zen-like quality to this work, if you can find reward in staying in the moment and in giving up what you love because someone else's need is greater. Sounds good in theory, but I counseled a volunteer who was coming up on the separation and she was crying and angry, and she said, "Just because I'm not blind!" She said, "What if he never swims again? Swimming's his favorite thing." I said, "You know how dogs' paws paddle in their sleep?" Dreams: the place most of us get what we need.

There is another side to this; it makes a pretty picture. The folks who raise the pups and then have to give them up? When the dogs get old and retire, the raisers can get them back. They can take them in as elderly dogs and coddle them in their well-earned rest. Raise enough puppies over the years—a steady stream of dear ones returning home.

Fran doesn't hold a grudge. She says she liked the invitation, and we walk together to the office to have it copied.

There are people whose goodness brings them to do this work, and there are those of us who come here *for* it. Both ways work.

Although, metaphorically, I am still in the lake, priding myself on a strong Australian crawl while nearby a hammerhead waits. Never mind the fact that this ravenous shark, in real life, is found in warm seas. It is with me in the lake where I mourn my lost status as someone who doesn't cause problems, and prove again that life is one long medley of prayers that we are not exposed, and try to convince myself that people who seem to suffer are not, in fact, unhappy, and want to be persuaded by the Japanese poem: "The barn burned down./ Now I can see the moon."

Did I invite this? It is like sitting in prayers at school when the headmistress says, "Who dropped lunch papers on the hockey field?" and although you went home for lunch, you think, *I did, I did.*

EMERGENCY

Denis Johnson

I'd been working in the emergency room for about three weeks, I guess. This was in 1973, before the summer ended. With nothing to do on the overnight shift but batch the insurance reports from the daytime shifts, I just started wandering around, over to the coronary-care unit, down to the cafeteria, et cetera, looking for Georgie, the orderly, a pretty good friend of mine. He often stole pills from the cabinets.

He was running over the tiled floor of the operating room with a mop. "Are you still doing that?" I said.

"Jesus, there's a lot of blood here," he complained.

"Where?" The floor looked clean enough to me.

"What the hell were they doing in here?" he asked me.

"They were performing surgery, Georgie," I told him.

"There's so much goop inside of us, man," he said, "and it all wants to get out." He leaned his mop against a cabinet.

"What are you crying for?" I didn't understand.

He stood still, raised both arms slowly behind his head, and tightened his ponytail. Then he grabbed the mop and started making broad random arcs with it, trembling and weeping and moving all around the place really fast. "What am I *crying* for?" he said. "Jesus. Wow, oh boy, perfect."

I was hanging out in the E.R. with fat, quivering Nurse. One of the Family Service doctors that nobody liked came in looking for Georgie to wipe up after him. "Where's Georgie?" this guy asked.

"Georgie's in O.R.," Nurse said.

"Again?"

"No," Nurse said. "Still."

"Still? Doing what?"

"Cleaning the floor."

"Again?"

"No," Nurse said again. "Still."

Back in O.R., Georgie dropped his mop and bent over in the posture of a child soiling its diapers. He stared down with his mouth open in terror.

He said, "What am I going to do about these fucking *shoes,* man?"

"Whatever you stole," I said, "I guess you already ate it all, right?"

"Listen to how they squish," he said, walking around carefully on his heels.

"Let me check your pockets, man."

He stood still a minute, and I found his stash. I left him two of each, whatever they were. "Shift is about half over," I told him.

"Good. Because I really, really, really need a drink," he said. "Will you please help me get this blood mopped up?"

Around 3:30 a.m. a guy with a knife in his eye came in, led by Georgie.

"I hope *you* didn't do that to him," Nurse said.

"Me?" Georgie said. "No. He was like this."

"My wife did it," the man said. The blade was buried to the hilt in the outside corner of his left eye. It was a hunting knife kind of thing.

"Who brought you in?" Nurse said.

"Nobody. I just walked down. It's only three blocks," the man said.

Nurse peered at him. "We'd better get you lying down."

"Okay, I'm certainly ready for something like that," the man said.

She peered a bit longer into his face.

"Is your other eye," she said, "a glass eye?"

"It's plastic, or something artificial like that," he said.

"And you can see out of *this* eye?" she asked, meaning the wounded one.

"I can see. But I can't make a fist out of my left hand because this knife is doing something to my brain."

"My God," Nurse said.

"I guess I'd better get the doctor," I said.

"There you go," Nurse agreed.

They got him lying down, and Georgie says to the patient, "Name?"

"Terrence Weber."

"Your face is dark. I can't see what you're saying."

"Georgie," I said.

"What are you saying, man? I can't see."

Nurse came over, and Georgie said to her, "His face is dark."

She leaned over the patient. "How long ago did this happen, Terry?" she shouted down into his face.

"Just a while ago. My wife did it. I was asleep," the patient said.

"Do you want the police?"

He thought about it and finally said, "Not unless I die."

Nurse went to the wall intercom and buzzed the doctor on duty, the Family Service person. "Got a surprise for you," she said over the intercom. He took his time getting down the hall to her, because he knew she hated Family Service and her happy tone of voice could only mean something beyond his competence and potentially humiliating.

He peeked into the trauma room and saw the situation: the

clerk—that is, me—standing next to the orderly, Georgie, both of us on drugs, looking down at a patient with a knife sticking up out of his face.

"What seems to be the trouble?" he said.

The doctor gathered the three of us around him in the office and said, "Here's the situation. We've got to get a team here, an entire team. I want a good eye man. A great eye man. The best eye man. I want a brain surgeon. And I want a really good gas man, get me a genius. I'm not touching that head. I'm just going to watch this one. I know my limits. We'll just get him prepped and sit tight. Orderly!"

"Do you mean me?" Georgie said. "Should I get him prepped?"

"Is this a hospital?" the doctor asked. "Is this the emergency room? Is that a patient? Are you the orderly?"

I dialled the hospital operator and told her to get me the eye man and the brain man and the gas man.

Georgie could be heard across the hall, washing his hands and singing a Neil Young song that went "Hello, cowgirl in the sand. Is this place at your command?"

"That person is not right, not at all, not one bit," the doctor said.

"As long as my instructions are audible to him it doesn't concern me," Nurse insisted, spooning stuff up out of a little Dixie cup. "I've got my own life and the protection of my family to think of."

"Well, okay, okay. Don't chew my head off," the doctor said.

The eye man was on vacation or something. While the hospital's operator called around to find someone else just as good, the other specialists were hurrying through the night to join us. I stood around looking at charts and chewing up more of Georgie's pills. Some of them tasted the way urine smells, some of them burned, some of them tasted like chalk. Various nurses, and two physicians who'd been tending somebody in I.C.U., were hanging out down here with us now.

Everybody had a different idea about exactly how to approach the problem of removing the knife from Terrence Weber's brain. But when Georgie came in from prepping the patient—from shaving the patient's eyebrow and disinfecting the area around the wound, and so on—he seemed to be holding the hunting knife in his left hand.

The talk just dropped off a cliff.

"Where," the doctor asked finally, "did you get that?"

Nobody said one thing more, not for quite a long time.

After a while, one of the I.C.U. nurses said, "Your shoelace is untied." Georgie laid the knife on a chart and bent down to fix his shoe.

There were twenty more minutes left to get through.

"How's the guy doing?" I asked.

"Who?" Georgie said.

It turned out that Terrence Weber still had excellent vision in the one good eye, and acceptable motor and reflex, despite his earlier motor complaint. "His vitals are normal," Nurse said. "There's nothing wrong with the guy. It's one of those things."

After a while you forget it's summer. You don't remember what the morning is. I'd worked two doubles with eight hours off in between, which I'd spent sleeping on a gurney in the nurse's station. Georgie's pills were making me feel like a giant helium-filled balloon, but I was wide awake. Georgie and I went out to the lot, to his orange pickup.

We lay down on a stretch of dusty plywood in the back of the truck with the daylight knocking against our eyelids and the fragrance of alfalfa thickening on our tongues.

"I want to go to church," Georgie said.

"Let's go to the county fair."

"I'd like to worship. I would."

"They have these injured hawks and eagles there. From the Humane Society," I said.

"I need a quiet chapel about now."

Georgie and I had a terrific time driving around. For a while the day was clear and peaceful. It was one of the moments you stay in, to hell with all the troubles of before and after. The sky is blue and the dead are coming back. Later in the afternoon, with sad resignation, the county fair bares its breasts. A champion of the drug LSD, a very famous guru of the love generation, is being interviewed amid a TV crew off to the left of the poultry cages. His eyeballs look like he bought them in a joke shop. It doesn't occur to me, as I pity this extraterrestrial, that in my life I've taken as much as he has.

After that, we got lost. We drove for hours, literally hours, but we couldn't find the road back to town.

Georgie started to complain. "That was the worst fair I've been to. Where were the rides?"

"They had rides," I said.

"I didn't see one ride."

A jackrabbit scurried out in front of us, and we hit it.

"There was a merry-go-round, a Ferris wheel, and a thing called the Hammer that people were bent over vomiting from after they got off," I said. "Are you completely blind?"

"What was that?"

"A rabbit."

"Something thumped."

"You hit him. *He* thumped."

Georgie stood on the brake pedal. "Rabbit stew."

He threw the truck in reverse and zigzagged back toward the rabbit. "Where's my hunting knife?" He almost ran over the poor animal a second time.

"We'll camp in the wilderness," he said. "In the morning we'll breakfast on its haunches." He was waving Terrence Weber's hunting knife around in what I was sure was a dangerous way.

In a minute he was standing at the edge of the fields, cutting the scrawny little thing up, tossing away its organs. "I should have been a doctor," he cried.

A family in a big Dodge, the only car we'd seen for a long time, slowed down and gawked out the windows as they passed by. The father said, "What is it, a snake?"

"No, it's not a snake," Georgie said. "It's a rabbit with babies inside it."

"Babies!" the mother said, and the father sped the car forward, over the protests of several little kids in the back.

Georgie came back to my side of the truck with his shirtfront stretched out in front of him as if he were carrying apples in it, or some such, but they were, in fact, slimy miniature bunnies. "No way I'm eating those things," I told him.

"Take them, take them. I gotta drive, take them," he said, dumping them in my lap and getting in on his side of the truck. He started driving along faster and faster, with a look of glory on his face. "We killed the mother and saved the children," he said.

"It's getting late," I said. "Let's get back to town."

"You bet." Sixty, seventy, eighty-five, just topping ninety.

"These rabbits better be kept warm." One at a time I slid the little things in between my shirt buttons and nestled them against my belly. "They're hardly moving," I told Georgie.

"We'll get some milk and sugar and all that, and we'll raise them up ourselves. They'll get as big as gorillas."

The road we were lost on cut straight through the middle of the world. It was still daytime, but the sun had no more power than an ornament or a sponge. In this light the truck's hood, which had been bright orange, had turned a deep blue.

Georgie let us drift to the shoulder of the road, slowly, slowly, as if he'd fallen asleep or given up trying to find his way.

"What is it?"

"We can't go on. I don't have any headlights," Georgie said.

We parked under a strange sky with a faint image of a quarter-moon superimposed on it.

There was a little woods beside us. This day had been dry and hot, the buck pines and what-all simmering patiently, but as we sat there smoking cigarettes it started to get very cold.

"The summer's over," I said.

That was the year when arctic clouds moved down over the Midwest and we had two weeks of winter in September.

"Do you realize it's going to snow?" Georgie asked me.

He was right, a gun-blue storm was shaping up. We got out and walked around idiotically. The beautiful chill! That sudden crispness, and the tang of evergreen stabbing us!

The gusts of snow twisted themselves around our heads while the night fell. I couldn't find the truck. We just kept getting more and more lost. I kept calling, "Georgie, can you see?" and he kept saying, "See what? See what?"

The only light visible was a streak of sunset flickering below the hem of the clouds. We headed that way.

We bumped softly down a hill toward an open field that seemed to be a military graveyard, filled with rows and rows of austere, identical markers over soldiers' graves. I'd never before come across this cemetery. On the farther side of the field, just beyond the curtains of snow, the sky was torn away and the angels were descending out of a brilliant blue summer, their huge faces streaked with light and full of pity. The sight of them cut through my heart and down the knuckles of my spine, and if there'd been anything in my bowels I would have messed my pants from fear.

Georgie opened his arms and cried out, "It's the drive-in, man!"

"The drive-in . . ." I wasn't sure what these words meant.

"They're showing movies in a fucking blizzard!" Georgie screamed.

"I see. I thought it was something else," I said.

We walked carefully down there and climbed through the busted fence and stood in the very back. The speakers, which I'd mistaken for grave markers, muttered in unison. Then there was tinkly music, of which I could very nearly make out the tune. Famous movie stars rode bicycles beside a river, laughing out of their gigantic, lovely mouths. If anybody had come to see this show, they'd left when the weather started. Not one car remained, not even a broken-down one from last week, or one left here because it was out of gas. In a couple of minutes, in the middle of a whirling square dance, the screen turned black, the cinematic summer ended, the snow went dark, there was nothing but my breath.

"I'm starting to get my eyes back," Georgie said in another minute.

A general greyness was giving birth to various shapes, it was true. "But which ones are close and which ones are far off?" I begged him to tell me.

By trial and error, with a lot of walking back and forth in wet shoes, we found the truck and sat inside it shivering.

"Let's get out of here," I said.

"We can't go anywhere without headlights."

"We've gotta get back. We're a long way from home."

"No, we're not."

"We must have come three hundred miles."

"We're right outside town, Fuckhead. We've just been driving around and around."

"This is no place to camp. I hear the Interstate over there."

"We'll just stay here till it gets late. We can drive home late. We'll be invisible."

We listened to the big rigs going from San Francisco to Pennsylvania along the Interstate, like shudders down a long hacksaw blade, while the snow buried us.

Eventually Georgie said, "We better get some milk for those bunnies."

"We don't have *milk*," I said.

"We'll mix sugar up with it."

"Will you forget about this milk all of a sudden?"

"They're mammals, man."

"Forget about those rabbits."

"Where are they, anyway?"

"You're not listening to me. I said, 'Forget the rabbits.'"

"Where are they?"

The truth was I'd forgotten all about them, and they were dead.

"They slid around behind me and got squashed," I said tearfully.

"They slid around *behind*?"

He watched while I pried them out from behind my back.

I picked them out one at a time and held them in my hands and we looked at them. There were eight. They weren't any bigger than my fingers, but everything was there.

Little feet! Eyelids! Even whiskers! "Deceased," I said.

Georgie asked, "Does everything you touch turn to shit? Does this happen to you every time?"

"No wonder they call me Fuckhead."

"It's a name that's going to stick."

"I realize that."

"'Fuckhead' is gonna ride you to your grave."

"I just said so. I agreed with you in advance," I said.

Or maybe that wasn't the time it snowed. Maybe it was the time we slept in the truck and I rolled over on the bunnies and flattened them. It doesn't matter. What's important for me to remember now is that early the next morning the snow was melted off the windshield and the daylight woke me up. A mist covered everything and, with the sunshine, was beginning to grow sharp and strange. The bunnies weren't a problem yet, or they'd already been a problem and were already forgotten, and there was nothing on my mind. I felt the beauty of the morning. I could understand how a drowning man might suddenly feel a deep thirst being quenched. Or how the slave might become a friend to his master. Georgie slept with his face right on the steering wheel.

I saw bits of snow resembling an abundance of blossoms on the stems of the drive-in speakers—no, revealing the blossoms that were always there. A bull elk stood still in the pasture beyond the fence, giving off an air of authority and stupidity. And a coyote jogged across the pasture and faded away among the saplings.

That afternoon we got back to work in time to resume everything as if it had never stopped happening and we'd never been anywhere else.

"The Lord," the intercom said, "is my shepherd." It did that each evening because this was a Catholic hospital. "Our Father, who art in Heaven," and so on.

"Yeah, yeah," Nurse said.

The man with the knife in his head, Terrence Weber, was released around suppertime. They'd kept him overnight and given him an eyepatch—all for no reason, really.

He stopped off at E.R. to say goodbye. "Well, those pills they gave me make everything taste terrible," he said.

"It could have been worse," Nurse said.

"Even my tongue."

"It's just a miracle you didn't end up sightless or at least dead," she reminded him.

The patient recognized me. He acknowledged me with a smile. "I was peeping on the lady next door while she was out there sunbathing," he said. "My wife decided to blind me."

He shook Georgie's hand. Georgie didn't know him. "Who are you supposed to be?" he asked Terrence Weber.

Some hours before that, Georgie had said something that had suddenly and completely explained the difference between us. We'd been driving back toward town, along the Old Highway, through the flatness. We picked up a hitchhiker, a boy I knew. We stopped the truck and the boy climbed slowly up out of the fields as out of the mouth of a volcano. His name was Hardee. He looked even worse than we probably did.

"We got messed up and slept in the truck all night," I told Hardee.

"I had a feeling," Hardee said. "Either that or, you know, driving a thousand miles."

"That too," I said.

"Or you're sick or diseased or something."

"Who's this guy?" Georgie asked.

"This is Hardee. He lived with me last summer. I found him on the doorstep. What happened to your dog?" I asked Hardee.

"He's still down there."

"Yeah, I heard you went to Texas."

"I was working on a bee farm," Hardee said.

"Wow. Do those things sting you?"

"Not like you'd think," Hardee said. "You're part of their daily drill. It's all part of a harmony."

Outside, the same identical stretch of ground repeatedly rolled past our faces. The day was cloudless, blinding. But Georgie said, "Look at that," pointing straight ahead of us.

One star was so hot it showed, bright and blue, in the empty sky.

"I recognized you right away," I told Hardee. "But what happened to your hair? Who chopped it off?"

"I hate to say."

"Don't tell me."

"They drafted me."

"Oh no."

"Oh yeah. I'm AWOL. I'm bad AWOL. I got to get to Canada."

"Oh, that's terrible," I said to Hardee.

"Don't worry," Georgie said. "We'll get you there."

"How?"

"Somehow. I think I know some people. Don't worry. You're on your way to Canada."

That world! These days it's all been erased and they've rolled it up like a scroll and put it away somewhere. Yes, I can touch it with my fingers. But where is it?

After a while Hardee asked Georgie, "What do you do for a job," and Georgie said, "I save lives."

from **BELOVED**

Toni Morrison

She made the pastry dough and thought she ought to tell Ella and John to stop on by because three pies, maybe four, were too much to keep for one's own. Sethe thought they might as well back it up with a couple of chickens. Stamp allowed that perch and catfish were jumping into the boat—didn't even have to drop a line.

From Denver's two thrilled eyes it grew to a feast for ninety people. 124 shook with their voices far into the night. Ninety people who ate so well, and laughed so much, it made them angry. They woke up the next morning and remembered the meal-fried perch that Stamp Paid handled with a hickory twig, holding his left palm out against the spit and pop of the boiling grease; the corn pudding made with cream; tired, overfed children asleep in the grass, tiny bones of roasted rabbit still in their hands—and got angry.

Baby Suggs' three (maybe four) pies grew to ten (maybe twelve). Sethe's two hens became five turkeys. The one block of ice brought all the way from Cincinnati—over which they poured mashed watermelon mixed with sugar and mint to make a punch—became a wagonload of ice cakes for a washtub full of strawberry shrug. 124, rocking with laughter, goodwill and food for ninety, made them angry. Too much, they thought. Where does she get it all, Baby Suggs, holy? Why is she and hers always the center of things? How come she always knows exactly what to do and when? Giving advice; passing messages; healing the sick, hiding fugitives, loving, cooking, cooking, loving, preaching, singing, dancing and loving everybody like it was her job and hers alone.

Now to take two buckets of blackberries and make ten, maybe twelve, pies; to have turkey enough for the whole town pretty near, new peas in September, fresh cream but no cow, ice *and* sugar, batter bread, bread pudding, raised bread, shortbread—it made them mad. Loaves and fishes were His powers—they did not belong to an ex-slave who had probably never carried one hundred pounds to the scale, or picked okra with a baby on her back. Who had never been lashed by a ten-year-old whiteboy as God knows they had. Who had not even escaped slavery—had, in fact, been *bought out* of it by a doting son and *driven* to the Ohio River in a wagon—free papers folded between her breasts (driven by the very man who had been her master, who also paid her resettlement fee—name of Garner), and rented a house with *two* floors *and* a well from the Bodwins—the white brother and sister who gave Stamp Paid, Ella and John clothes, goods and gear for runaways because they hated slavery worse than they hated slaves.

It made them furious. They swallowed baking soda, the morning after, to calm the stomach violence caused by the bounty, the reckless generosity on display at 124. Whispered to each other in the yards about fat rats, doom and uncalled-for pride.

The scent of their disapproval lay heavy in the air. Baby Suggs woke to it and wondered what it was as she boiled hominy for her grandchildren. Later, as she stood in the garden, chopping at the tight soil over the roots of the pepper plants, she smelled it again. She lifted her head and looked around. Behind her some yards to the left Sethe squatted in the pole beans. Her shoulders were distorted by the greased flannel under her dress to encourage the healing of her back. Near her in a bushel basket was the three-week-old baby. Baby Suggs, holy, looked up. The sky was blue and clear. Not one touch of death in the definite green of the leaves. She could hear birds and, faintly, the stream way down in the meadow. The puppy, Here Boy, was burying the last bones from yesterday's party. From somewhere at the side of the house came the voices of Buglar, Howard and the crawling girl. Nothing seemed amiss—yet the smell of disapproval was sharp. Back beyond the vegetable garden, closer to the stream but in full sun, she had planted corn. Much as they'd picked for the party, there were still ears ripening, which she could see from where she stood. Baby Suggs leaned back into the peppers and the squash vines with her hoe. Carefully, with the blade at just the right angle, she cut through a stalk of insistent rue. Its flowers she stuck through a split in her hat; the rest she tossed aside. The quiet clok clok clok of wood splitting reminded her that Stamp was doing the chore he promised to the night before. She sighed at her work and, a moment later, straightened up to sniff the disapproval once again. Resting on the handle of the hoe, she concentrated. She was accustomed to the knowledge that nobody prayed for her—but this free-floating repulsion was new. It wasn't whitefolks—that much she could tell—so it must be colored ones. And then she knew. Her friends and neighbors were angry at her because she had overstepped, given too much, offended them by excess.

Baby closed her eyes. Perhaps they were right. Suddenly, behind the disapproving odor, way way back behind it, she smelled another thing. Dark and coming. Something she couldn't get at because the other odor hid it.

She squeezed her eyes tight to see what it was but all she could make out was high-topped shoes she didn't like the look of.

Thwarted yet wondering, she chopped away with the hoe. What could it be? This dark and coming thing. What was left to hurt her now? News of Halle's death? No. She had been prepared for that better than she had for his life. The last of her children, whom she barely glanced at when he was born because it wasn't worth the trouble to try to learn features you would never see change into adulthood anyway. Seven times she had done that: held a little foot; examined the fat fingertips with her own— fingers she never saw become the male or female hands a mother would recognize anywhere. She didn't know to this day what their permanent teeth looked like; or how they held their heads when they walked. Did Patty lose her lisp? What color did Famous' skin finally take? Was that a cleft in Johnny's chin or just a dimple that would disappear soon's his jawbone changed? Four girls, and the last time she saw them there was no hair under their arms. Does Ardelia still love the burned bottom of bread? All seven were gone or dead. What would be the point of looking too hard at that youngest one? But for some reason they let her keep him. He was with her—everywhere.

When she hurt her hip in Carolina she was a real bargain (costing less than Halle, who was ten then) for Mr. Garner, who took them both to Kentucky to a farm he called Sweet Home. Because of the hip she jerked like a three-legged dog when she walked. But at Sweet Home there wasn't a rice field or tobacco patch in sight, and nobody, but nobody, knocked her down. Not once. Lilian Garner called her Jenny for some reason but she never pushed, hit or called her mean names. Even when she slipped in cow dung and broke every egg in her apron, nobody said you-black-bitch-what's-the-matter-with-you and nobody knocked her down.

Sweet Home was tiny compared to the places she had been. Mr. Garner, Mrs. Garner, herself, Halle, and four boys, over half named Paul, made up the entire population. Mrs. Garner hummed when she worked; Mr. Garner acted like the world was a toy he was supposed to have fun with. Neither wanted her in the field—Mr. Garner's boys, including Halle, did all of that— which was a blessing since she could not have managed it anyway. What she did was stand beside the humming Lillian Garner while the two of them cooked, preserved, washed, ironed, made candles, clothes, soap and cider; fed chickens, pigs, dogs and geese; milked cows, churned butter, rendered fat, laid fires. . . . Nothing to it. And nobody knocked her down.

Her hip hurt every single day—but she never spoke of it. Only Halle, who had watched her movements closely for the last four years, knew that to get in and out of bed she had to lift her thigh with both hands, which was why he spoke to Mr. Garner about buying her out of there so she could sit down for a change. Sweet boy. The one person who did something hard for her: gave her his work, his life and now his children, whose voices she could just make out as she stood in the garden wondering what was the dark and coming thing behind the scent of disapproval. Sweet Home was a marked improvement. No question. And no matter, for the sadness was at her center, the desolated center where the self that was no self made its home. Sad as it was that she did not know where her children were buried or what they looked like if alive, fact was she knew more about them than she knew about herself, having never had the map to discover what she was like.

Could she sing? (Was it nice to hear when she did?) Was she pretty? Was she a good friend? Could she have been a loving mother? A faithful wife? Have I got a sister and does she favor me? If my mother knew me would she like me?

In Lillian Garner's house, exempted from the field work that broke her hip and the exhaustion that drugged her mind; in Lillian Garner's house where nobody knocked her down (or up), she listened to the whitewoman humming at her work; watched her face light up when Mr. Garner came in and thought, It's better here, but I'm not. The Garners, it seemed to her, ran a special kind of slavery, treating them like paid labor, listening to what they said, teaching what they wanted known. And he didn't stud his boys. Never brought them to her cabin with directions to "lay down with her," like they did in Carolina, or rented their sex out on other farms. It surprised and pleased her, but worried her too. Would he pick women for them or what did he think was going to happen when those boys ran smack into their nature? Some danger he was courting and he surely knew it. In fact, his order for them not to leave Sweet Home, except in his company, was not so much because of the law, but the danger of men-bred slaves on the loose.

Baby Suggs talked as little as she could get away with because what was there to say that the roots of her tongue could manage? So the whitewoman, finding her new slave excellent if silent help, hummed to herself while she worked.

When Mr. Garner agreed to the arrangements with Halle, and when Halle looked like it meant more to him that she go free than anything in the world, she let herself be taken 'cross the river. Of the two hard things—standing on her feet till she dropped or leaving her last and probably only living child—she chose the hard thing that made him happy, and never put to him the question she put to herself: What for? What does a sixty-odd-year-old slavewoman who walks like a three-legged dog need freedom for? And when she stepped foot on free ground she could not believe that Halle knew what she didn't; that Halle, who had never drawn one free breath, knew that there was nothing like it in this world. It scared her.

Something's the matter. What's the matter? What's the matter? she asked herself. She didn't know what she looked like and was not curious. But suddenly she saw her hands and thought with a clarity as simple as it was dazzling, "These hands belong to me. These *my* hands." Next she felt a knocking in her chest and discovered something else new: her own heartbeat. Had it been there all along? This pounding thing? She felt like a fool and began to laugh out loud. Mr. Garner looked over his shoulder at her with wide brown eyes and smiled himself. "What's funny, Jenny?"

She couldn't stop laughing. "My heart's beating," she said.

And it was true.

Mr. Garner laughed. "Nothing to be scared of, Jenny. Just keep your same ways, you'll be all right."

She covered her mouth to keep from laughing too loud.

"These people I'm taking you to will give you what help you need. Name of Bodwin. A brother and a sister. Scots. I been knowing them for twenty years or more."

Baby Suggs thought it was a good time to ask him something she had long wanted to know.

"Mr. Garner," she said, "why you all call me Jenny?"

"'Cause that what's on your sales ticket, gal. Ain't that your name? What you call yourself?"

"Nothing," she said. "I don't call myself nothing."

Mr. Garner went red with laughter. "When I took you out of Carolina, Whitlow called you Jenny and Jenny Whitlow is what his bill said. Didn't he call you Jenny?"

"No, sir. If he did I didn't hear it."

"What did you answer to?"

"Anything, but Suggs is what my husband name."

"You got married, Jenny? I didn't know it."

"Manner of speaking."

"You know where he is, this husband?"

"No, sir."

"Is that Halle's daddy?"

"No, sir."

"Why you call him Suggs, then? His bill of sale says Whitlow too, just like yours."

"Suggs is my name, sir. From my husband. He didn't call me Jenny."

"What he call you?"

"Baby."

"Well," said Mr. Garner, going pink again, "if I was you I'd stick to Jenny Whitlow. Mrs. Baby Suggs ain't no name for a freed Negro."

Maybe not, she thought, but Baby Suggs was all she had left of the "husband" she claimed. A serious, melancholy man who taught her how to make shoes. The two of them made a pact: whichever one got a chance to run would take it; together if possible, alone if not, and no looking back. He got his chance, and since she never heard otherwise she believed he made it. Now how could he find or hear tell of her if she was calling herself some bill-of-sale name?

She couldn't get over the city. More people than Carolina and enough whitefolks to stop the breath. Two-story buildings everywhere, and walkways made of perfectly cut slats of wood. Roads wide as Garner's whole house.

"This is a city of water," said Mr. Garner. "Everything travels by water and what the rivers can't carry the canals take. A queen of a city, Jenny. Everything you ever dreamed of, they make it right here. Iron stoves, buttons, ships, shirts, hairbrushes, paint, steam engines, books. A sewer system make your eyes bug out. Oh, this is a city, all right. If you have to live in a city—this is it."

The Bodwins lived right in the center of a street full of houses and trees. Mr. Garner leaped out and tied his horse to a solid iron post.

"Here we are."

Baby picked up her bundle and with great difficulty, caused by her hip and the hours of sitting in a wagon, climbed down. Mr. Garner was up the walk and on the porch before she touched ground, but she got a peep at a Negro girl's face at the open door before she followed a path to the back of the house. She waited what seemed a long time before this same girl opened the kitchen door and offered her a seat by the window.

"Can I get you anything to eat, ma'am?" the girl asked.

"No, darling. I'd look favorable on some water though." The girl went to the sink and pumped a cupful of water. She placed it in Baby Suggs' hand. "I'm Janey, ma'am."

Baby, marveling at the sink, drank every drop of water although it tasted like a serious medicine. "Suggs," she said, blotting her lips with the back of her hand. "Baby Suggs."

"Glad to meet you, Mrs. Suggs. You going to be staying here?"

"I don't know where I'll be. Mr. Garner—that's him what brought me here—he say he arrange something for me." And then, "I'm free, you know."

Janey smiled. "Yes, ma'am."

"Your people live around here?"

"Yes, ma'am. All us live out on Bluestone."

"We scattered," said Baby Suggs, "but maybe not for long."

Great God, she thought, where do I start? Get somebody to write old Whitlow. See who took Patty and Rosa Lee. Somebody name Dunn got Ardelia and went West, she heard. No point in trying for Tyree or John. They cut thirty years ago and, if she searched too hard and they were hiding, finding them would do them more harm than good. Nancy and Famous died in a ship off the Virginia coast before it set sail for Savannah. That much she knew. The overseer at Whitlow's place brought her the news, more from a wish to have his way with her than from the kindness of his heart. The captain waited three weeks in port, to get a full cargo before setting off. Of the slaves in the hold who didn't make it, he said, two were Whitlow pickaninnies name of . . .

But she knew their names. She knew, and covered her ears with her fists to keep from hearing them come from his mouth.

Janey heated some milk and poured it in a bowl next to a plate of cornbread. After some coaxing, Baby Suggs came to the table and sat down. She crumbled the bread into the hot milk and discovered she was hungrier than she had ever been in her life and that was saying something.

"They going to miss this?"

"No," said Janey. "Eat all you want; it's ours."

"Anybody else live here?"

"Just me. Mr. Woodruff, he does the outside chores. He comes by two, three days a week."

"Just you two?"

"Yes, ma'am. I do the cooking and washing."

"Maybe your people know of somebody looking for help."

"I be sure to ask, but I know they take women at the slaughterhouse."

"Doing what?"

"I don't know."

"Something men don't want to do, I reckon."

"My cousin say you get all the meat you want, plus twenty-five cents the hour. She make summer sausage."

Baby Suggs lifted her hand to the top of her head. Money? Money? They would pay her money every single day? Money?

"Where is this here slaughterhouse?" she asked.

Before Janey could answer, the Bodwins came in to the kitchen with a grinning Mr. Garner behind. Undeniably brother and sister, both dressed in gray with faces too young for their snow-white hair.

"Did you give her anything to eat, Janey?" asked the brother.

"Yes, sir."

"Keep your seat, Jenny," said the sister, and that good news got better.

When they asked what work she could do, instead of reeling off the hundreds of tasks she had performed, she asked about the slaughterhouse. She was too old for that, they said.

"She's the best cobbler you ever see," said Mr. Garner.

"Cobbler?" Sister Bodwin raised her black thick eyebrows. "Who taught you that?"

"Was a slave taught me," said Baby Suggs.

"New boots, or just repair?"

"New, old, anything."

"Well," said Brother Bodwin, "that'll be something, but you'll need more."

"What about taking in wash?" asked Sister Bodwin.

"Yes, ma'am."

"Two cents a pound."

"Yes, ma'am. But where's the in?"

"What?"

"You said 'take in wash.' Where is the 'in'? Where I'm going to be."

"Oh, just listen to this, Jenny," said Mr. Garner. "These two angels got a house for you. Place they own out a ways."

It had belonged to their grandparents before they moved in

town. Recently it had been rented out to a whole parcel of Negroes, who had left the state. It was too big a house for Jenny alone, they said (two rooms upstairs, two down), but it was the best and the only thing they could do. In return for laundry, some seamstress work, a little canning and so on (oh shoes, too), they would permit her to stay there. Provided she was clean. The past parcel of colored wasn't. Baby Suggs agreed to the situation, sorry to see the money go but excited about a house with steps—never mind she couldn't climb them. Mr. Garner told the Bodwins that she was a right fine cook as well as a fine cobbler and showed his belly and the sample on his feet. Everybody laughed.

"Anything you need, let us know," said the sister. "We don't hold with slavery, even Garner's kind."

"Tell em, Jenny. You live any better on any place before mine?"

"No, sir," she said. "No place."

"How long was you at Sweet Home?"

"Ten year, I believe."

"Ever go hungry?"

"No, sir."

"Cold?"

"No, sir."

"Anybody lay a hand on you?"

"No, sir."

"Did I let Halle buy you or not?"

"Yes, sir, you did," she said, thinking, But you got my boy and I'm all broke down. You be renting him out to pay for me way after I'm gone to Glory.

Woodruff, they said, would carry her out there, they said, and all three disappeared through the kitchen door.

"I have to fix the supper now," said Janey.

"I'll help," said Baby Suggs. "You too short to reach the fire."

It was dark when Woodruff clicked the horse into a trot. He was a young man with a heavy beard and a burned place on his jaw the beard did not hide.

"You born up here?" Baby Suggs asked him.

"No, ma'am. Virginia. Been here a couple years."

"I see."

"You going to a nice house. Big too. A preacher and his family was in there. Eighteen children."

"Have mercy. Where they go?"

"Took off to Illinois. Bishop Allen gave him a congregation up there. Big."

"What churches around here? I ain't set foot in one in ten years."

"How come?"

"Wasn't none. I dislike the place I was before this last one, but I did get to church every Sunday some kind of way. I bet the Lord done forgot who I am by now."

"Go see Reverend Pike, ma'am. He'll reacquaint you."

"I won't need him for that. I can make my own acquaintance. What I need him for is to reacquaint me with my children. He can read and write, I reckon?"

"Sure."

"Good, 'cause I got a lot of digging up to do." But the news they dug up was so pitiful she quit. After two years of messages written by the preacher's hand, two years of washing, sewing, canning, cobbling, gardening, and sitting in churches, all she found out was that the Whitlow place was gone and that you couldn't write to "a man named Dunn" if all you knew was that he went West. The good news, however, was that Halle got married and had a baby coming. She fixed on that and her own brand of preaching, having made up her mind about what to do with the heart that started beating the minute she crossed the Ohio River. And it worked out, worked out just fine, until she got proud and let herself be overwhelmed by the sight of her daughter-in-law and Halle's children—one of whom was born on the way—and have a celebration of blackberries that put Christmas to shame. Now she stood in the garden smelling disapproval, feeling a dark and coming thing, and seeing high-topped shoes that she didn't like the look of at all. At all.

from **AMERICAN PASTORAL**

Philip Roth

A tiny, bone-white girl who looked half Merry's age but claimed to be some six years older, a Miss Rita Cohen, came to the Swede four months after Merry's disappearance. She was dressed like Dr. King's successor, Ralph Abernathy, in freedom-rider overalls and ugly big shoes, and a bush of wiry hair emphatically framed her bland baby face. He should have recognized immediately who she was—for the four months he had been waiting for just such a person—but she was so tiny, so young, so ineffectual-looking that he could barely believe she was at the University of Pennsylvania's Wharton School of Business and Finance (doing a thesis on the leather industry in Newark, New Jersey), let alone the provocateur who was Merry's mentor in world revolution.

On the day she showed up at the factory, the Swede had not known that Rita Cohen had undertaken some fancy footwork—in and out through the basement door beneath the loading dock—so as to elude the surveillance team the FBI had assigned to observe from Central Avenue the arrival and departure of everyone visiting his office.

Three, four times a year someone either called or wrote to ask permission to see the plant. In the old days, Lou Levov, busy as he might be, always made time for the Newark school classes, or Boy Scout troops, or visiting notables chaperoned by a functionary from City Hall or the Chamber of Commerce. Though the Swede didn't get nearly the pleasure his father did from being an authority on the glove trade, though he wouldn't claim his father's authority on anything pertaining to the leather industry—pertaining to anything else, either—occasionally he did assist a student by answering questions over the phone or, if the student struck him as especially serious, by offering a brief tour.

Of course, had he known beforehand that this student was no student but his fugitive daughter's emissary, he would never have arranged their meeting to take place at the factory. Why Rita hadn't explained to the Swede whose emissary she was, said nothing about Merry until the tour had been concluded, was undoubtedly so she could size up the Swede first; or maybe she said nothing for so long the better to enjoy toying with him. Maybe she just enjoyed the power. Maybe she was just another politician and the enjoyment of power lay behind much of what she did.

Because the Swede's desk was separated from the making department by glass partitions, he and the women at the machines could command a clear view of one another. He had instituted this arrangement so as to wrest relief from the mechanical racket while maintaining access between himself and the floor. His father had refused to be confined to any office, glass-enclosed or otherwise: just planted his desk in the middle of the making room's two hundred sewing machines—royalty right at the heart of the overcrowded hive, the swarm around him whining its buzz-saw bee buzz while he talked to his customers and his contractors on the phone and simultaneously plowed through his paperwork. Only from out on the floor, he claimed, could he distinguish within the contrapuntal din the sound of a Singer on the fritz and with his screwdriver be over the machine before the girl had even alerted her forelady to the trouble. Vicky, Newark Maid's elderly black forelady, so testified (with her brand of wry admiration) at his retirement banquet. While everything was running without a hitch, Lou was impatient, fidgety—in a word, said Vicky, the insufferable boss—but when a cutter came around to complain about the foreman, when the foreman came around to complain about a cutter, when skins arrived months late or in damaged condition or were of poor quality, when he discovered a lining contractor cheating him on the yield or a shipping clerk robbing him blind, when he determined that the glove slitter with the red Corvette and the sunglasses was, on the side, a bookie running a numbers game among the employees, then he was in his element and in his intimitable way set out to make things right—so that when they *were* right, said the next-to-last speaker, the proud son, introducing his father in the longest, most laudatory of the evening's jocular encomiums, "he could begin driving himself—and the rest of us—nuts with worrying again. But then, always expecting the worst, he was never disappointed for long. Never caught off guard either. All of which goes to show that, like everything else at Newark Maid, worrying *works*. Ladies and gentlemen, the man who has been my lifelong teacher—and not just in the art of worrying—the man who has made of my life a lifelong education, a difficult education sometimes but always a profitable one, who explained to me when I was a boy of five the secret of making a product perfect—'You work at it,' he told me—ladies and gentlemen, a man who has worked at it and succeeded at it since the day he went off to begin tanning hides at the age of fourteen, the glover's glover, who knows more about the glove business than anybody else alive, Mr. Newark Maid, my father, Lou Levov." "Look," began Mr. Newark Maid, "don't let anybody kid you tonight. I enjoy working, I enjoy the glove business, I enjoy the challenge, I don't like the idea of retiring, I think it's the first step to the grave. But none of that bothers me for one big reason—because I am the luckiest man in the world. And lucky because of one word. The biggest little word there is: family. If I was being pushed out by a competitor, I wouldn't be standing here smiling—you know me, I would be standing here shouting. But who I am being pushed out by is my own beloved son. I have been blessed with the most wonderful family a man could want: a wonderful wife, two wonderful boys, wonderful grandchildren. . . ."

The Swede had Vicky bring a sheepskin into the office and he gave it to the Wharton girl to feel.

"This has been pickled but it hasn't been tanned," he told her. "It's a hair sheepskin. Doesn't have wool like a domestic sheep but hair."

"What happens to the hair?" she asked him. "Does it get used?"

"Good question. The hair is used to make carpet. Up in Amsterdam, New York. Bigelow. Mohawk. But the primary value is the skins. The hair is a by-product, and how you get the hair off the skin and all the rest of it is another story entirely. Before synthetics came along, the hair mostly went into cheap carpets. There's a company who brokered all the hair from the tanneries to the carpetmakers, but you don't want to go into that," he said, observing how before they'd really even begun she'd filled with notes the top sheet of a fresh yellow legal pad. "Though if you do," he added, touched by—and attracted by—her thoroughness, "because I suppose it does all sort of tie together, I could send you to talk to those people. I think the family is still around. It's a niche that not many people know about. It's interesting. It's *all* interesting. You've settled on an interesting subject, young lady."

"I think I have," she said, warmly smiling over at him.

"Anyway, this skin"—he'd taken it back from her and was stroking it with the side of a thumb as you might stroke the cat to get the purr going—"is called a cabretta in the industry's terminology. Small sheep. Little sheep. They only live twenty or thirty degrees north and south of the equator. They're sort of on a semi-wild grazing basis—families in an African village will each own four or five sheep, and they'll all be flocked together and put out in the bush. What you were holding in your hand isn't raw anymore. We buy them in what's called the pickled stage. The hair's been removed and the preprocessing has been done to preserve them to get here. We used to bring them in raw—huge bales tied with rope and so on, skins just dried in the air. I actually have a ship's manifest—it's somewhere here, I can find it for you if you want to see it—a copy of a ship's manifest from 1790, in which skins were landed in Boston similar to what we were bringing in up to last year. And from the same ports in Africa."

It could have been his father talking to her. For all he knew, every word of every sentence uttered by him he had heard from his father's mouth before he'd finished grade school, and then two or three thousand times again during the decades they'd run the business together. Trade talk was a tradition in glove families going back hundreds of years—in the best of them, the father passed the secrets on to the son along with all the history and all the lore. It was true in the tanneries, where the tanning process is like cooking and the recipes are handed down from the father to the son, and it was true in the glove shops and it was true on the cutting-room floor. The old Italian cutters would train their sons and no one else, and those sons accepted the tutorial from their fathers as he had accepted the tutorial from his. Beginning when he was a kid of five and extending into his maturity, the father as the authority was unopposed: accepting his authority was one and the same with extracting from him the wisdom that had made Newark Maid manufacturer of the country's best ladies' glove. The Swede quickly came to love in the same wholehearted way the very things his father did and, at the factory, to think more or less as he did. And to sound as he did—if not on every last subject, then whenever a conversation came around to leather or Newark or gloves.

Not since Merry had disappeared had he felt anything like this loquacious. Right up to that morning, all he'd been wanting was to weep or to hide; but because there was Dawn to nurse and a business to tend to and his parents to prop up, because everybody else was paralyzed by disbelief and shattered to the core, neither inclination had as yet eroded the protective front he provided the family and presented to the world. But now words were sweeping him on, buoying him up, his *father's* words released by the sight of this tiny girl studiously taking them down. She was nearly as small, he thought, as the kids from Merry's third-grade class, who'd been bused the thirty-eight miles from their rural schoolhouse one day back in the late fifties so that Merry's daddy could show them how he made gloves, show them especially Merry's magical spot, the laying-off table, where, at the end of the making process, the men shaped and pressed each and every glove by pulling it carefully down over steam-heated brass hands veneered in chrome. The hands were dangerously hot and they were shiny and they stuck straight up from the table in a row, thin-looking as hands that had been flattened in a mangle and then amputated, beautifully amputated hands afloat in space like the souls of the dead. As a little girl, Merry was captivated by their enigma, called them "the pancake hands." Merry as a little girl saying to her classmates, "You want to make five dollars a dozen," which was what glovemakers were always saying and what she'd been hearing since she was born—five dollars a dozen, that was what you shot for, regardless. Merry whispering to the teacher, "People cheating on piece rates is always a problem. My daddy had to fire one man. He was stealing time," and the Swede telling her, "Honey, let Daddy conduct the tour, okay?" Merry as a little girl reveling in the dazzling idea of stealing *time*. Merry flitting from floor to floor, so proud and proprietary, flaunting her familiarity with all the employees, unaware as yet of the desecration of dignity inherent to the ruthless exploitation of the worker by the profit-hungry boss who unjustly owns the means of production.

No wonder he felt so untamed, craving to spill over with talk. Momentarily it was *then* again—nothing blown up, nothing ruined. As a family they still flew the flight of the immigrant rocket, the upward, unbroken immigrant trajectory from slave-driven great-grandfather to self-driven grandfather to self-confident, accomplished, independent father to the highest high flier of them all, the fourth-generation child for whom America was to be heaven itself. No wonder he couldn't shut up. It was impossible to shut up. The Swede was giving in to the ordinary human wish to live once again in the past—to spend a self-deluding, harmless few moments back in the wholesome striving of the past, when the family endured by a truth in no way grounded in abetting destruction but rather in eluding and outlasting destruction, overcoming its mysterious inroads by creating the utopia of a rational existence.

He heard her asking, "How many come in a shipment?"

"How many skins? A couple of thousand dozen skins."

"A bale is how many?"

He liked finding that she was interested in every last detail. Yes, talking to this attentive student up from Wharton, he was suddenly able to like something as he had not been able to like anything, to bear anything, even to understand anything he'd come up against for four lifeless months. He'd felt himself instead to be perishing of everything. "Oh, a hundred and twenty skins," he replied.

She continued taking notes as she asked, "They come right to your shipping department?"

"They come to the tannery. The tannery is a contractor. We buy the material and then we give it to them, and we give them the process to use and then they convert it into leather for us. My grandfather and my father worked in the tannery right here in Newark. So did I, for six months, when I started in the business. Ever been inside a tannery?"

"Not yet."

"Well, you've got to go to a tannery if you're going to write about leather. I'll set that up for you if you'd like that. They're primitive places. The technology has improved things, but what you'll see isn't that different from what you would have seen hundreds of years ago. Awful work. Said to be the oldest industry of which relics have been found anywhere. Six-thousand-year-old relics of tanning found somewhere—Turkey, I believe. First clothing was just skins that were tanned by smoking them. I told you it was an interesting subject once you get into it. My father is the leather scholar. He's who you should be talking to, but he's living in Florida now. Start my father off about gloves and he'll talk for two days running. That's typical, by the way. Glovemen love the trade and everything about it. Tell me, have you ever seen anything manufactured, Miss Cohen?"

"I can't say I have."

"Never seen anything made?"

"Saw my mother make a cake when I was a kid."

He laughed. She had made him laugh. A feisty innocent, eager to learn. His daughter was easily a foot taller than Rita Cohen, fair where she was dark, but otherwise Rita Cohen, homely little thing though she was, had begun to remind him of Merry before her repugnance set in and she began to become their enemy. The good-natured intelligence that would just waft out of her and into the house when she came home from school overbrimming with what she'd learned in class. How she remembered everything. Everything neatly taken down in her notebook and memorized overnight.

"I'll tell you what we're going to do. We're going to bring you right through the whole process. Come on. We're going to make you a pair of gloves and you're going to watch them being made from start to finish. What size do you wear?"

"I don't know. Small."

He'd gotten up from the desk and come around and taken hold of her hand. "Very small. I'm guessing you're a four." He'd already got from the top drawer of his desk a measuring tape with a D ring at one end, and now he put it around her hand, threaded the other end through the D ring, and pulled the tape around her palm. "We'll see what kind of guesser I am. Close your hand." She made a fist, causing the hand to slightly expand, and he read the size in French inches. "Four it is. In a ladies' size that's as small as they come. Anything smaller is a child's. Come on. I'll show you how it's done."

He felt as though he'd stepped right back into the mouth of the past as they started, side by side, up the wooden steps of the old stairwell. He heard himself telling her (while simultaneously hearing his father telling her), "You always sort your skins at the northern side of the factory, where there's no direct sunlight. That way you can really study the skins for quality. Where the sunlight comes in you can't see. The cutting room and the sorting, always on the northern side. Sorting at the top. The second floor the cutting. And the first floor, where you came, the making. Bottom floor finishing and shipping. We're going to work our way from the top down."

That they did. And he was happy. He could not help himself. It was not right. It was not real. Something must be done to stop this. But she was busy taking notes, and he could not stop—a girl who knew the value of hard work and paying attention, and interested in the right things, interested in the preparation of leather and the manufacture of gloves, and to stop himself was impossible.

When someone is suffering as the Swede was suffering, asking him to be undeluded by a momentary uplifting, however dubious its rationale, is asking an awful lot.

In the cutting room, there were twenty-five men at work, about six to a table, and the Swede led her over to the oldest of them, whom he introduced as "the Master," a small, bald fellow with a hearing aid who continued working at a rectangular piece of leather—"That's the piece the glove is made from," said the Swede, "called a trank"—working at it with a ruler and shears all the time that the Swede was telling her just who this Master was. With a light heart. Still floating free. Doing nothing to stop it. Letting his father's patter flow.

The cutting room was where the Swede had got inspired to follow his father into gloves, the place where he believed he'd grown from a boy into a man. The cutting room, up high and full of light, had been his favorite spot in the factory since he was just a kid and the old European cutters came to work identically dressed in three-piece suits, starched white shirts, ties, suspenders, and cuff links. Each cutter would carefully remove the suit coat and hang it in the closet, but no one in the Swede's memory had ever removed the tie, and only a very few descended to the informality of removing the vest, let alone turning up shirtsleeves, before donning a fresh white apron and getting down to the first skin, unrolling it from the dampened muslin cloth and beginning the work of stretching. The wall of big windows to the north illuminated the hardwood cutting tables with the cool, even light you needed for grading and matching and cutting skins. The polished smoothness of the table's rounded edge, worked smooth over the years from all the animal skins stretched across it and pulled to length, was so provocative to the boy that he always had to restrain himself from rushing to press the concavity of his cheek against the convexity of the wood—restrained himself until he was alone. There was a blurry line of footprints worn into the wood floor where the men stood all day at the cutting tables, and when no one else was up there he liked to go and stand with his shoes where the floor was worn away. Watching the cutters work, he knew that they were the elite and that they knew it and the boss knew it. Though they considered themselves to be men more aristocratic than anyone around, including the boss, a cutter's working hand was proudly calloused from cutting with his big, heavy shears. Beneath those white shirts were arms and chests and shoulders full of a workingman's strength—powerful they had to be, to pull and pull on leather all their lives, to squeeze out of every skin every inch of leather there was.

A lot of licking went on, a lot of saliva went into every glove, but, as his father joked, "The customer never knows it." The cutter would spit into the dry inking material in which he rubbed the brush for the stencil that numbered the pieces he cut from each trank. Having cut a pair of gloves, he would touch his finger to his tongue so as to wet the numbered pieces, to stick them together before they were rubber-banded for the sewing forelady and the sewers. What the boy never got over were those first German cutters employed by Newark Maid, who used to keep a schooner of beer beside them and sip from it, they said, "to keep the whistle wet" and their saliva flowing. Quickly enough Lou Levov had done away with the beer, but the saliva? No. Nobody could want to do away with the saliva. That was part and parcel of all that they loved, the son and heir no less than the founding father.

"Harry can cut a glove as good as any of them." Harry, the Master, stood directly beside the Swede, indifferent to his boss's words and doing his work. "He's only been forty-one years with Newark Maid but he works at it. The cutter has to visualize how the skin is going to realize itself into the maximum number of gloves. Then he has to cut it. Takes great skill to cut a glove right. Table cutting is an art. No two skins are alike. The skins all come in different according to each animal's diet and age, every one different as far as stretchability goes, and the skill involved in making every glove come out like every other is amazing. Same thing with the sewing. Kind of work people don't want to do anymore. You can't just take a sewer who knows how to run a traditional sewing machine, or knows how to sew dresses, and start her here on gloves. She has to go through a three- or four-month training process, has to have finger dexterity, has to have patience, and it's six months before she's proficient and reaches even eighty percent efficiency. Glove sewing is a tremendously complicated procedure. If you want to make a better glove, you have to spend money and train workers. Takes a lot of hard work and attention, all the twists and turns where the finger crotches are sewn—it's very hard. In the days when my father first opened a glove shop, the people were in it for life—Harry's the last of them. This cutting room is one of the last in this hemisphere. Our production is still always full. We still have people here who know what they're doing. Nobody cuts gloves this way anymore, not in this country, where hardly anybody's left to cut them, and not anywhere else either, except maybe in a little family-run shop in Naples or Grenoble. These were people, the people who worked here, who were in it for life. They were born into the glove industry and they died in the glove industry. Today we're constantly retraining people. Today our economy is such that people take a job here and if something comes along for another fifty cents an hour, they're gone."

She wrote all this down.

"When I first came into the business and my father sent me up here to learn how to cut, all I did was stand right here at the cutting table and watch this guy. I learned this business in the old-fashioned way. From the ground up. My father started me literally sweeping the floors. Went through every single department, getting a feel for each operation and why it was being done. From Harry I learned how to cut a glove. I wouldn't say I was a proficient glove cutter. If I cut two, three pairs a day it was a lot, but I learned the rudimentary principles—right, Harry? A demanding teacher, this fellow. When he shows you how to do something, he goes all the way. Learning from Harry almost made me yearn for my old man. First day I came up here Harry set me straight—he told me that down where he lived boys would come to his door and say, 'Could you teach me to be a glove cutter?' and he would tell them, 'You've got to pay me fifteen thousand first, because that's how much time and leather you're going to destroy till you get to the point where you can make the minimum wage.' I watched him for a full two months before he let me anywhere near a hide. An average table cutter will cut three, three and a half dozen a day. A good, fast table cutter will cut five dozen a day. Harry was cutting five and a half dozen a day. 'You think I'm good?' he told me. 'You should have seen my dad.' Then he told me about his father and the tall man from Barnum and Bailey. Remember, Harry?" Harry nodded. "When the Barnum and Bailey circus came to Newark . . . this is 1917, 1918?" Harry nodded again without stopping his work. "Well, they came to town and they had a tall man, approaching nine feet or so, and Harry's father saw him one day in the street, walking along the street, at Broad and Market, and he got so excited he ran over to the tall man and he took his shoelace off his own shoe, measured the guy's hand right out there on the street, and he went home and made up a perfect

size-seventeen pair of gloves. Harry's father cut it and his mom
sewed it, and they went over to the circus and gave the gloves to
the tall man, and the whole family got free seats, and a big story
about Harry's dad ran in the *Newark News* the next day."

Harry corrected him. "The *Star-Eagle*."

"Right, before it became the *Ledger*."

"Wonderful," the girl said, laughing. "Your father must have
been very skilled."

"Couldn't speak a word of English," Harry told her.

"He couldn't? Well, that just goes to show, you don't have to
know English," she said, "to cut a perfect pair of gloves for a man
nine feet tall."

Harry didn't laugh but the Swede did, laughed and put his arm
around her. "This is Rita. We're going to make her a dress glove,
size four. Black or brown, honey?"

"Brown?"

From a wrapped-up bundle of hides dampening beside Harry,
he picked one out in a pale shade of brown. "This is a tough color
to get," the Swede told her. "British tan. You can see, there's all
sorts of variation in the color—see how light it is there, how dark
it is down there? Okay. This is sheepskin. What you saw in my office was pickled. This has been tanned. This is leather. But you
can still see the animal. If you were to look at the animal," he said,
"here it is—the head, the butt, the front legs, the hind legs, and
here's the back, where the leather is harder and thicker, as it is
over our own backbones. . . ."

Honey. He began calling her honey up in the cutting room and
he could not stop, and this even before he understood that by
standing beside her he was as close to Merry as he had been since
the general store blew up and his honey disappeared. This is a
French ruler, it's about an inch longer than an American ruler. . . .
This is called a spud knife, dull, beveled to an edge but not
sharp. . . . Now he's pulling the trank down like that, to the length
again—Harry likes to bet you that he'll pull it right down to the
pattern without even touching the pattern, but I don't bet him be-

cause I don't like losing. . . . This is called a fourchette. . . . See, all meticulously done. . . . He's going to cut yours and give it to me so we can take it down to the making department. . . . This is called the slitter, honey. Only mechanical process in the whole thing. A press and a die, and the slitter will take about four tranks at a time. . . .

"Wow. This is an elaborate process," said Rita.

"That it is. Hard really to make money in the glove business because it's so labor-intensive—a time-consuming process, many operations to be coordinated. Most of the glove businesses have been family businesses. From father to son. Very traditional business. A product is a product to most manufacturers. The guy who makes them doesn't know anything about them. The glove business isn't like that. This business has a long, long history."

"Do other people feel the romance of the glove business the way you do, Mr. Levov? You really are mad for this place and all the processes. I guess that's what makes you a happy man."

"Am I?" he asked, and felt as though he were going to be dissected, cut into by a knife, opened up and all his misery revealed. "I guess I am."

"Are you the last of the Mohicans?"

"No, most of them, I believe, in this business have that same feeling for the tradition, that same love. Because it does require a love and a legacy to motivate somebody to stay in a business like this. You have to have strong ties to it to be able to stick it out. Come on," he said, having managed momentarily to quash everything that was shadowing him and menacing him, succeeded still to be able to speak with great precision despite her telling him he was a happy man. "Let's go back to the making room."

This is the silking, that's a story in itself, but this is what she's going to do first. . . . This is called a piqué machine, it sews the finest stitch, called piqué, requires far more skill than the other stitches. . . . This is called a polishing machine and that is called a stretcher and you are called honey and I am called Daddy and this is called living and the other is called dying and this is called madness and this is called mourning and this is called hell, pure hell, and you have to have strong ties to be able to stick it out, this is called trying-to-go-on-as-though-nothing-has-happened and this is called paying-the-full-price-but-in-God's-name-for-what, this is called wanting-to-be-dead-and-wanting-to-find-her-and-to-kill-her-and-to-save-her-from-whatever-she-is-going-through-wherever-on-earth-she-may-be-at-this-moment, this unbridled outpouring is called blotting-out-everything *and it does not work, I am half insane, the shattering force of that bomb is too great. . . .* And then they were back at his office again, waiting for Rita's gloves to come from the finishing department, and he was repeating to her a favorite observation of his father's, one that his father had read somewhere and always used to impress visitors, and he heard himself repeating it, word for word, as his own. If only he could get her to stay and not go, if he could keep on talking about gloves to her, about gloves, about skins, about his horrible riddle, implore her, beg her, *Don't leave me alone with this horrible riddle. . . .* "Monkeys, gorillas, they have brains and we have a brain, but they don't have this thing, the thumb. They can't move it opposite the way we do. The inner digit on the hand of man, that might be the distinguishing physical feature between ourselves and the rest of the animals. And the glove protects that inner digit. The ladies' glove, the welder's glove, the rubber glove, the baseball glove, et cetera. This is the root of humanity, this opposable thumb. It enables us to make tools and build cities and everything else. More than the brain. Maybe some other animals have bigger brains in proportion to their bodies than we have. I don't know. But the hand itself is an intricate thing. It moves. There is no other part of a human being that is clothed that is such a complex moving structure. . . ." And that was when Vicky popped in the door with the size-four finished gloves. "Here's your pair of gloves," Vicky said, and gave them to the boss, who looked them over and then leaned across the desk to show them to the girl. "See the seams? The width of the sewing at the edge of the leather—that's where the quality workmanship is. This margin is probably about a thirty-second of an inch between the stitching and the edge. And that requires a high skill level, far higher than normal. If a glove is not well sewn, this edge might come to an eighth of an inch. It also will not be straight. Look at how straight these seams are. This is why a Newark Maid glove is a good glove, Rita. Because of the straight seams. Because of the fine leather. It's well tanned. It's soft. It's pliable. Smells like the inside of a new car. I love good leather, I love fine gloves, and I was brought up on the idea of making the best glove possible. It's in my blood, and nothing gives me greater pleasure"—he clutched at his own effusiveness the way a sick person clutches at any sign of health, no matter how minute—"than giving you these lovely gloves. Here," he said, "with our compliments," and, smiling, he presented the gloves to the girl, who excitedly pulled them onto her little hands—"Slowly, slowly . . . always draw on a pair of gloves by the fingers," he told her, "afterward the thumb, then draw the wrist down in place . . . always the first time draw them on slowly"—and she looked up and, smiling back at him with the pleasure that any child takes in receiving a gift, showed him with her hands in the air how beautiful the gloves looked, how beautifully they fit. "Close your hand, make a fist," the Swede said. "Feel how the glove expands where your hand expands and nicely adjusts to your size? That's what the cutter does when he does his job right—no stretch left in the length, he's pulled that all out at the table because you don't want the fingers to stretch, but an exactly measured amount of hidden stretch left in the width. That stretch in the width is a precise calculation."

"Yes, yes, it's wonderful, absolutely perfect," she told him, opening and closing her hands in turn. "God bless the precise calculators of this world," she said, laughing, "who leave stretch hidden in the width," and only after Vicky had shut the door to his glass-enclosed office and headed back into the racket of the making department did Rita add, very softly, "She wants her Audrey Hepburn scrapbook."

from **"PASTORALIA"**

George Saunders

I have to admit I'm not feeling my best. Not that I'm doing so bad. Not that I really have anything to complain about. Not that I would actually verbally complain if I did have something to complain about. No. Because I'm Thinking Positive/Saying Positive. I'm sitting back on my haunches, waiting for people to poke in their heads. Although it's been thirteen days since anyone poked in their head and Janet's speaking English to me more and more, which is partly why I feel so, you know, crummy.

"Jeez," she says first thing this morning. "I'm so tired of roast goat I could scream."

What am I supposed to say to that? It puts me in a bad spot. She thinks I'm a goody-goody and that her speaking English makes me uncomfortable. And she's right. It does. Because we've got it good. Every morning, a new goat, just killed, sits in our Big Slot. In our Little Slot, a book of matches. That's better than some. Some are required to catch wild hares in snares. Some are required to wear pioneer garb while cutting the heads off chickens. But not us. I just have to haul the dead goat out of the Big Slot and skin it with a sharp flint. Janet just has to make the fire. So things are pretty good. Not as good as in the old days, but then again, not so bad.

In the old days, when heads were constantly poking in, we liked what we did. Really hammed it up. Had little grunting fights. Whenever I was about to toss a handful of dirt in her face I'd pound a rock against a rock in rage. That way she knew to close her eyes. Sometimes she did this kind of crude weaving. It was like: Roots of Weaving. Sometimes we'd go down to Russian Peasant Farm for a barbecue, I remember there was Murray and Leon, Leon was dating Eileen, Eileen was the one with all the cats, but now, with the big decline in heads poking in, the Russian Peasants are all elsewhere, some to Administration but most not, Eileen's cats have gone wild, and honest to God sometimes I worry I'll go to the Big Slot and find it goatless.

This morning I go to the Big Slot and find it goatless. Instead of a goat there's a note:

Hold on, hold on, it says. *The goat's coming, for crissake. Don't get all snooty.*

The problem is, what am I supposed to do during the time when I'm supposed to be skinning the goat with the flint? I decide to pretend to be desperately ill. I rock in a corner and moan. This gets old. Skinning the goat with the flint takes the better part of an hour. No way am I rocking and moaning for an hour.

Janet comes in from her Separate Area and her eyebrows go up.

"No freaking goat?" she says.

I make some guttural sounds and some motions meaning: Big rain come down, and boom, make goats run, goats now away, away in high hills, and as my fear was great, I did not follow.

Janet scratches under her armpit and makes a sound like a monkey, then lights a cigarette.

"What a bunch of shit," she says. "Why you insist, I'll never know. Who's here? Do you see anyone here but us?"

I gesture to her to put out the cigarette and make the fire. She gestures to me to kiss her butt.

"Why am I making a fire?" she says. "A fire in advance of a goat. Is this like a wishful fire? Like a hopeful fire? No, sorry, I've had it. What would I do in the real world if there was thunder and so on and our goats actually ran away? Maybe I'd mourn, like cut myself with that flint, or maybe I'd kick your ass for being so stupid as to leave the goats out in the rain. What, they didn't put it in the Big Slot?"

I scowl at her and shake my head.

"Well, did you at least check the Little Slot?" she says. "Maybe it was a small goat and they really crammed it in. Maybe for once they gave us a nice quail or something."

I give her a look, then walk off in a rolling gait to check the Little Slot.

Nothing.

"Well, freak this," she says. "I'm going to walk right out of here and see what the hell is up."

But she won't. She knows it and I know it. She sits on her log and smokes and together we wait to hear a clunk in the Big Slot.

About lunch we hit the Reserve Crackers. About dinner we again hit the Reserve Crackers.

No heads poke in and there's no clunk in either the Big or Little Slot.

Then the quality of light changes and she stands at the door of her Separate Area.

"No goat tomorrow, I'm out of here and down the hill," she says. "I swear to God. You watch."

I go into my Separate Area and put on my footies. I have some cocoa and take out a Daily Partner Performance Evaluation Form.

Do I note any attitudinal difficulties? I do not. How do I rate my Partner overall? Very good. Are there any Situations which require Mediation?

There are not.

I fax it in.

Next morning, no goat. Also no note. Janet sits on her log and smokes and together we wait to hear a clunk in the Big Slot.

No heads poke in and there's no clunk in either the Big or Little Slot.

About lunch we hit the Reserve Crackers. About dinner we again hit the Reserve Crackers.

Then the quality of light changes and she stands at the door of her Separate Area.

"Crackers, crackers, crackers!" she says pitifully. "Jesus, I wish you'd talk to me. I don't see why you won't. I'm about to go bonkers. We could at least talk. At least have some fun. Maybe play some Scrabble."

Scrabble.

I wave good night and give her a grunt.

"Bastard," she says, and hits me with the flint. She's a good thrower and I almost say ow. Instead I make a horselike sound of fury and consider pinning her to the floor in an effort to make her submit to my superior power etc. etc. Then I go into my Separate Area. I put on my footies and tidy up. I have some cocoa. I take out a Daily Partner Performance Evaluation Form.

Do I note any attitudinal difficulties? I do not. How do I rate my Partner overall? Very good. Are there any Situations which require Mediation?

There are not.

I fax it in.

In the morning in the Big Slot there's a nice fat goat. Also a note:

Ha ha! it says. *Sorry about the no goat and all. A little mix-up. In the future, when you look in here for a goat, what you will find on every occasion is a goat, and not a note. Or maybe both. Ha ha! Happy eating! Everything's fine!*

I skin the goat briskly with the flint. Janet comes in, smiles when she sees the goat, and makes, very quickly, a nice little fire, and does not say one English word all morning and even traces a few of our pictographs with a wettened finger, as if awestruck at their splendid beauty and so on.

Around noon she comes over and looks at the cut on my arm, from where she threw the flint.

"You gonna live?" she says. "Sorry, man, really sorry, I just like lost it."

I give her a look. She cans the English, then starts wailing in grief and sort of hunkers down in apology.

The goat tastes super after two days of crackers.

I have a nap by the fire and for once she doesn't walk around singing pop hits in English, only mumbles unintelligibly and pretends to be catching and eating small bugs.

Her way of saying sorry.

No one pokes their head in.

Once, back in the days when people still poked their heads in, this guy poked his head in.

"Whoa," he said. "These are some very cramped living quarters. This really makes you appreciate the way we live now. Do you have call-waiting? Do you know how to make a nice mushroom cream sauce? Ha ha! I pity you guys. And also, and yet, I thank you guys, who were my precursors, right? Is that the spirit? Is that your point? You weren't ignorant on purpose? You were doing the best you could? Just like I am? Probably someday some guy representing me will be in there, and some punk who I'm precursor of will be hooting at me, asking why my shoes were made out of dead cows and so forth? Because in that future time, wearing dead skin on your feet, no, they won't do that. That will seem to them like barbarity, just like you dragging that broad around by her hair seems to us like barbarity, although to me, not that much, after living with my wife fifteen years. Ha ha! Have a good one!"

I never drag Janet around by the hair.

Too cliché.

Just then his wife poked in her head.

"Stinks in there," she said, and yanked her head out.

"That's the roasting goat," her husband said. "Everything wasn't all prettied up. When you ate meat, it was like you were eating actual meat, the flesh of a dead animal, an animal that maybe had been licking your hand just a few hours before."

"I would never do that," said the wife.

"You do it now, bozo!" said the man. "You just pay someone to do the dirty work. The slaughtering? The skinning?"

"I do not either," said the wife.

We couldn't see them, only hear them through the place where the heads poke in.

"Ever heard of a slaughterhouse?" the husband said. "Ha ha! Gotcha! What do you think goes on in there? Some guy you never met kills and flays a cow with what you might term big old cow eyes, so you can have your shoes and I can have my steak and my shoes!"

"That's different," she said. "Those animals were raised for slaughter. That's what they were made for. Plus I cook them in an oven, I don't squat there in my underwear with smelly smoke blowing all over me."

"Thank heaven for small favors," he said. "Joking! I'm joking. You squatting in your underwear is not such a bad mental picture, believe me."

"Plus where do they poop," she said.

"Ask them," said the husband. "Ask them where they poop, if you so choose. You paid your dime. That is certainly your prerogative."

"I don't believe I will," said the wife.

"Well, I'm not shy," he said.

Then there was no sound from the head-hole for quite some time. Possibly they were quietly discussing it.

"Okay, so where do you poop?" asked the husband, poking his head in.

"We have disposable bags that mount on a sort of rack," said Janet. "The septic doesn't come up this far."

"Ah," he said. "They poop in bags that mount on racks."

"Wonderful," said his wife. "I'm the richer for that information."

"But hold on," the husband said. "In the old times, like when the cave was real and all, where then did they go? I take it there were no disposal bags in those times, if I'm right."

"In those times they just went out in the woods," said Janet.

"Ah," he said. "That makes sense."

You see what I mean about Janet? When addressed directly we're supposed to cower shrieking in the corner but instead she answers twice in English?

I gave her a look.

"Oh, he's okay," she whispered. "He's no narc. I can tell."

In a minute in came a paper airplane: our Client Vignette Evaluation.

Under *Overall Impression* he'd written: *A-okay! Very nice.*

Under *Learning Value* he'd written: *We learned where they pooped. Both old days and now.*

I added it to our pile, then went into my Separate Area and put on my footies. I filled out my Daily Partner Performance Evaluation Form. Did I note any attitudinal difficulties? I did not. How did I rate my Partner overall? Very good. Were there any Situations which required Mediation?

There were not.

I faxed it in.

This morning is the morning I empty our Human Refuse bags and the trash bags and the bag from the bottom of the sleek metal hole where Janet puts her used feminine items.

For this I get an extra sixty a month. Plus it's always nice to get out of the cave.

I knock on the door of her Separate Area.

"Who is it?" she asks, playing dumb.

She knows very well who it is. I stick in my arm and wave around a trash bag.

"Go for it," she says.

She's in there washing her armpits with a washcloth. The room smells like her, only more so. I add the trash from her wicker basket to my big white bag. I add her bag of used feminine items to my big white bag. I take three bags labeled Caution Human Refuse from the corner and add them to my big pink bag labeled Caution Human Refuse.

I mime to her that I dreamed of a herd that covered the plain like the grass of the earth, they were as numerous as grasshoppers and yet the meat of their humps resembled each a tiny mountain etc. etc., and sharpen my spear and try to look like I'm going into a sort of prehunt trance.

"Are you going?" she shouts. "Are you going now? Is that what you're saying?"

I nod.

"Christ, so go already," she says. "Have fun. Bring back some mints."

She has worked very hard these many months to hollow out a rock in which to hide her mints and her smokes. Mints mints mints. Smokes smokes smokes. No matter how long we're in here together I will never get the hots for her. She's fifty and has large feet and sloping shoulders and a pinched little face and chews with her mouth open. Sometimes she puts on big ugly glasses in the cave and does a crossword: very verboten.

Out I go, with the white regular trash bag in one hand and our mutual big pink Human Refuse bag in the other.

.   .   .

Next morning in the Big Slot is a goat and in the Little Slot a rabbit and a note addressed to Distribution:

Please accept this extra food as a token of what our esteem is like, the note says. *Please know that each one of you is very special to us, and are never forgotten about. Please know that if each one of you could be kept, you would be, if that would benefit everyone. But it wouldn't, or we would do it, wouldn't we, we would keep every one of you. But as we meld into our sleeker new organization, what an excellent opportunity to adjust our Staff Mix. And so, although in this time of scarcity and challenge, some must perhaps go, the upside of this is, some must stay, and perhaps it will be you. Let us hope it will be you, each and every one of you, but no, as stated previously, it won't, that is impossible. So just enjoy the treats provided, and don't worry, and wait for your supervisor to contact you, and if he or she doesn't, know with relief that the Staff Remixing has passed by your door. Although it is only honest to inform you that some who make the first pass may indeed be removed in the second, or maybe even a third, depending on how the Remixing goes, although if anyone is removed in both the first and second pass, that will be a redundant screw-up, please ignore. We will only remove each of you once. If that many times! Some of you will be removed never, the better ones of you. But we find ourselves in a too-many-Indians situation and so must first cut some Indians and then, later, possibly, some chiefs. But not yet, because that is harder, because that is us. Soon, but not yet, we have to decide which of us to remove, and that is so very hard, because we are so very useful. Not that we are saying we chiefs are more useful than you Indians, but certainly we do make some very difficult decisions that perhaps you Indians would find hard to make, keeping you up nights, such as which of you to remove. But don't worry about us, we've been doing this for years, only first and foremost remember that what we are doing, all of us, chiefs and Indians both, is a fun privilege, how many would like to do what we do, in the entertainment field.*

"Jeez," says Janet. "Let the freaking canning begin."

I give her a look.

"Oh all right all right," she says. "Ooga mooga. Ooga ooga mooga. Is that better?"

She can be as snotty as she likes but a Remixing is nothing to sneeze at.

I skin and roast the goat and rabbit. After breakfast she puts on her Walkman and starts a letter to her sister: very verboten. I work on the pictographs. I mean I kneel while pretending to paint them by dipping my crude dry brush into the splotches of hard colorful plastic meant to look like paint made from squashed berries.

Around noon the fax in my Separate Area makes the sound it makes when a fax is coming in.

Getting it would require leaving the cave and entering my Separate Area during working hours.

"Christ, go get it," Janet says. "Are you nuts? It might be from Louise."

I go get it.

It's from Louise.

Nelson doing better today, it says. *Not much new swelling. Played trucks and ate 3 pcs bologna. Asked about you. No temperature, good range of motion in both legs and arms. Visa is up to $6800, should I transfer to new card w/ lower interest rate?*

Sounds good, I fax back. *How are other kids?*

Kids are kids are kids, she faxes back. *Driving me nuts. Always talking.*

Miss you, I fax, and she faxes back the necessary Signature Card.

I sign the card. I fax the card.

Nelson's three. Three months ago his muscles stiffened up. The medicine they put him on to loosen his muscles did somewhat loosen them, but also it caused his muscles to swell. Otherwise he's fine, only he's stiff and swollen and it hurts when he moves. They have a name for what they originally thought he had, but when the medication made him swell up, Dr. Evans had to admit that whatever he had, it wasn't what they'd originally thought it was.

So we're watching him closely.

I return to the cave.

"How are things?" Janet says.

I grimace.

"Well, shit," she says. "You know I'm freaking rooting for you guys."

Sometimes she can be pretty nice.

First thing next morning Greg Nordstrom pokes his head in and asks me to brunch.

Which is a first.

"How about me?" says Janet.

"Ha ha!" says Nordstrom. "Not you. Not today. Maybe soon, however!"

I follow him out.

Very bright sun.

About fifty feet from the cave there's a red paper screen that says Patience! Under Construction, and we go behind it.

"You'll be getting your proxy forms in your Slot soon," he says, spreading out some bagels on a blanket. "Fill out the proxy as you see fit, everything's fine, just vote, do it boldly, exert your choice, it has to do with your stock option. Are you vested? Great to be vested. Just wait until you are. It really feels like a Benefit. You'll see why they call Benefits Benefits, when every month, ka-ching, that option money kicks up a notch. Man, we're lucky."

"Yes," I say.

"I am and you are," he says. "Not everyone is. Some aren't. Those being removed in the Staff Remixing, no. But you're not being removed. At least I don't think so. Now Janet, I have some concerns about Janet, I don't know what they're going to do about Janet. It's not me, it's them, but what can I do? How is she? Is she okay? How have you found her? I want you to speak frankly. Are there problems? Problems we can maybe help correct? How is she? Nice? Reliable? It's not negative to point out a defect. Actually, it's positive, because then the defect can be fixed. What's negative is to withhold valuable info. Are you? Withholding valuable info? I hope not. Are you being negative? Is she a bit of a pain? Please tell me. I want you to. If you admit she's a bit of a pain, I'll write down how positive you were. Look, you know and I know she's got some performance issues, so what an exciting opportunity, for you to admit it and me to hear it loud and clear. Super!"

For six years she's been telling me about her Pap smears and her kid in rehab and her mother in Fort Wayne who has a bad valve and can't stand up or her lungs fill with blood etc. etc.

"I haven't really noticed any problems," I say.

"Blah blah blah," he says. "What kind of praise is that? Empty praise? Is it empty praise? I'd caution against empty praise. Because empty praise is what? Is like what? Is a lie. And a lie is what? Is negative. You're like the opposite of that little boy who cried Wolf. You're like that little boy who cried No Wolf, when a wolf was in fact chewing on his leg, by the name of Janet. Because what have I recently seen? Having seen your Daily Partner Performance Evaluation Forms, I haven't seen on them a single discouraging word. Not one. Did you ever note a single attitudinal difficulty? You did not. How did you rate your Partner overall? Very good, always, every single day. Were there ever any Situations which required Mediation? There were not, even when, in one instance, she told a guy where you folks pooped. In English. In the cave. I have documentation, because I read that guy's Client Vignette Evaluation."

It gets very quiet. The wind blows and the paper screen tips up a bit. The bagels look good but we're not eating them.

"Look," he says. "I know it's hard to be objective about people we come to daily know, but in the big picture, who benefits when the truth is not told? Does Janet? How can Janet know she's not being her best self if someone doesn't tell her, then right away afterwards harshly discipline her? And with Janet not being her best self, is the organization healthier? And with the organization not being healthier, and the organization being that thing that ultimately puts the food in your face, you can easily see that, by lying about Janet's behavior, you are taking the food out of your own face. Who puts the cash in your hand to buy that food in your face? We do. What do we want of you? We want you to tell the truth. That's it. That is all."

We sit awhile in silence.

"Very simple," he says. "A nonbrainer."

A white fuzzy thing lands in my arm hair. I pick it out.

Down it falls.

"Sad," he says. "Sad is all it is. We live in a beautiful world, full of beautiful challenges and flowers and birds and super people, but also a few regrettable bad apples, such as that questionable Janet. Do I hate her? Do I want her killed? Gosh no, I think she's super, I want her to be praised while getting a hot oil massage, she has some very nice traits. But guess what, I'm not paying her to have nice traits, I'm paying her to do consistently good work. Is she? Doing consistently good work? She is not. And here are you, saddled with a subpar colleague. Poor you. She's stopping your rise and growth. People are talking about you in our lounge. Look, I know you feel Janet's not so great. She's a lump to you. I see it in your eye. And that must chafe. Because you are good. Very good. One of our best. And she's bad, very bad, one of our worst, sometimes I could just slap her for what she's doing to you."

"She's a friend," I say.

"You know what it's like, to me?" he says. "The Bible. Remember that part in the Bible when Christ or God says that any group or organization of two or more of us is a body? I think that is so true. Our body has a rotten toe by the name of Janet, who is turning black and stinking up the joint, and next to that bad stinking toe lives her friend the good nonstinker toe, who for some reason insists on holding its tongue, if a toe can be said to have a tongue. Speak up, little toe, let the brain know the state of the rot, so we can rush down what is necessary to stop Janet from stinking. What will be needed? We do not yet know. Maybe some antiseptic, maybe a nice sharp saw with which to lop off Janet. For us to know, what must you do? Tell the truth. Start generating frank and nonbiased assessments of this subpar colleague. That's it. That is all. Did you or did you not in your Employment Agreement agree to complete, every day, an accurate Daily Partner Performance Evaluation Form? You did. You signed in triplicate. I have a copy in my dossier. But enough mean and sad talk, I know my point has been gotten. Gotten by you. Now for the fun. The eating. Eating the good food I have broughten. That's fun, isn't it? I think that's fun."

We start to eat. It's fun.

"Broughten," he says. "The good food I have broughten. Is it brought or broughten?"

"Brought," I say.

"The good food I have brought," he says. "Broughten."

Back in the cave Janet's made a nice fire.

"So what did numbnuts want?" she says. "Are you fired?"

I shake my head no.

"Is he in love with you?" she says. "Does he want to go out with you?"

I shake my head no.

"Is he in love with me?" she says. "Does he want to go out with me? Am I fired?"

I do not shake my head no.

"Wait a minute, wait a minute, go back," she says. "I'm fired?"

I shake my head no.

"But I'm in the shit?" she says. "I'm somewhat in the shit?"

I shrug.

"Will you freaking talk to me?" she says. "This is important. Don't be a dick for once."

I do not consider myself a dick and I do not appreciate being called a dick, in the cave, in English, and the truth is, if she would try a little harder not to talk in the cave, she would not be so much in the shit.

I hold up one finger, like: Wait a sec. Then I go into my Separate Area and write her a note:

Nordstrom is unhappy with you, it says. *And unhappy with me*

*because I have been lying for you on my DPPEFs. So I am going
to start telling the truth. And as you know, if I tell the truth about
you, you will be a goner, unless you start acting better. Therefore
please start acting better. Sorry I couldn't say this in the cave, but
as you know, we are not supposed to speak English in the cave. I
enjoy working with you. We just have to get this thing straightened out.*

Sitting on her log she reads my note.

"Time to pull head out of ass, I guess," she says.

I give her a thumbs-up.

Next morning I go to the Big Slot and find it goatless. Also there
is no note.

Janet comes out and hands me a note and makes, very quickly,
a nice little fire.

I really apreciate what you did, her note says. *That you tole me
the truth. Your a real pal and are going to see how good I can be.*

For breakfast I count out twenty Reserve Crackers each. Afterward I work on the pictographs and she pretends to catch and
eat small bugs. For lunch I count out twenty Reserve Crackers
each. After lunch I pretend to sharpen my spear and she sits at
my feet speaking long strings of unintelligible sounds.

No one pokes their head in.

When the quality of light changes she stands at the door of
her Separate Area and sort of wiggles her eyebrows, like: Pretty
good, eh?

I go into my Separate Area. I take out a Daily Partner Performance Evaluation Form.

For once it's easy.

Do I note any attitudinal difficulties? I do not. How do I rate
my Partner overall? Very good. Are there any Situations which require Mediation?

There are not.

I fax it in.

from **WALDEN TWO**

B. F. Skinner

We found space near the windows of a small lounge and drew up chairs so that we could look out over the slowly darkening landscape. Frazier seemed to have no particular discussion prepared and he had begun to look a little tired. Castle must have been full of things to say, but he apparently felt that I should open the conversation.

"We are grateful for your kindness," I said to Frazier, "not only in asking us to visit Walden Two but in giving us so much of your time. I'm afraid it's something of an imposition."

"On the contrary," said Frazier. "I'm fully paid for talking with you. Two labor-credits are allowed each day for taking charge of guests of Walden Two. I can use only one of them, but it's a bargain even so, because I'm more than fairly paid by your company."

"Labor-credits?" I said.

"I'm sorry. I had forgotten. Labor-credits are a sort of money. But they're not coins or bills—just entries in a ledger. All goods and services are free, as you saw in the dining room this evening. Each of us pays for what he uses with twelve hundred labor-credits each year—say, four credits for each workday. We change the value according to the needs of the community. At two hours of work per credit—an eight-hour day—we could operate at a handsome profit. We're satisfied to keep just a shade beyond breaking even. The profit system is bad even when the worker gets the profits, because the strain of overwork isn't relieved by even a large reward. All we ask is to make expenses, with a slight margin of safety; we adjust the value of the labor-credit accordingly. At present it's about one hour of work per credit."

"Your members work only four hours a day?" I said. There was an overtone of outraged virtue in my voice, as if I had asked if they were all adulterous.

"On the average," Frazier replied casually. In spite of our obvious interest he went on at once to another point. "A credit system also makes it possible to evaluate a job in terms of the willingness of the members to undertake it. After all, a man isn't doing more or less than his share because of the time he puts in; it's what he's doing that counts. So we simply assign different credit values to different kinds of work, and adjust them from time to time on the basis of demand. Bellamy suggested the principle in *Looking Backward*."

"An unpleasant job like cleaning sewers has a high value, I suppose," I said.

"Exactly. Somewhere around one and a half credits per hour. The sewer man works a little over two hours a day. Pleasanter jobs have lower values—say point seven or point eight. That means five hours a day, or even more. Working in the flower gardens has a very low value—point one. No one makes a living at it, but many people like to spend a little time that way, and we give them credit. In the long run, when the values have been adjusted, all kinds of work are equally desirable. If they weren't, there would be a demand for the more desirable, and the credit value would be changed. Once in a while we manipulate a preference, if some job seems to be avoided without cause."

"I suppose you put phonographs in your dormitories which repeat 'I like to work in sewers. Sewers are lots of fun,'" said Castle.

"No, Walden Two isn't that kind of brave new world," said Frazier. "We don't *propagandize*. That's a basic principle. I don't deny that it would be possible. We could make the heaviest work appear most honorable and desirable. Something of the sort has always been done by well-organized governments—to facilitate the recruiting of armies, for example. But not here. You may say that we propagandize *all* labor, if you like, but I see no objection to that. If we can make work pleasanter by proper training, why shouldn't we? But I digress."

"What about the knowledge and skill required in many jobs?" said Castle. "Doesn't that interfere with free bidding? Certainly you can't allow just anyone to work as a doctor."

"No, of course not. The principle has to be modified where long training is needed. Still, the preferences of the community as a whole determine the final value. If our doctors were conspicuously overworked *according to our standards*, it would be hard to get young people to choose that profession. We must see to it that there are enough doctors to bring the average schedule within range of the Walden Two standard."

"What if nobody wanted to be a doctor?" I said.

"Our trouble is the other way round."

"I thought as much," said Castle. "Too many of your young members will want to go into interesting lines in spite of the work load. What do you do, then?"

"Let them know how many places will be available, and let them decide. We're glad to have more than enough doctors, of course, and could always find some sort of work for them, but we can't offer more of a strictly medical practice than our disgustingly good health affords."

"Then you don't offer complete personal freedom, do you?" said Castle, with ill-concealed excitement. "You haven't really resolved the conflict between a *laissez-faire* and a planned society."

"I think we have. Yes. But you must know more about our educational system before I can show you how. The fact is, it's very unlikely that anyone at Walden Two will set his heart on a course of action so firmly that he'll be unhappy if it isn't open to him. That's as true of the choice of a girl as of a profession. Personal jealousy is almost unknown among us, and for a simple reason: we provide a broad experience and many attractive alternatives. The tender sentiment of the 'one and only' has less to do with constancy of heart than with singleness of opportunity. The chances are that our superfluous young premedic will find other courses open to him which will very soon prove equally attractive."

"There's another case, too," I said. "You must have some sort of government. I don't see how you can permit a free choice of jobs there."

"Our only government is a Board of Planners," said Frazier, with a change of tone which suggested that I had set off another standard harangue. "The name goes back to the days when Walden Two existed only on paper. There are six Planners, usually three men and three women. The sexes are on such equal terms here that no one guards equality very jealously. They may serve for ten years, but no longer. Three of us who've been on the Board since the beginning retire this year.

"The Planners are charged with the success of the community. They make policies, review the work of the Managers, keep an eye on the state of the nation in general. They also have certain judicial functions. They're allowed six hundred credits a year for their services, which leaves two credits still due each day. At least one must be worked out in straight physical labor. That's why I can claim only one credit for acting as your Virgil through *il paradiso*."

"It was Beatrice," I corrected.

"How do you choose your Planners?" said Rodge.

"The Board selects a replacement from a pair of names supplied by the Managers."

"The members don't vote for them?" said Castle.

"*No,*" said Frazier emphatically.

"What are Managers?" I said hastily.

"What the name implies: specialists in charge of the divisions and services of Walden Two. There are Managers of Food, Health, Play, Arts, Dentistry, Dairy, various industries, Supply,

Labor, Nursery School, Advanced Education, and dozens of others. They requisition labor according to their needs, and their job is the managerial function which survives after they've assigned as much as possible to others. They're the hardest workers among us. It's an exceptional person who seeks and finds a place as Manager. He must have ability and a real concern for the welfare of the community."

"*They* are elected by the members, I suppose?" said Castle, but it was obvious that he hoped for nothing of the sort.

"The Managers aren't honorific personages, but carefully trained and tested specialists. How could the members gauge their ability? No, these are very much like Civil Service jobs. You work up to be a Manager—through intermediate positions which carry a good deal of responsibility and provide the necessary apprenticeship."

"Then the members have no voice whatsoever," said Castle in a carefully controlled voice, as if he were filing the point away for future use.

"Nor do they wish to have," said Frazier flatly.

"Do you count your professional people as Managers?" I said, again hastily.

"Some of them. The Manager of Health is one of our doctors—Mr. Meyerson. But the word 'profession' has little meaning here. All professional training is paid for by the community and is looked upon as part of our common capital, exactly like any other tool."

"Mr. Meyerson?" I said. "Your doctor is not an M.D.? Not a real physician?"

"As real as they come, with a degree from a top-ranking medical school. But we don't use honorific titles. Why call him *Doctor* Meyerson? We don't call our Dairy Manager *Dairyman* Larson. The medical profession has been slow to give up the chicanery of prescientific medicine. It's abandoning the hocus-pocus of the ciphered prescription, but the honorific title is still too dear. In Walden Two—"

"Then you distinguish only Planners, Managers, and Workers," I said to prevent what threatened to be a major distraction.

"And Scientists. The community supports a certain amount of research. Experiments are in progress in plant and animal breeding, the control of infant behavior, educational processes of several sorts, and the use of some of our raw materials. Scientists receive the same labor-credits as Managers—two or three per day depending upon the work."

"No pure science?" exclaimed Castle with mock surprise.

"Only in our spare time," said Frazier. "And I shan't be much disturbed by your elevated eyebrows until you show me where any other condition prevails. Our policy is better than that of your educational institutions, where the would-be scientist pays his way by teaching."

"Have you forgotten our centers of pure research?" I said.

"Pure? If you mean completely unshackled with respect to means and ends, I challenge you to name five. It's otherwise pay-as-you-go. Do you know of any 'pure' scientist in our universities who wouldn't settle for two hours of physical labor each day instead of the soul-searching work he's now compelled to do in the name of education?"

I had no ready answer, for I had to consider the cultural engineering needed to equate the two possibilities. My silence began to seem significant, and I cast about for a question along a different line.

"Why should everyone engage in menial work?" I asked. "Isn't that really a misuse of manpower if a man has special talents or abilities?"

"There's no misuse. Some of us would be smart enough to get along without doing physical work, but we're also smart enough to know that in the long run it would mean trouble. A leisure class would grow like a cancer until the strain upon the rest of the community became intolerable. We might escape the consequences in our own lifetime, but we couldn't visualize a permanent society on such a plan. The really intelligent man doesn't want to feel that his work is being done by anyone else. He's sensitive enough to be disturbed by slight resentments which, multiplied a million-fold, mean his downfall. Perhaps he remembers his own reactions when others have imposed on him; perhaps he has had a more severe ethical training. Call it conscience, if you like." He threw his head back and studied the ceiling. When he resumed, his tone was dramatically far-away.

"That's the virtue of Walden Two which pleases me most. I was never happy in being waited on. I could never enjoy the fleshpots for thinking of what might be going on below stairs." It was obviously a borrowed expression, for Frazier's early life had not been affluent. But he suddenly continued in a loud, clear voice which could leave no doubt of his sincerity, "Here a man can hold up his head and say, 'I've done my share!' "

He seemed ashamed of his excitement, of his show of sentiment, and I felt a strange affection for him. Castle missed the overtones and broke in abruptly.

"But can't superior ability be held in check so it won't lead to tyranny? And isn't it possible to convince the menial laborer that he's only doing the kind of work for which he's best suited and that the smart fellow is really working, too?"

"Provided the smart fellow is really working," Frazier answered, rallying himself with an effort. "Nobody resents the fact that our Planners and Managers could wear white collars if they wished. But you're quite right: with adequate cultural design a society might run smoothly, even though the physical work were not evenly distributed. It might even be possible, through such engineering, to sustain a small leisure class without serious danger. A well-organized society is so efficient and productive that a small area of waste is unimportant. A caste system of brains and brawn could be made to work because it's in the interest of brains to make it fair to brawn."

"Then why insist upon universal brawn?" said Castle impatiently.

"Simply because brains and brawn are never exclusive. No one of us is all brains or all brawn, and our lives must be adjusted accordingly. It's fatal to forget the minority element—fatal to treat brawn as if there were no brains, and perhaps more speedily fatal to treat brains as if there were no brawn. One or two hours of physical work each day is a health measure. Men have always lived by their muscles—you can tell that from their physiques. We mustn't let our big muscles atrophy just because we've devised superior ways of using the little ones. We haven't yet evolved a pure Man Thinking. Ask any doctor about the occupational diseases of the unoccupied. Because of certain cultural prejudices which Veblen might have noted, the doctor can prescribe nothing more than golf, or a mechanical horse, or chopping wood, provided the patient has no real need for wood. But what the doctor would like to say is 'Go to work!'

"But there's a better reason why brains must not neglect brawn," Frazier continued. "Nowadays it's the smart fellow, the small-muscle user, who finds himself in the position of governor. In Walden Two he makes plans, obtains materials, devises codes, evaluates trends, conducts experiments. In work of this sort the manager must keep an eye on the managed, must understand his needs, must experience his lot. That's why our Planners, Managers, and Scientists are required to work out some of their labor-credits in menial tasks. It's our constitutional guarantee that the problems of the big-muscle user won't be forgotten."

We fell silent. Our reflections in the windows mingled confusingly with the last traces of daylight in the southern sky. Finally Castle roused himself.

"But four hours a day!" he said. "I can't take that seriously. Think of the struggle to get a forty-hour week! What would our industrialists not give for your secret. Or our politicians! Mr. Frazier, we're all compelled to admire the life you are showing us, but I feel somehow as if you were exhibiting a lovely lady floating in midair. You've even passed a hoop about her to emphasize your wizardry. Now, when you pretend to tell us how the trick is done, we're told that the lady is supported by a slender thread: The explanation is as hard to accept as the illusion. Where's your proof?"

"The proof of an accomplished fact? Don't be absurd! But perhaps I can satisfy you by telling you how we knew it could be done before we tried."

"That would be something," said Castle dryly.

"Very well, then," said Frazier. "Let's take a standard seven-day week of eight hours a day. (The forty-hour week hasn't reached into every walk of life. Many a farmer would call it a vacation.) That's nearly 3000 hours per year. Our plan was to reduce it to 1500. Actually we did better than that, but how were we sure we could cut it in half? Will an answer to that satisfy you?"

"It will astonish me," said Castle.

"Very well, then," said Frazier quickly, as if he had actually been spurred on by Castle's remark. "First of all we have the obvious fact that four is more than half of eight. We work more skillfully and faster during the first four hours of the day. The eventual effect of a four-hour day is enormous, provided the rest of a man's time isn't spent too strenuously. Let's take a conservative estimate, to allow for tasks which can't be speeded up, and say that our four hours are the equivalent of five out of the usual eight. Do you agree?"

"I should be contentious if I didn't," said Castle. "But you're a long way from eight."

"Secondly," said Frazier, with a satisfied smile which promised that eight would be reached in due time, "we have the extra motivation that comes when a man is working for himself instead of for a profit-taking boss. That's a true 'incentive wage' and the effect is prodigious. Waste is avoided, workmanship is better, deliberate slowdowns unheard of. Shall we say that four hours for oneself are worth six out of eight for the other fellow?"

"And I hope you will point out," I said, "that the four are no harder than the six. Loafing doesn't really make a job easier. Boredom's more exhausting than heavy work. But what about the other two?"

"Let me remind you that not all Americans capable of working are now employed," said Frazier. "We're really comparing eight hours a day on the part or *some* with four hours on the part of practically *all*. In Walden Two we have no leisure class, no prematurely aged or occupationally disabled, no drunkenness, no criminals, far fewer sick. We have no unemployment due to bad planning. No one is paid to sit idle for the sake of maintaining labor standards. Our children work at an early age—moderately, but happily. What will you settle for, Mr. Castle? May I add another hour to my six?"

"I'm afraid I should let you add more than that," said Castle, laughing with surprising good nature.

"But let's be conservative," said Frazier, obviously pleased, "and say that when every potential worker puts in four hours for himself we have the equivalent of perhaps two-thirds of all available workers putting in seven out of eight hours for somebody else. Now, what about those who are actually at work? Are they working to the best advantage? Have they been carefully selected for the work they are doing? Are they making the best use of labor-saving machines and methods? What percentage of the farms in America are mechanized as we are here? Do the workers welcome and improve upon labor-saving devices and methods? How many good workers are free to move on to more productive levels? How much education do workers receive to make them as efficient as possible?"

"I can't let you claim much credit for a better use of manpower," said Castle, "if you give your members a free choice of jobs."

"It's an extravagance, you're right," said Frazier. "In another generation we shall do better; our educational system will see to that. I agree. Add nothing for the waste due to misplaced talents." He was silent a moment, as if calculating whether he could afford to make this concession.

"You still have an hour to account for," I reminded him.

"I know, I know," he said. "Well, how much of the machinery of distribution have we eliminated—with the release of how many men? How many jobs have we simply eliminated? Walk down any city street. How often will you find people really usefully engaged? There's a bank. And beyond it a loan company. And an advertising agency. And over there an insurance office. And another." It was not effective showmanship, but Frazier seemed content to make his point at the cost of some personal dignity. "We have a hard time explaining insurance to our children. Insurance against what? And there's a funeral home—a crematory disposes of our ashes as it sees fit." He threw off this subject with a shake of the head. "And there and there the ubiquitous bars and taverns, equally useless. Drinking isn't prohibited in Walden Two, but we all give it up as soon as we gratify the needs which are responsible for the habit in the world at large."

"If I may be permitted to interrupt this little tour," I said, "what are those needs?"

"Well, why do you drink?" said Frazier.

"I don't—a great deal. But I like a cocktail before dinner. In fact, my company isn't worth much until I've had one."

"On the contrary, I find it delightful," said Frazier.

"It's different here," I said, falling into his trap. Frazier and Castle laughed raucously.

"Of course it's different here!" Frazier shouted. "You need your cocktail to counteract the fatigue and boredom of a mismanaged society. Here we need no antidotes. No opiates. But why else do you drink? Or why does anyone?—since I can see you're not a typical case."

"Why—to forget one's troubles—" I stammered. "Of course, I see what you will say to that. But to get away, let's say, or to get a change—to lower one's inhibitions. You do have inhibitions, don't you? Perhaps someone else can help me out." I turned tactlessly to Barbara, who looked away.

Frazier chuckled quietly for a moment, and struck out again.

"Let me point out a few businesses which we haven't elimi-nated, but certainly streamlined with respect to manpower," he said. "The big department stores, the meat markets, the corner drugstores, the groceries, the automobile display rooms, the furniture stores, the shoe stores, the candy stores, all staffed with unnecessary people doing unnecessary things. Half the restaurants can be closed for good. And there's a beauty parlor and there a movie palace. And over there a dance hall, and there a bowling alley. And all the time busses and streetcars are whizzing by, carrying people to and fro from one useless spot to another."

It was a bad show but a devastating argument.

"Take your last hour and welcome," said Castle when he saw that Frazier was resting from his labors. "I should have taken your word for it. After all, as you say, it's an accomplished fact."

"Would you like to see me make it *ten* hours?" said Frazier. He smiled boyishly and we all laughed. "I haven't mentioned our most dramatic saving in manpower."

"Then you still have a chance to get away from the book," I said. "I must confess that I'm not quite so impressed as Mr. Castle. Most of what you have said so far is fairly standard criticism of our economic system. You've been pretty close to the professors."

"Of course I have. Even the professors know all this. The economics of a community are child's play."

"What about those two extra hours?" I said, deciding to let the insinuation pass.

Frazier waited a moment, looking from one of us to another.

"*Cherchez la femme!*" he said at last. He stopped to enjoy our puzzlement. "The women! The women! What do you suppose they've been doing all this time? There's our greatest achievement! We have industrialized housewifery!" He pronounced it "huzzifry" again, and this time I got the reference. "Some of our women are still engaged in activities which would have been part of their jobs as housewives, but they work more efficiently and happily. And at least half of them are available for other work."

Frazier sat back with evident satisfaction. Castle roused himself.

"I'm worried," he said bluntly. "You've made a four-hour day seem convincing by pointing to a large part of the population not gainfully employed. But many of those people don't live as well as you. Our present average production may need only four hours per day per man—but that won't do. It must be something more than the average. You'd better leave the unproductive sharecropper out of it. He neither produces *nor consumes*—poor devil."

"It's true, we enjoy a high standard of living," said Frazier. "But our personal wealth is actually very small. The goods we consume don't come to much in dollars and cents. We practice the Thoreauvian principle of avoiding unnecessary possessions. Thoreau pointed out that the average Concord laborer worked ten or fifteen years of his life just to have a roof over his head. We could say ten weeks and be on the safe side. Our food is plentiful and healthful, but not expensive. There's little or no spoilage or waste in distribution or storage, and none due to miscalculated needs. The same is true of other staples. We don't feel the pressure of promotional devices which stimulate unnecessary consumption. We have some automobiles and trucks, but far fewer than the hundred family cars and the many business vehicles we should own if we weren't living in a community. Our radio installation is far less expensive than the three or four hundred sets we should otherwise be operating—even if some of us were radioless sharecroppers.

"No, Mr. Castle, we strike for economic freedom at this very point—by devising a very high standard of living with a low consumption of goods. We consume *less* than the average American."

It was now quite dark outside, and very still. Only the faint rhythmic song of frogs and peepers could be heard through the ventilating louvers. The building itself had grown quiet. No one else had been in the lounge for some time, and several of the lights had been frugally turned off. A pleasant drowsiness was creeping over me.

"You know, of course," Frazier said with a frown, "that this is by far the least interesting side of Walden Two." He seemed to have been seized with a sudden fear that we were bored. "And the least important, too—absolutely the least important. How'd we get started on it, anyway?"

"You confessed that you would be paid for talking to us," I said. "And very much underpaid, I may add. I don't know what the dollars-and-cents value of one labor-credit may be, but it's a most inadequate measure of an enjoyable evening."

The others murmured assent, and Frazier smiled with obvious delight.

"While you're in that mood," he said, "I should tell you that you'll be permitted to contribute labor-credits while you're here, too. We ask only two per day, since you're not acquiring a legal interest in the community or clothing yourselves at our expense."

"Fair enough," I said, but rather taken aback.

"We don't begrudge you the food you consume or the space you occupy, nor are we afraid of the effect of idleness upon the morale of our members. We ask you to work because we should feel inhospitable if you didn't. Be frank, now. No matter how warmly we welcomed you, wouldn't you soon feel that you ought to leave? But a couple of hours a day will fully pay for the services the community renders and incidentally do you a lot of good. And you may stay as long as you like with no fear of sponging. And because I receive a credit each day for acting as your guide, you needn't feel that you're imposing on me."

"What's to prevent some visitor—say, a writer—from putting in his two hours and staying on for good?" I asked. "He would find ample time for his trade and buy his own clothes and secure his own future without being a member."

"We've no objection, but we should ask that one half of any money made during his stay be turned over to Walden Two."

"Oh ho!" cried Castle. "Then it would be possible for a member to accumulate a private fortune—by writing books, say, in his spare time."

"Whatever for?" Frazier said. It seemed like genuine surprise, but his tone changed immediately. "As it happens, it isn't possible. *All* money earned by members belongs to the community.

Part of our foreign exchange comes from private enterprises of that sort."

"Rather unfair to the member as compared with the guest, isn't it?" said Castle.

"What's unfair about it? What does the member want money for? Remember, the guest doesn't receive medical services, clothing, or security against old age or ill-health."

Frazier had risen as he was speaking, and we all followed his example promptly. It was clear that we had had enough for one day.

"I shouldn't be acting in the interests of the community," said Frazier, "if I kept you from your beds any longer. We expect a full day's work from you tomorrow morning. Can you find your way to your rooms?"

We made arrangements to meet at ten the next day and parted. Castle and I led the way down the silent, dimly lighted Walk. Presently we found that we were alone. Our companions, for reasons best known to themselves, had turned off and gone outside.

"I wonder what their two hours will be worth tomorrow?" said Castle. "Enemies of the people, I suppose you'd call them."

from **THREE LIVES**

Gertrude Stein

The Life of the Good Anna

Anna Federner, this good Anna, was of solid lower middle-class south german stock.

When she was seventeen years old she went to service in a bourgeois family, in the large city near her native town, but she did not stay there long. One day her mistress offered her maid—that was Anna—to a friend, to see her home. Anna felt herself to be a servant, not a maid, and so she promptly left the place.

Anna had always a firm old world sense of what was the right way for a girl to do.

No argument could bring her to sit an evening in the empty parlour, although the smell of paint when they were fixing up the kitchen made her very sick, and tired as she always was, she never would sit down during the long talks she held with Miss Mathilda. A girl was a girl and should act always like a girl, both as to giving all respect and as to what she had to eat.

A little time after she left this service, Anna and her mother made the voyage to America. They came second-class, but it was for them a long and dreary journey. The mother was already ill with consumption.

They landed in a pleasant town in the far South and there the mother slowly died.

Anna was now alone and she made her way to Bridgepoint where an older half brother was already settled. This brother was a heavy, lumbering, good natured german man, full of the infirmity that comes of excess of body.

He was a baker and married and fairly well to do.

Anna liked her brother well enough but was never in any way dependent on him.

When she arrived in Bridgepoint, she took service with Miss Mary Wadsmith.

Miss Mary Wadsmith was a large, fair, helpless woman, burdened with the care of two young children. They had been left her by her brother and his wife who had died within a few months of each other.

Anna soon had the household altogether in her charge.

Anna found her place with large, abundant women, for such were always lazy, careless or all helpless, and so the burden of their lives could fall on Anna, and give her just content. Anna's superiors must be always these large helpless women, or be men, for none others could give themselves to be made so comfortable and free.

Anna had no strong natural feeling to love children, as she had to love cats and dogs, and a large mistress. She never became deeply fond of Edgar and Jane Wadsmith. She naturally preferred the boy, for boys love always better to be done for and made comfortable and full of eating, while in the little girl she had to meet the feminine, the subtle opposition, showing so early always in a young girl's nature.

For the summer, the Wadsmiths had a pleasant house out in the country, and the winter months they spent in hotel apartments in the city.

Gradually it came to Anna to take the whole direction of their movements, to make all the decisions as to their journeying to and fro, and for the arranging of the places where they were to live.

Anna had been with Miss Mary for three years, when little Jane began to raise her strength in opposition. Jane was a neat, pleasant little girl, pretty and sweet with a young girl's charm, and with two blonde braids carefully plaited down her back.

Miss Mary, like her Anna, had no strong natural feeling to love children, but she was fond of these two young ones of her blood, and yielded docilely to the stronger power in the really pleasing little girl. Anna always preferred the rougher handling of the boy, while Miss Mary found the gentle force and the sweet domination of the girl to please her better.

In a spring when all the preparations for the moving had been made, Miss Mary and Jane went together to the country home, and Anna, after finishing up the city matters was to follow them in a few days with Edgar, whose vacation had not yet begun.

Many times during the preparation for this summer, Jane had met Anna with sharp resistance, in opposition to her ways. It was simple for little Jane to give unpleasant orders, not from herself but from Miss Mary, large, docile, helpless Miss Mary Wadsmith who could never think out any orders to give Anna from herself.

Anna's eyes grew slowly sharper, harder, and her lower teeth thrust a little forward and pressing strongly up, framed always more slowly the "Yes, Miss Jane," to the quick, "Oh Anna! Miss Mary says she wants you to do it so!"

On the day of their migration, Miss Mary had been already put into the carriage. "Oh, Anna!" cried little Jane running back into the house, "Miss Mary says that you are to bring along the blue dressings out of her room and mine." Anna's body stiffened, "We never use them in the summer, Miss Jane," she said thickly. "Yes Anna, but Miss Mary thinks it would be nice, and she told me to tell you not to forget, good-by!" and the little girl skipped lightly down the steps into the carriage and they drove away.

Anna stood still on the steps, her eyes hard and sharp and shining, and her body and her face stiff with resentment. And then she went into the house, giving the door a shattering slam.

Anna was very hard to live with in those next three days. Even

Baby, the new puppy, the pride of Anna's heart, a present from her friend the widow, Mrs. Lehntman—even this pretty little black and tan felt the heat of Anna's scorching flame. And Edgar, who had looked forward to these days, to be for him filled full of freedom and of things to eat—he could not rest a moment in Anna's bitter sight.

On the third day, Anna and Edgar went to the Wadsmith country home. The blue dressings out of the two rooms remained behind.

All the way, Edgar sat in front with the colored man and drove. It was an early spring day in the South. The fields and woods were heavy from the soaking rains. The horses dragged the carriage slowly over the long road, sticky with brown clay and rough with masses of stones thrown here and there to be broken and trodden into place by passing teams. Over and through the soaking earth was the feathery new spring growth of little flowers, of young leaves and of ferns. The tree tops were all bright with reds and yellows, with brilliant gleaming whites and gorgeous greens. All the lower air was full of the damp haze rising from heavy soaking water on the earth, mingled with a warm and pleasant smell from the blue smoke of the spring fires in all the open fields. And above all this was the clear, upper air, and the songs of birds and the joy of sunshine and of lengthening days.

The languor and the stir, the warmth and weight and the strong feel of life from the deep centres of the earth that comes always with the early, soaking spring, when it is not answered with an active fervent joy, gives always anger, irritation and unrest.

To Anna alone there in the carriage, drawing always nearer to the struggle with her mistress, the warmth, the slowness, the jolting over stones, the steaming from the horses, the cries of men and animals and birds, and the new life all round about were simply maddening. "Baby! if you don't lie still, I think I kill you. I can't stand it any more like this."

At this time Anna, about twenty-seven years of age, was not yet all thin and worn. The sharp bony edges and corners of her head and face were still rounded out with flesh, but already the temper and the humor showed sharply in her clean blue eyes, and the thinning was begun about the lower jaw, that was so often strained with the upward pressure of resolve.

To-day, alone there in the carriage, she was all stiff and yet all trembling with the sore effort of decision and revolt.

As the carriage turned into the Wadsmith gate, little Jane ran out to see. She just looked at Anna's face; she did not say a word about blue dressings.

Anna got down from the carriage with little Baby in her arms. She took out all the goods that she had brought and the carriage drove away. Anna left everything on the porch, and went in to where Miss Mary Wadsmith was sitting by the fire.

Miss Mary was sitting in a large armchair by the fire. All the nooks and crannies of the chair were filled full of her soft and spreading body. She was dressed in a black satin morning gown, the sleeves, great monster things, were heavy with the mass of her soft flesh. She sat there always, large, helpless, gentle. She had a fair, soft, regular, good-looking face, with pleasant, empty, grey-blue eyes, and heavy sleepy lids.

Behind Miss Mary was the little Jane, nervous and jerky with excitement as she saw Anna come into the room.

"Miss Mary," Anna began. She had stopped just within the door, her body and her face stiff with repression, her teeth closed hard and the white lights flashing sharply in the pale, clean blue of her eyes. Her bearing was full of the strange coquetry of anger and of fear, the stiffness, the bridling, the suggestive movement underneath the rigidness of forced control, all the queer ways the passions have to show themselves all one.

"Miss Mary," the words came slowly with thick utterance and with jerks, but always firm and strong. "Miss Mary, I can't stand it any more like this. When you tell me anything to do, I do it. I do everything I can and you know I work myself sick for you. The blue dressings in your room makes too much work to have for summer. Miss Jane don't know what work is. If you want to do things like that I go away."

Anna stopped still. Her words had not the strength of meaning they were meant to have, but the power in the mood of Anna's soul frightened and awed Miss Mary through and through.

Like in all large and helpless women, Miss Mary's heart beat weakly in the soft and helpless mass it had to govern. Little Jane's excitements had already tried her strength. Now she grew pale and fainted quite away.

"Miss Mary!" cried Anna running to her mistress and supporting all her helpless weight back in the chair. Little Jane, distracted, flew about as Anna ordered, bringing smelling salts and brandy and vinegar and water and chafing poor Miss Mary's wrists.

Miss Mary slowly opened her mild eyes. Anna sent the weeping little Jane out of the room. She herself managed to get Miss Mary quiet on the couch.

There was never a word more said about blue dressings.

Anna had conquered, and a few days later little Jane gave her a green parrot to make peace.

For six more years little Jane and Anna lived in the same house. They were careful and respectful to each other to the end.

Anna liked the parrot very well. She was fond of cats too and of horses, but best of all animals she loved the dog and best of all dogs, little Baby, the first gift from her friend, the widow Mrs. Lehntman.

The widow Mrs. Lehntman was the romance in Anna's life.

Anna met her first at the house of her half brother, the baker, who had known the late Mr. Lehntman, a small grocer, very well.

Mrs. Lehntman had been for many years a midwife. Since her husband's death she had herself and two young children to support.

Mrs. Lehntman was a good looking woman. She had a plump well rounded body, clear olive skin, bright dark eyes and crisp black curling hair. She was pleasant, magnetic, efficient and good. She was very attractive, very generous and very amiable.

She was a few years older than our good Anna, who was soon entirely subdued by her magnetic, sympathetic charm.

Mrs. Lehntman in her work loved best to deliver young girls who were in trouble. She would take these into her own house and care for them in secret, till they could guiltlessly go home or back to work, and then slowly pay her the money for their care. And so through this new friend Anna led a wider and more entertaining life, and often she used up her savings in helping Mrs. Lehntman through those times when she was giving very much more than she got.

It was through Mrs. Lehntman that Anna met Dr. Shonjen who employed her when at last it had to be that she must go away from her Miss Mary Wadsmith.

During the last years with her Miss Mary, Anna's health was very bad, as indeed it always was from that time on until the end of her strong life.

Anna was a medium sized, thin, hard working, worrying woman.

She had always had bad headaches and now they came more often and more wearing.

Her face grew thin, more bony and more worn, her skin stained itself pale yellow, as it does with working sickly women, and the clear blue of her eyes went pale.

Her back troubled her a good deal, too. She was always tired at her work and her temper grew more difficult and fretful.

Miss Mary Wadsmith often tried to make Anna see a little to herself, and get a doctor, and the little Jane, now blossoming into a pretty, sweet young woman, did her best to make Anna do things for her good. Anna was stubborn always to Miss Jane, and fearful of interference in her ways. Miss Mary Wadsmith's mild advice she easily could always turn aside.

Mrs. Lehntman was the only one who had any power over Anna. She induced her to let Dr. Shonjen take her in his care.

No one but a Dr. Shonjen could have brought a good and german Anna first to stop her work and then submit herself to operation, but he knew so well how to deal with german and poor people. Cheery, jovial, hearty, full of jokes that made much fun and yet were full of simple common sense and reasoning courage, he could persuade even a good Anna to do things that were for her own good.

Edgar had now been for some years away from home, first at a school and then at work to prepare himself to be a civil engineer. Miss Mary and Jane promised to take a trip for all the time that Anna was away and so there would be no need for Anna's work, nor for a new girl to take Anna's place.

Anna's mind was thus a little set at rest. She gave herself to Mrs. Lehntman and the doctor to do what they thought best to make her well and strong.

Anna endured the operation very well, and was patient, almost docile, in the slow recovery of her working strength. But when she was once more at work for her Miss Mary Wadsmith, all the good effect of these several months of rest were soon worked and worried well away.

For all the rest of her strong working life Anna was never really well. She had bad headaches all the time and she was always thin and worn.

She worked away her appetite, her health and strength, and always for the sake of those who begged her not to work so hard. To her thinking, in her stubborn, faithful, german soul, this was the right way for a girl to do.

Anna's life with Miss Mary Wadsmith was now drawing to an end.

Miss Jane, now altogether a young lady, had come out into the world. Soon she would become engaged and then be married, and then perhaps Miss Mary Wadsmith would make her home with her.

In such a household Anna was certain that she would never take a place. Miss Jane was always careful and respectful and very good to Anna, but never could Anna be a girl in a household where Miss Jane would be the head. This much was very certain in her mind, and so these last two years with her Miss Mary were not as happy as before.

The change came very soon.

Miss Jane became engaged and in a few months was to marry a man from out of town, from Curden, an hour's railway ride from Bridgepoint.

Poor Miss Mary Wadsmith did not know the strong resolve Anna had made to live apart from her when this new household should be formed. Anna found it very hard to speak to her Miss Mary of this change.

The preparations for the wedding went on day and night.

Anna worked and sewed hard to make it all go well.

Miss Mary was much fluttered, but content and happy with Anna to make everything so easy for them all.

Anna worked so all the time to drown her sorrow and her conscience too, for somehow it was not right to leave Miss Mary so. But what else could she do? She could not live as her Miss Mary's girl, in a house where Miss Jane would be the head.

The wedding day grew always nearer. At last it came and passed.

The young people went on their wedding trip, and Anna and Miss Mary were left behind to pack up all the things.

Even yet poor Anna had not had the strength to tell Miss Mary her resolve, but now it had to be.

Anna every spare minute ran to her friend Mrs. Lehntman for comfort and advice. She begged her friend to be with her when she told the news to Miss Mary.

Perhaps if Mrs. Lehntman had not been in Bridgepoint, Anna would have tried to live in the new house. Mrs. Lehntman did not urge her to this thing nor even give her this advice, but feeling for Mrs. Lehntman as she did made even faithful Anna not quite so strong in her dependence on Miss Mary's need as she would otherwise have been.

Remember, Mrs. Lehntman was the romance in Anna's life.

All the packing was now done and in a few days Miss Mary was to go to the new house, where the young people were ready for her coming.

At last Anna had to speak.

Mrs. Lehntman agreed to go with her and help to make the matter clear to poor Miss Mary.

The two women came together to Miss Mary Wadsmith sitting placid by the fire in the empty living room. Miss Mary had seen Mrs. Lehntman many times before, and so her coming in with Anna raised no suspicion in her mind.

It was very hard for the two women to begin.

It must be very gently done, this telling to Miss Mary of the change. She must not be shocked by suddenness or with excitement.

Anna was all stiff, and inside all a quiver with shame, anxiety and grief. Even courageous Mrs. Lehntman, efficient, impulsive and complacent as she was and not deeply concerned in the event, felt awkward, abashed and almost guilty in that large, mild, helpless presence. And at her side to make her feel the power of it all, was the intense conviction of poor Anna, struggling to be unfeeling, self righteous and suppressed.

"Miss Mary"—with Anna when things had to come they came always sharp and short—"Miss Mary, Mrs. Lehntman has come here with me, so I can tell you about not staying with you there in Curden. Of course I go help you to get settled and then I think I come back and stay right here in Bridgepoint. You know my brother he is here and all his family, and I think it would be not right to go away from them so far, and you know you don't want me now so much Miss Mary when you are all together there in Curden."

Miss Mary Wadsmith was puzzled. She did not understand what Anna meant by what she said.

"Why Anna of course you can come to see your brother whenever you like to, and I will always pay your fare. I thought you understood all about that, and we will be very glad to have your nieces come to stay with you as often as they like. There will always be room enough in a big house like Mr. Goldthwaite's."

It was now for Mrs. Lehntman to begin her work.

"Miss Wadsmith does not understand just what you mean

Anna," she began. "Miss Wadsmith, Anna feels how good and kind you are, and she talks about it all the time, and what you do for her in every way you can, and she is very grateful and never would want to go away from you, only she thinks it would be better now that Mrs. Goldthwaite has this big new house and will want to manage it in her own way, she thinks perhaps it would be better if Mrs. Goldthwaite had all new servants with her to begin with, and not a girl like Anna who knew her when she was a little girl. That is what Anna feels about it now, and she asked me and I said to her that I thought it would be better for you all and you knew she liked you so much and that you were so good to her, and you would understand how she thought it would be better in the new house if she stayed on here in Bridgepoint, anyway for a little while until Mrs. Goldthwaite was used to her new house. Isn't that it Anna that you wanted Miss Wadsmith to know?"

"Oh Anna," Miss Mary Wadsmith said it slowly and in a grieved tone of surprise that was very hard for the good Anna to endure, "Oh Anna, I didn't think that you would ever want to leave me after all these years."

"Miss Mary!" it came in one tense jerky burst, "Miss Mary it's only working under Miss Jane now would make me leave you so. I know how good you are and I work myself sick for you and for Mr. Edgar and for Miss Jane too, only Miss Jane she will want everything different from like the way we always did, and you know Miss Mary I can't have Miss Jane watching at me all the time, and every minute something new. Miss Mary, it would be very bad and Miss Jane don't really want me to come with you to the new house, I know that all the time. Please Miss Mary don't feel bad about it or think I ever want to go away from you if I could do things right for you the way they ought to be."

Poor Miss Mary. Struggling was not a thing for her to do. Anna would surely yield if she would struggle, but struggling was too much work and too much worry for peaceful Miss Mary to endure. If Anna would do so she must. Poor Miss Mary Wadsmith sighed, looked wistfully at Anna and then gave it up.

"You must do as you think best Anna," she said at last letting all of her soft self sink back into the chair. "I am very sorry and so I am sure will be Miss Jane when she hears what you have thought it best to do. It was very good of Mrs. Lehntman to come with you and I am sure she does it for your good. I suppose you want to go out a little now. Come back in an hour Anna and help me go to bed." Miss Mary closed her eyes and rested still and placid by the fire.

The two women went away.

This was the end of Anna's service with Miss Mary Wadsmith, and soon her new life taking care of Dr. Shonjen was begun.

from **NO LEASE ON LIFE**

Lynne Tillman

A few enemies were strays, accidental acquaintances. Accidents are sometimes dressed up as people. She'd had sex with some accidents. Accidents were always waiting to happen. Maybe she'd looked at someone funny once. Maybe she'd sided with someone in an unimportant bar argument and another person she hadn't even noticed became enraged. This person was plotting against her secretly. She had a few secret enemies.

A couple of her enemies were blatant. They were disappointed, dangerously overweight men. She worked with them one week on, one week off, in the proofroom. She read proof with them. It was an outdated occupation. The two fat men taught her not to sympathize automatically with unhappy people. The emotionally crippled and downtrodden can be vicious. She worked with a lot of miserable people. There were many miserable people in the company, misery wants company. Proofreading didn't make her miserable. She liked focusing on typos and misspellings, on periods, commas, quotation marks, neutral characters in her life.

Five out of ten working days she rolled out of bed and over to the proofroom and worked late into the night. Ten hours, twelve hours, silver time, golden time, good overtime. The first time she saw the proofroom, she was in the building to take a proofreading test. She'd prepared and memorized the symbols, for delete, add, cap, small cap, wrong font. They were listed in any adequate dictionary.

Elizabeth didn't know it, but on the way to the test, she passed her future co-workers. They were sitting in a small room, with no door, at a long table, reading aloud to each other. Doing hot reads, she learned after she had the job. When you read silently to yourself, it's a cold read. It was confusing, six voices going simultaneously, people reading business articles to each other. Others were eating take-out food from different restaurants, but all the restaurants used the same plastic or Styrofoam containers. Some were reading the paper. Some were waiting for copy to come through a slot in the wall.

> There's a field of ostriches. They all have their heads stuck in the ground. Another ostrich comes along. He looks around and says, Hey, where is everybody?

The proofreaders were low down in the company. It was obvious from their exposed quarters. The proofroom was similar to a stall in a barn, there was no privacy. No door, no windows. Company status was exhibited by the size of the office, the number of windows, closeness to the boss, a door that shuts others out. Status used to be access to the telephone, but now even janitors in the company had remotes.

The proofroom had one phone for twelve people. Even though proofreaders might do nothing for hours, might be waiting for the editors to edit, for the writers to finish writing or the fact checkers to check facts, they weren't supposed to be in touch with the outside world.

During their work time they were supposed to be available. They were supposed to be ready for copy that dropped through a slot in the wall like slop thrown at pigs or food shoved under the door for prisoners in isolation. When the pages would finally drop through the slot into the metal basket, they produced a swishing sound. All the proofreaders would hear it. The person nearest the slot in the wall was the supervisor or the next in command. One of them took the copy out of the basket, logged it in, and handed it out.

The proofreaders were a despised minority, a rung above the lowest group, the mailroom workers. The mailroom was in the basement. The mailroom workers were male, mostly black or Hispanic. Occasionally, when Elizabeth mailed one of her own letters and didn't want it routed through the system, because she wasn't supposed to use the company's system, she hand-delivered it to the mailroom. She went down in the elevator. She saw the black and Hispanic men. They were always surprised when one of the people from above came down. They stopped sorting the mail briefly to take in her presence, or anyone's. Though she was a nothing in the company's eyes, she still came from the world above, two floors up. It was pathetic.

The proofreaders were white, college graduates, middle-class misfits who accepted inferior jobs and were not ambitious. They had no future except the copy desk. The copy desk was allowed to change sentences. Proofreaders could only correct mistakes in spelling or find errors in fact. Any other change had to be reported to the desk. The proofreaders were beneath the desk, beneath contempt. The proofreaders were also beneath the janitors, who called the head of the company Boss. The janitors lived in houses in the suburbs and had two cars.

Elizabeth had won the steady part-time job over many applicants. She'd scored high on the test and the head of the room liked her best. Elizabeth had worn black socks with heels, a black jacket, and black pants to her interview. The socks made her a weirdo in the supervisor's eyes. The supervisor decided she'd fit in with the room. The proofreaders referred to their quarters as "the room." It was a correctional facility, Roy said.

A doctor said to his patient: I've got some good news and some bad news. The bad news is that you have two weeks left to live. The good news is that I fucked my secretary this morning.

Elizabeth joined the proofroom with reluctance. She was getting older, freelance didn't cut it anymore, and the room provided health insurance. If she was hit by a car or contracted HIV or MS, she was covered. The company also had a pension plan.

The room didn't let outside light in, it kept them separated from the world. While Elizabeth did hot reads and cold reads, even while she focused on the little black marks on shiny white paper, she deliberately thought about other things. She tested herself. It was possible to catch mistakes without being resigned. She never entirely submitted to the page at hand.

Elizabeth liked some of her fellow workers. Even one of the disappointed fat men had his moments. Everyone does. The other disappointed fat man was her sole implacable foe. He was unattractive and self-righteous. He collected stamps. He was easy to hate, and he hated her. He despised her. She could see it in his eyes. He was a company boy. Every time Elizabeth used the company mail, he was offended, outraged. She flaunted it in front of him whenever she could. She liked having him as an enemy.

—Enemies last longer than friends, enemies define you, friends don't, Elizabeth said to Roy.
—They're both under dickheads in the dictionary.
—Dickheads won't be in there.

from **THE HOUSE OF MIRTH**

Edith Wharton

The end of it was that, after anxious inquiry and much delib-eration, Mrs. Fisher and Gerty, for once oddly united in their ef-fort to help their friend, decided on placing her in the work-room of Mme. Regina's renowned millinery establishment. Even this arrangement was not effected without considerable negotiation, for Mme. Regina had a strong prejudice against untrained assis-tance, and was induced to yield only by the fact that she owed the patronage of Mrs. Bry and Mrs. Gormer to Carry Fisher's influ-ence. She had been willing from the first to employ Lily in the show-room: as a displayer of hats, a fashionable beauty might be a valuable asset. But to this suggestion Miss Bart opposed a neg-ative which Gerty emphatically supported, while Mrs. Fisher, in-wardly unconvinced, but resigned to this latest proof of Lily's unreason, agreed that perhaps in the end it would be more useful that she should learn the trade. To Regina's work-room Lily was therefore committed by her friends, and there Mrs. Fisher left her with a sigh of relief, while Gerty's watchfulness continued to hover over her at a distance.

Lily had taken up her work early in January. It was now two months later, and she was still being rebuked for her inability to sew spangles on a hat-frame. As she returned to her work she heard a titter pass down the tables. She knew she was an object of criticism and amusement to the other work-women. They were, of course, aware of her history—the exact situation of every girl in the room was known and freely discussed by all the others—but the knowledge did not produce in them any awkward sense of class distinction: it merely explained why her untutored fingers were still blundering over the rudiments of the trade. Lily had no desire that they should recognize any social difference in her; but she had hoped to be received as their equal, and perhaps before long to show herself their superior by a special deftness of touch, and it was humiliating to find that, after two months of drudgery, she still betrayed her lack of early training. Remote was the day when she might aspire to exercise the talents she felt confident of possessing; only experienced workers were entrusted with the delicate art of shaping and trimming the hat, and the forewoman still held her inexorably to the routine of preparatory work.

She began to rip the spangles from the frame, listening absently to the buzz of talk which rose and fell with the coming and going of Miss Haines's active figure. The air was closer than usual, because Miss Haines, who had a cold, had not allowed a window to be opened even during the noon recess; and Lily's head was so heavy with the weight of a sleepless night that the chatter of her companions had the incoherence of a dream.

"I *told* her he'd never look at her again; and he didn't. I wouldn't have, either—I think she acted real mean to him. He took her to the Arion Ball, and had a hack for her both ways . . . She's taken ten bottles, and her headaches don't seem no better—but she's written a testimonial to say the first bottle cured her, and she got five dollars and her picture in the paper . . . Mrs. Trenor's hat? The one with the green Paradise? Here, Miss Haines—it'll be ready right off . . . That was one of the Trenor girls here yesterday with Mrs. George Dorset. How'd I know? Why, Madam sent for me to alter the flower in that Virot hat—the blue tulle: she's tall and slight, with her hair fuzzed out—a good deal like Mamie Leach, on'y thinner . . ."

On and on it flowed, a current of meaningless sound, on which, startlingly enough, a familiar name now and then floated to the surface. It was the strangest part of Lily's strange experience, the hearing of these names, the seeing the fragmentary and distorted image of the world she had lived in reflected in the mirror of the working-girls' minds. She had never before suspected the mixture of insatiable curiosity and contemptuous freedom with which she and her kind were discussed in this under-world of toilers who lived on their vanity and self-indulgence. Every girl in Mme. Regina's work-room knew to whom the headgear in her hands was destined, and had her opinion of its future wearer, and a definite knowledge of the latter's place in the social system. That Lily was a star fallen from that sky did not, after the first stir of curiosity had subsided, materially add to their interest in her. She had fallen, she had "gone under," and true to the ideal of their race, they were awed only by success—by the gross tangible image of material achievement. The consciousness of her different point of view merely kept them at a little distance from her, as though she were a foreigner with whom it was an effort to talk.

"Miss Bart, if you can't sew those spangles on more regular I guess you'd better give the hat to Miss Kilroy."

Lily looked down ruefully at her handiwork. The forewoman was right: the sewing-on of the spangles was inexcusably bad. What made her so much more clumsy than usual? Was it a growing distaste for her task, or actual physical disability? She felt tired and confused: it was an effort to put her thoughts together. She rose and handed the hat to Miss Kilroy, who took it with a suppressed smile.

"I'm sorry; I'm afraid I am not well," she said to the forewoman.

Miss Haines offered no comment. From the first she had augured ill of Mme. Regina's consenting to include a fashionable apprentice among her workers. In that temple of art no raw beginners were wanted, and Miss Haines would have been more than human had she not taken a certain pleasure in seeing her forebodings confirmed.

"You'd better go back to binding edges," she said drily.

Lily slipped out last among the band of liberated work-women. She did not care to be mingled in their noisy dispersal: once in the street, she always felt an irresistible return to her old standpoint, an instinctive shrinking from all that was unpolished and promiscuous. In the days—how distant they now seemed!—when she had visited the Girls' Club with Gerty Farish, she had felt an enlightened interest in the working classes; but that was because she looked down on them from above, from the happy altitude of her grace and her beneficence. Now that she was on a level with them, the point of view was less interesting.

She felt a touch on her arm, and met the penitent eye of Miss Kilroy.

"Miss Bart, I guess you can sew those spangles on as well as I can when you're feeling right. Miss Haines didn't act fair to you."

Lily's color rose at the unexpected advance: it was a long time since real kindness had looked at her from any eyes but Gerty's.

"Oh, thank you: I'm not particularly well, but Miss Haines was right. I *am* clumsy."

"Well, it's mean work for anybody with a headache." Miss Kilroy paused irresolutely. "You ought to go right home and lay down. Ever try orangeine?"

"Thank you." Lily held out her hand. "It's very kind of you—I mean to go home."

She looked gratefully at Miss Kilroy, but neither knew what more to say. Lily was aware that the other was on the point of offering to go home with her, but she wanted to be alone and silent—even kindness, the sort of kindness that Miss Kilroy could give, would have jarred on her just then.

"Thank you," she repeated as she turned away.

She struck westward through the dreary March twilight, toward the street where her boarding-house stood. She had resolutely refused Gerty's offer of hospitality. Something of her mother's fierce shrinking from observation and sympathy was beginning to develop in her, and the promiscuity of small quarters and close intimacy seemed, on the whole, less endurable than the solitude of a hall bedroom in a house where she could come and go unremarked among other workers. For a while she had been sustained by this desire for privacy and independence; but now, perhaps from increasing physical weariness, the lassitude brought about by hours of unwonted confinement, she was beginning to feel acutely the ugliness and discomfort of her surroundings. The day's task done, she dreaded to return to her narrow room, with its blotched wall-paper and shabby paint; and she hated every step of the walk thither, through the degradation of a New York street in the last stages of decline from fashion to commerce.

But what she dreaded most of all was having to pass the chemist's at the corner of Sixth Avenue. She had meant to take another street: she had usually done so of late. But to-day her steps were irresistibly drawn toward the flaring plate-glass corner; she tried to take the lower crossing, but a laden dray crowded her back, and she struck across the street obliquely, reaching the sidewalk just opposite the chemist's door.

Over the counter she caught the eye of the clerk who had waited on her before, and slipped the prescription into his hand. There could be no question about the prescription: it was a copy of one of Mrs. Hatch's, obligingly furnished by that lady's chemist. Lily was confident that the clerk would fill it without hesitation; yet the nervous dread of a refusal, or even of an expression of doubt, communicated itself to her restless hands as she affected to examine the bottles of perfume stacked on the glass case before her.

The clerk had read the prescription without comment; but in the act of handing out the bottle he paused.

"You don't want to increase the dose, you know," he remarked.

Lily's heart contracted. What did he mean by looking at her in that way?

"Of course not," she murmured, holding out her hand.

"That's all right: it's a queer-acting drug. A drop or two more, and off you go—the doctors don't know why."

The dread lest he should question her, or keep the bottle back, choked the murmur of acquiescence in her throat; and when at length she emerged safely from the shop she was almost dizzy with the intensity of her relief. The mere touch of the packet thrilled her tired nerves with the delicious promise of a night of sleep, and in the reaction from her momentary fear she felt as if the first fumes of drowsiness were already stealing over her.

from **JOHN HENRY DAYS**

Colson Whitehead

It is odd because it is just him and L'il Bob working the tunnel.
John Henry and his partner always work with a second team. It
keeps the productivity up. Two pairs of men boring twin holes
into the mountain and singing to their work. The sound of the
hammer is percussion, each blow a footfall into the mountain to
the other side. But today he does not know why they are alone in
the darkness and why they do not sing. He cannot see L'il Bob's
face and cannot move his mouth to talk to him. To find out what
is happening. It is as if neither can stop. Their labor pulls them
like a stream and it is all they can do to stay afloat. It seems they
have been at this hole forever. He cannot seem to get the bit
deeper. The mountain has grown harder. They have hit the mountain's heart and the mountain is using all of its ancient will to prevent their violence against its self. It works against them. Then
with one blow John Henry feels something give and with the next
blow the bit sinks in deep, deeper than he has ever driven before.
John Henry thinks, we've hit the western cut. The two ends of the
tunnel have met. He is about to cheer. They have won Captain
Johnson's bonus. Then the blood comes.

The blood is black until the candlelight hits it and it turns deep
red. He can see then that it is blood. It should have been light

from the western cut that came through the hole but it is blood.
The black then red spray erupts from around the drill. He steps
back. He still cannot speak. He looks at L'il Bob and sees his partner's head turn. L'il Bob blinks through the blood on his face and
then he grins. John Henry cannot stop him from what he is about
to do. L'il Bob's fingers open and the bit flies from the hole and
the spray of blood becomes a geyser. The force of the blood
pushes John Henry backward. He falls on the timber planks and
when he wipes his eyes free L'il Bob is gone. The blood of the
mountain pours into the cut. Out east. He thinks the planks are
bobbing in it beneath him, and then he looks and sees that the
rock around him is now flesh. The red shale glistens like animal
meat. Ridges formed by the blasting are now tracings of sinew.
Veins and arteries. It is a living breathing mountain and he is in its
angry guts. The heart of the mountain pours itself over him. The
blood is up to his neck. Then the blood spray blinds him again
and he is awake.

When he wakened he was grateful for a moment and then he
realized it was still dark. He had traveled through a series of fever
dreams all night. They were coupled together like train cars. He
knew that the caboose contained morning and each time he fell
asleep he hoped that this time he would step into it. But he
opened the door to the next car and stepped again into nightmare.
He did not know what time it was. The camp was quiet. Every
one else slept off their labor. He had lost two days' wages laid up
in bed. It was all he could do to crawl to the outhouse and the
outhouse stank with his stink. He shivered and his blanket was
damp with fever sweat. John Henry could not get warm no matter what he did and the blanket chilled him even more. He was
laid up with fever. It was the longest night he could remember.
He prayed for morning.

He wakened to the bustle of the other men getting ready to go
back into the mountain. L'il Bob came into his shanty looking
worried. He carried a bucket of water and his blanket for John
Henry to use while he was working. L'il Bob asked his friend was

he coming back to work that day and John Henry tried to sit up. His head exploded with worms and he was too dizzy, he fell back to the bed like a felled tree. L'il Bob put the blanket on his friend and told him that he'd tell the boss John Henry is sick again. The shaker complained about Jesse, John Henry's replacement. He's slow and stupid, L'il Bob told his friend. You're twice as fast as him, he said. John Henry closed his eyes and his eyes rolled beneath their lids and when he woke up again he could tell from the sunlight it was about noon. He was grateful he did not dream again.

He got sick the day after Tommy died. The sun had just slipped behind the mountain. The smoke from the latest blasting had stopped sneaking out the tunnel and it was time to go back in to see how much the blast had advanced the heading. John Henry sat on a crate and rubbed tallow into the handle of his sledge. He waited for the sheen that said he had put enough oil in. That morning he had felt the blows travel up his arms and rock his shoulders and knew that the handle was getting stiff. He had to limber it up or else he'd be sore when he sat down that night, the pain would creep on him like floodwater over a bank. When Tommy said he was heading back in to start mucking out the rock from the blast, John Henry looked down at the handle of his hammer. He had not finished and Tommy went ahead. John Henry saw his friend walk into the heading and felt the first chill of his fever. The old man led a mule cart into the tunnel and that was the last John Henry saw of him alive. He rubbed the sheep fat into the wood while both the mule and the man were killed by the loose, falling rock. When John Henry went inside to see where it happened, he was not surprised to see that it was near the crag that haunted him. The beak of shale was still there, snickering, telling him something. They buried Tommy and the mule together in the fill of the eastern cut. That night after midnight John Henry's chill had become a fever.

He was sick and afraid. The fever will pass but the mountain will not. He pulled the blankets over his head. John Henry heard the clink of hammers on drills, he was too far away from them to hear them for real but he heard them anyway. Sometimes the clinking matched the beat of his heart for a whole minute and then they fell away from each other. The rhythms met again when he least expected it and it was like he was one with the labor. The doctor came in and said Captain Johnson wanted him to check on John Henry. The doctor opened a packet and dropped the white dust into water and gave it to the fevered man. The doctor said, you should be able to work tomorrow. The company can't afford to keep on men who won't work, he said. Then he disappeared into the afternoon light. John Henry's big body shivered.

He knew the mountain was going to kill him the first time he saw it. The railroad put out word it needed men to dig a tunnel and hitched a flatcar for Negro workers to a westbound train. The men filed into the old car and sat on seats fashioned from nail kegs. In the Negro workers' car the men sized each other up and talked about the ride. It was the first time any of them had been on a train. They spat tobacco to the floor. The train took them as far as the tracks went and a wagon took them the rest of the way to the mountain. The wagon arrived at the grading camp and John Henry saw the mountain heaped up to Heaven and knew right then that he had lied. He had told Abby that when he returned they would get married. John Henry would save his wages and come back a rich man. Or rich enough to start a life with her. He had carried water in the mines when he was a slave. The mining company leased him from Reynolds when he reached the age of six. By that time a slaveowner could not get insurance on his slaves any more because too many died in the mines and the insurance companies were no longer going to insure slaves. Reynolds didn't want to lose his investment so he only leased children to the mining company, with the order that his slaves were not allowed to do anything dangerous. They could carry water or learn a blacksmith's trade but no more. John Henry carried water to miners before the Proclamation and when he heard about the work on the tunnel he knew he was going. He knew about being inside mountains, the coolness inside rock. But that first day, he saw the mountain and knew that this one was different. It will kill him.

He fell asleep again and woke again. He might have slept for two minutes or two hours. If his hammer had not needed some tallow he would have walked in with Tommy. They would have stood side by side and John Henry would have been killed too. Tommy's death was a message. God was telling him to prepare. The mountain will take him. Sooner or later. Tomorrow he would go back to work.

After the shift L'il Bob came to see John Henry. He brought food and water. For the first time since Tommy died he felt like eating and he wolfed it down. L'il Bob complained about Jesse. The fool nearly hit him today. Not once but twice. L'il Bob had to tell him to watch what he was doing. John Henry said he'd be back in the mountain again tomorrow and not to worry about Jesse no more. L'il Bob said this city man in city clothes came into Captain Johnson's office today. They talked for a long time and then the city man left. L'il Bob said he was from a mechanical company trying to sell Captain Johnson on one of their steam drills. One of the bosses said them steam drills can do the work of a whole team of drivers and they're cheaper too. The steam drill is better and faster and cheaper. Pretty soon they're going to replace all the men, L'il Bob said, do you believe that? Do you think Captain Johnson is going to get one of those things? L'il Bob asked.

The day in the mountain was almost done. The blood in his arms kept time better than any clock. The stacks of lead in his arms kept track of his labor better than the wheels inside a watch or the foreman's whistle. It was almost time to lay down his hammer when one of the runners came in telling all of them to come outside and see. The runner clasped his palms to his knees and panted, pushing each word up out of his body. John Henry and

L'il Bob and the other team assumed there had been another accident and another death. The work had gone too peacefully for too long and they were due for grief. His partner tossed his bit to the dirt and John Henry slung his sledge over his shoulder and they walked across the planks toward the sun. John Henry was near the mouth of the tunnel when he heard laughter behind him. He twisted his body and saw only the crag of rock behind him, craning down from roof. He had never before seen that the blasting had opened two shiny stones in the crag's rock face. The stones glinted like cruel eyes. As he stepped out into the thick dusk he knew it would never again taunt him. It had delivered its message.

The bosses and the crews and Captain Johnson stood around a long cart. The planks of the cart were fresh-cut wood and the tarp had seen little rain. Everything the railroad brought to the site aged fast. Years of calluses formed in days, newborn aches immediately felt ancient and lifelong. This thing that had gathered the men was new. The horses were well-fed and handsomely groomed. Not mules. They had never hauled exploded and blasted rock, the insides of mountains. The white tarp draped over a shape that was unfamiliar. It propped up fabric and bulged beneath the tarp but its true shape was impossible to tell. A man talked while his fingers snapped in the air like sparks. He wore the clothes of a city man, a carpetbagger, and was so clean shaven his face glowed like bleached bones. One of the men next to John Henry said it was a man from Burleigh company come to sell the Captain on a steam drill. The steeldriver and his partner shouldered up to the front to hear what he had to say. L'il Bob said, I told you it was coming. I told you it was coming.

The steam drill had been the talk of the work camp for the last few days. After dinner one night, before the men dispersed into gambling or sleep, one of the graders, a red-skinned man named Jefferson, said he knew of one of those things. He had seen it with his own eyes. He had been a blacksmith on the Hoosac Tunnel job in Massachusetts before coming down here to this mountain. Before the steam drill, he said, they could not find purchase in the rock. The work was slow. But then the bosses brought in one of them Burlee machines and the rock was more like sand once that machine got on it. It was powered by steam and it drank more water than a man but it didn't need food and worked twice as fast as a man. L'il Bob said Jefferson was one ignorant nigger, talking about that rickety thing like he looked up to it. But over the days and nights the talk returned again and again to the steam drill and many of the men were curious. Their speculations swarmed in the air like gnats at twilight. John Henry kept silent with his back to the mountain that was always there.

The salesman talked of tunnels up and down this line. He spread his arms as if he held all between the oceans between his palms. He talked of tunnels up and down railroad lines all across the country. Then he tucked his thumbs into his vest pockets and strummed his chest with thin fingers like spider legs. Captain Johnson reached for his pocket watch when the salesman from Burleigh started talking about feet per day, pennies per inch and advancing the heading. Most of this talk went in one ear and out the other ear of the men but they understood the meaning. They had all dealt with the doubletalk of merchants before. L'il Bob said I told you it was coming. All around them the work had stopped before this talk and even some of the men from the western cut had made their way around to see. Boss and water boy, black man and white man came to see the invention.

The salesman pulled back the tarp to reveal the thing he had ferried there. From the city to the country over those long roads. It was a strange creature. The trunk of it was the engine, and it stood on four slim steel struts. Sticking out the side of it like a broken rib was a handle where a man could control what happened inside. Black hoses like tails came out of the rear end and connected to a big, round boiler. And the snout of the thing, that was the drill. It gleamed. The men shifted on their feet. They did not sigh or gasp in astonishment. It was a curious sight and it kept their mouths shut. In their minds they put it inside the mountain, up against the rock. The salesman hopped onto the cart and rubbed the flank of the engine. He said it was eight horsepower. A device like this made quick work of the Hoosac, he said. A mountain like this will fall just as easily before it. He had been in camps on every line you have heard of and when they saw what the machine could do, they marveled, he said. He talked about the machine as a man would talk about a great man. One who had accomplished great things. Captain Johnson stared up at the steam drill and nodded. Then he looked at John Henry as if he expected the steeldriver to open his mouth and speak.

John Henry looked at the dirt and then back at the thing in the cart. It had steel that was stronger than his muscles and bones. The blood in his heart was nothing compared to the steam of the boiler. It had the power of eight horses. He felt the men around him turn toward him and look at him. He kept his eyes on the thing in the cart. Lord, he had not thought that it would be so soon. But he had known it would come. He looked at the thing in the cart and saw tomorrows. Tomorrows and all the tomorrows after all those tomorrows because he understood as he had always understood that that was what this machine was going to take away from him. He saw the future, the very thing the machine would steal from him. Just as he stole from the mountain every day with his steel that which made the mountain what it was. The three of them were linked like brothers.

The salesman asked Captain Johnson if he wanted a demonstration of the steam drill for him and his men. It's a simple operation to set up a demonstration, he said. He withdrew a kerchief and wiped his brow. His men can watch him use the machine and learn how to work it, he said. Then Captain Johnson can see for himself what a boon the machine will be in fulfillment of his contract with the railroad and his obligations to the timetable. L'il Bob made a sound from his gut.

John Henry let the head of his hammer fall to the ground softly, easily, like it was the first leaf of autumn. Like it was only the first of many to fall and gliding down on sorrow. In that moment a cloud moved across the sky, taking the mountain into its shadow and in the same moment John Henry's heart as well. He nudged the man in front of him and walked up to the cart. The head of the hammer carved a line in the dirt behind him. All the men followed him with their eyes. He stood before Captain Johnson and the salesman and all the men and made a challenge. Then he hoisted his hammer onto his shoulder and stared into their faces. He was sure that no one could see him tremble but the mountain.

John Henry stood in the work camp with his sledge in his hands. He grasped it as a drowning man might cling to a branch in the currents of the spring thaw. No one saw him. Most of the men had gone on ahead. The camp was nearly empty. It was time to work but this was not an ordinary workday on the mountain. No one stalked the tunnels. The men were not grading or mucking or pounding spikes. They waited for the contest. They gathered at the mouth of the eastern cut to see the truth of the challenge. This afternoon the timetable did not matter, neither the seconds nor the inches, for the line had to be stalled before it could go on. Everything stopped before the words John Henry had said. Tools lay untouched and the horses' tails whipped lazily in the sun. No hands covered ears to keep out the sound of blasting, the ground did not shake with the violence they made inside the mountain. It was still, and it was time.

As he lay in his bed on his last night he heard the words of the men coming through the walls of his shanty. If John Henry wanted he could have put faces to the voices but he did not try. He knew all the men. Some were friends. Some were enemies. It did not matter where they stood with him as their talk swirled into one talk about the contest. They laid bets on whether a man could beat a machine. All of their wagers on John Henry before this time were rehearsals for this day. One voice came to him saying it was impossible. Another voice said John Henry was no kind of man like you and me but a demon and no machine was going to stop him. One voice laid down odds. The voice said, step right up and make your bet, men. He heard voices raised in anger and then the scrambling sound of men in the dirt fighting. There was more than money on the line. Each wager was a glimpse into the man who made it. There was more than wages on the line in this contest.

On his last night John Henry did not allow L'il Bob to see him. His friend was hurt by the words John Henry spoke to him, one foot on the dirt floor within and one foot on the dirt ground without, and he did not understand why his partner had forsaken him. But I have a plan, L'il Bob said. I can fix that machine so it won't do nothing but shake and squawk, he said. No plans are going to help me tomorrow, John Henry said. He told his partner to get Adams and L'il Bob asked why but John Henry would not tell him. Just get the man, he said. When the door closed he heard his friend's voice crying for Adams, Adams. It was not fair to his friend but he could find no other course in himself.

John Henry had wages saved. Even as he collected them through the long months to give to Abby he knew he would never present them to her in person, standing in front of her after so long, to show her what all the time away had brought them. He had lied about his return and the bills he stuffed into his hiding place were hope against the mountain. He did not drink. He did not gamble with money. When he gambled he put himself up as his winnings and in the long time in this place he had saved more money than any of his friends knew. He was the highest-paid steeldriver for what he could do with his arms. Captain Johnson gave him bonuses for steeldriving contests that he won with his arms. He trusted L'il Bob to send it on to her.

Adams could make letters and write. His hands had been chewed up from his labor on the tunnel but he could still write. He was the one the colored men came to when they wanted something written. He put on paper the stories and the lies they posted to their families and their women. When Adams showed up John Henry told him he wanted to write a letter, and the man departed to get his materials. In that time he composed again the words and in the middle of it he remembered that Adams had come to the mountain in the same car as he had. John Henry had first seen the man in the workers' car, across from him on the journey up here, as they sat on the nail kegs that were their seats and they all wondered what was waiting for them up here. Now John Henry knew. But none of that was going to go into the letter. L'il Bob could give her the details of the contest but he wanted to put other things in the letter. He warned Adams to keep his mouth shut about why he had called him there. When he looked into the man's eyes he knew he would not say anything. Adams was not one of the stupid and shiftless men the railroad company attracted. He had sense. When Adams left John Henry put the voices out of his mind and wept. With the salt in his mouth he said, never wear black wear blue, never wear black wear blue.

It was almost time. When he ate his breakfast that morning all the men he had worked alongside for so long looked at him over tin plates as they ate. His stare told them not to talk to him so they just looked at him, taking measure of him with their eyes. They wanted to know what was in him that was not in them. One man said that all the people from all around were coming down to the eastern cut to see the contest. The word had traveled beyond the work camps, beyond the hearths of the bosses, and everyone wanted to come and see the contest between the man and the machine. Another man said they were going to charge tickets to see. This was bigger than the black man against the white man and they were drawn by these new stakes. It was once in a lifetime. In this talk some of the men looked at John Henry and changed their wagers. Beating another man, beating twenty men was one thing and this was another. L'il Bob came over to John Henry, scraping food off his plate to give to his partner. He had a ridge of bruises along the right side of his face and John Henry knew it was because of him. L'il Bob had fought someone for saying John Henry would lose. The bruises did not need to be explained, them or anything else except the letter and the money he had saved. L'il Bob would follow his wishes and get it to her. When he finished eating he went back to his bed and waited for the sounds of the men to die out, to drift over to the tunnel.

John Henry stood in the camp with the sun on him. It was almost time. Down there they all waited. He spat at the ground and rolled back his shoulders. He looked up at the top of the mountain, where the treetops stretched with their little points, like a million fingers grasping at Heaven. The mountain was so tall and John Henry was so small. He drew a hand across his brow to put the sun out of his eyes and he looked up at the mountain, past the leaves and down the trunks and into the soil and into the rock heart of the mountain, he looked and addressed. There was no one to hear him but himself. He walked down the road with his hammer in his hand.

A WRESTLER WITH SHARKS

Richard Yates

Nobody had much respect for *The Labor Leader*. Even Finkel and Kramm, its owners, the two sour brothers-in-law who'd dreamed it up in the first place and who somehow managed to make a profit on it year after year—even they could take little pride in the thing. At least, that's what I used to suspect from the way they'd hump grudgingly around the office, shivering the bile-green partitions with their thumps and shouts, grabbing and tearing at galley proofs, breaking pencil points, dropping wet cigar butts on the floor and slamming telephones contemptuously into their cradles. *The Labor Leader* was all either of them would ever have for a life's work, and they seemed to hate it.

You couldn't blame them: the thing was a monster. In format it was a fat biweekly tabloid, badly printed, that spilled easily out of your hands and was very hard to put together again in the right order; in policy it called itself "An Independent Newspaper Pledged to the Spirit of the Trade Union Movement," but its real pitch was to be a kind of trade journal for union officials, who subscribed to it out of union funds and who must surely have been inclined to tolerate, rather than to want or need, whatever thin sustenance it gave to them. The *Leader*'s coverage of national events "from the labor angle" was certain to be stale, likely to be muddled, and often opaque with typographical errors; most of its dense columns were filled with flattering reports on the doings of the unions whose leaders were on the subscription list, often to the exclusion of much bigger news about those whose leaders weren't. And every issue carried scores of simpleminded ads urging "Harmony" in the names of various small industrial firms that Finkel and Kramm had been able to beg or browbeat into buying space—a compromise that would almost certainly have hobbled a real labor paper but that didn't, typically enough, seem to cramp the *Leader*'s style at all.

There was a fast turnover on the editorial staff. Whenever somebody quit, the *Leader* would advertise in the help-wanted section of the *Times,* offering a "moderate salary commensurate with experience." This always brought a good crowd to the sidewalk outside the *Leader*'s office, a gritty storefront on the lower fringe of the garment district, and Kramm, who was the editor (Finkel was the publisher), would keep them all waiting for half an hour before he picked up a sheaf of application forms, shot his cuffs, and gravely opened the door—I think he enjoyed this occasional chance to play the man of affairs.

"All right, take your time," he'd say, as they jostled inside and pressed against the wooden rail that shielded the inner offices. "Take your time, gentlemen." Then he would raise a hand and say, "May I have your attention, please?" And he'd begin to explain the job. Half the applicants would go away when he got to the part about the salary structure, and most of those who remained offered little competition to anyone who was sober, clean and able to construct an English sentence.

That's the way we'd all been hired, the six or eight of us who frowned under the *Leader*'s sickly fluorescent lights that winter, and most of us made no secret of our desire for better things. I went to work there a couple of weeks after losing my job on one of the metropolitan dailies, and stayed only until I was rescued the next spring by the big picture magazine that still employs me. The others had other explanations, which, like me, they spent a

great deal of time discussing: it was a great place for shrill and redundant hard-luck stories.

But Leon Sobel joined the staff about a month after I did, and
from the moment Kramm led him into the editorial room we all
knew he was going to be different. He stood among the messy
desks with the look of a man surveying new fields to conquer, and
when Kramm introduced him around (forgetting half our names)
he made a theatrically solemn business out of shaking hands. He
was about thirty-five, older than most of us, a very small, tense
man with black hair that seemed to explode from his skull and a
humorless thin-lipped face that was blotched with the scars of
acne. His eyebrows were always in motion when he talked, and
his eyes, not so much piercing as anxious to pierce, never left the
eyes of his listener.

The first thing I learned about him was that he'd never held an
office job before: he had been a sheet-metal worker all his adult
life. What's more, he hadn't come to the *Leader* out of need, like
the rest of us, but, as he put it, out of principle. To do so, in fact,
he had given up a factory job paying nearly twice the money.

"What'sa matter, don'tcha believe me?" he asked, after telling
me this.

"Well, it's not that," I said. "It's just that I—"

"Maybe you think I'm crazy," he said, and screwed up his face
into a canny smile.

I tried to protest, but he wouldn't have it. "Listen, don't worry,
McCabe. I'm called crazy a lotta times already. It don't bother me.
My wife says, 'Leon, you gotta expect it.' She says, 'People never
understand a man who wants something more outa life than just
money.' And she's right! She's right!"

"No," I said. "Wait a second. I—"

"People think you gotta be one of two things: either you're a
shark, or you gotta lay back and let the sharks eatcha alive—this
is the world. Me, I'm the kinda guy's gotta go out and wrestle with
the sharks. Why? I dunno why. This is crazy? Okay."

"Wait a second," I said. And I tried to explain that I had nothing whatever against his striking a blow for social justice, if that was what he had in mind; it was just that I thought *The Labor Leader* was about the least likely place in the world for him to do it.

But his shrug told me I was quibbling. "So?" he said. "It's a paper, isn't it? Well, I'm a writer. And what good's a writer if he don't get printed? Listen." He lifted one haunch and placed it on the edge of my desk—he was too short a man to do this gracefully, but the force of his argument helped him to bring it off. "Listen, McCabe. You're a young kid yet. I wanna tellya something. Know how many books I wrote already?" And now his hands came into play, as they always did sooner or later. Both stubby fists were thrust under my nose and allowed to shake there for a moment before they burst into a thicket of stiff, quivering fingers—only the thumb of one hand remained folded down. "Nine," he said, and the hands fell limp on his thigh, to rest until he needed them again. "Nine. Novels, philosophy, political theory—the entire gamut. And not one of 'em published. Believe me, I been around awhile."

"I believe you," I said.

"So finally I sat down and figured: What's the answer? And I figured this: the trouble with my books is, they tell the truth. And the truth is a funny thing, McCabe. People wanna read it, but they only wanna read it when it comes from somebody they already know their name. Am I right? So all right. I figure, I wanna write these books, first I gotta build up a name for myself. This is worth any sacrifice. This is the only way. You know something, McCabe? The last one I wrote took me two years?" Two fingers sprang up to illustrate the point, and dropped again. "Two years, working four, five hours every night and all day long on the weekends. And then you oughta seen the crap I got from the publishers. Every damn publisher in town. My wife cried. She says, 'But why, Leon? Why?' " Here his lips curled tight against his small, stained teeth, and the fist of one hand smacked the palm of the other on his thigh, but then he relaxed. "I told her, 'Listen, honey. You know why.' " And now he was smiling at me in quiet triumph.

"I says, 'This book told the truth. That's why.' " Then he winked, slid off my desk and walked away, erect and jaunty in his soiled sport shirt and his dark serge pants that hung loose and shiny in the seat. That was Sobel.

It took him a little while to loosen up in the job: for the first week or so, when he wasn't talking, he went at everything with a zeal and a fear of failure that disconcerted everyone but Finney, the managing editor. Like the rest of us, Sobel had a list of twelve or fifteen union offices around town, and the main part of his job was to keep in touch with them and write up whatever bits of news they gave out. As a rule there was nothing very exciting to write about. The average story ran two or three paragraphs with a single-column head:

PLUMBERS WIN
3¢ PAY HIKE

or something like that. But Sobel composed them all as carefully as sonnets, and after he'd turned one in he would sit chewing his lips in anxiety until Finney raised a forefinger and said, "C'mere a second, Sobel."

Then he'd go over and stand, nodding apologetically, while Finney pointed out some niggling grammatical flaw. "Never end a sentence with a preposition, Sobel. You don't wanna say, 'gave the plumbers new grounds to bargain on.' You wanna say, 'gave the plumbers new grounds on which to bargain.' "

Finney enjoyed these lectures. The annoying thing, from a spectator's point of view, was that Sobel took so long to learn what everyone else seemed to know instinctively: that Finney was scared of his own shadow and would back down on anything at all if you raised your voice. He was a frail, nervous man who dribbled on his chin when he got excited and raked trembling fingers through his thickly oiled hair, with the result that his fingers spread hair oil, like a spoor of his personality, to everything he touched: his clothes, his pencils, his telephone and his typewriter keys. I guess the main reason he was managing editor was that nobody else would submit to the bullying he took from Kramm: their editorial conferences always began with Kramm shouting "Finney! Finney!" from behind his partition, and Finney jumping like a squirrel to hurry inside. Then you'd hear the relentless drone of Kramm's demands and the quavering sputter of Finney's explanations, and it would end with a thump as Kramm socked his desk. "No, Finney. No, no, *no*! What's the matter with you? I gotta draw you a picture? All right, all right, get outa here, I'll do it myself." At first you might wonder why Finney took it—nobody could need a job that badly—but the answer lay in the fact that there were only three bylined pieces in *The Labor Leader*: a boiler-plated sports feature that we got from a syndicate, a ponderous column called "LABOR TODAY, by Julius Kramm," that ran facing the editorial page, and a double-column box in the back of the book with the heading:

BROADWAY BEAT
BY WEST FINNEY

There was even a thumbnail picture of him in the upper left-hand corner, hair slicked down and teeth bared in a confident smile. The text managed to work in a labor angle here and there—a paragraph on Actors' Equity, say, or the stagehands' union—but mostly he played it straight, in the manner of two or three real Broadway-and-nightclub columnists. "Heard about the new thrush at the Copa?" he would ask the labor leaders; then he'd give them her name, with a sly note about her bust and hip measurements and a folksy note about the state from which she "hailed," and he'd wind it up like this: "She's got the whole town talking, and turning up in droves. Their verdict, in which this department wholly concurs: the lady has class." No reader could have guessed that West Finney's shoes needed repair, that he got no complimentary tickets to anything and never went out except to take in a movie or to crouch over a liverwurst sandwich at the

Automat. He wrote the column on his own time and got extra money for it—the figure I heard was fifty dollars a month. So it was a mutually satisfactory deal: for that small sum Kramm held his whipping boy in absolute bondage; for that small torture Finney could paste clippings in a scrapbook, with all the contamination of *The Labor Leader* sheared away into the wastebasket of his furnished room, and whisper himself to sleep with dreams of ultimate freedom.

Anyway, this was the man who could make Sobel apologize for the grammar of his news stories, and it was a sad thing to watch. Of course, it couldn't go on forever, and one day it stopped.

Finney had called Sobel over to explain about split infinitives, and Sobel was wrinkling his brow in an effort to understand. Neither of them noticed that Kramm was standing in the doorway of his office a few feet away, listening, and looking at the wet end of his cigar as if it tasted terrible.

"Finney," he said. "You wanna be an English teacher, get a job in the high school."

Startled, Finney stuck a pencil behind his ear without noticing that another pencil was already there, and both pencils clattered to the floor. "Well, I—" he said. "Just thought I'd—"

"Finney, this does not interest me. Pick up your pencils and listen to me, please. For your information, Mr. Sobel is not supposed to be a literary Englishman. He is supposed to be a literate American, and this I believe he is. Do I make myself clear?"

And the look on Sobel's face as he walked back to his own desk was that of a man released from prison.

From that moment on he began to relax; or almost from that moment—what seemed to clinch the transformation was O'Leary's hat.

O'Leary was a recent City College graduate and one of the best men on the staff (he has since done very well; you'll often see his byline in one of the evening papers), and the hat he wore that winter was of the waterproof cloth kind that is sold in raincoat shops. There was nothing very dashing about it—in fact its floppiness made O'Leary's face look too thin—but Sobel must secretly have admired it as a symbol of journalism, or of nonconformity, for one morning he showed up in an identical one, brand new. It looked even worse on him than on O'Leary, particularly when worn with his lumpy brown overcoat, but he seemed to cherish it. He developed a whole new set of mannerisms to go with the hat: cocking it back, with a flip of the index finger as he settled down to make his morning phone calls ("This is Leon Sobel, of *The Labor Leader* . . ."), tugging it smartly forward as he left the office on a reporting assignment, twirling it onto a peg when he came back to write his story. At the end of the day, when he'd dropped the last of his copy into Finney's wire basket, he would shape the hat into a careless slant over one eyebrow, swing the overcoat around his shoulders and stride out with a loose salute of farewell, and I used to picture him studying his reflection in the black subway windows all the way home to the Bronx.

He seemed determined to love his work. He even brought in a snapshot of his family—a tired, abjectly smiling woman and two small sons—and fastened it to his desktop with cellophane tape. Nobody else ever left anything more personal than a book of matches in the office overnight.

One afternoon toward the end of February, Finney summoned me to his oily desk. "McCabe," he said. "Wanna do a column for us?"

"What kind of a column?"

"Labor gossip," he said. "Straight union items with a gossip or a chatter angle—little humor, personalities, stuff like that. Mr. Kramm thinks we need it, and I told him you'd be the best man for the job."

I can't deny that I was flattered (we are all conditioned by our surroundings, after all), but I was also suspicious. "Do I get a byline?"

He began to blink nervously. "Oh, no, no byline," he said. "Mr. Kramm wants this to be anonymous. See, the guys'll give you any items they turn up, and you'll just collect 'em and put 'em in shape. It's just something you can do on office time, part of your regular job. See what I mean?"

I saw what he meant. "Part of my regular salary too," I said. "Right?"

"That's right."

"No thanks," I told him, and then, feeling generous, I suggested that he try O'Leary.

"Nah, I already asked him," Finney said. "He don't wanna do it either. Nobody does."

I should have guessed, of course, that he'd been working down the list of everyone in the office. And to judge from the lateness of the day, I must have been close to the tail end.

Sobel fell in step with me as we left the building after work that night. He was wearing his overcoat cloak-style, the sleeves dangling, and holding his cloth hat in place as he hopped nimbly to avoid the furrows of dirty slush on the sidewalk. "Letcha in on a little secret, McCabe," he said. "I'm doin' a column for the paper. It's all arranged."

"Yeah?" I said. "Any money in it?"

"Money?" He winked. "I'll tell y' about that part. Let's get a cuppa coffee." He led me into the tiled and steaming brilliance of the Automat, and when we were settled at a damp corner table he explained everything. "Finney says no money, see? So I said okay. He says no byline either. I said okay." He winked again. "Playin' it smart."

"How do you mean?"

"How do I mean?" He always repeated your question like that, savoring it, holding his black eyebrows high while he made you wait for the answer. "Listen, I got this Finney figured out. *He* don't decide these things. You think he decides anything around that place? You better wise up, McCabe. Mr. *Kramm* makes the decisions. And Mr. Kramm is an intelligent man, don't kid yourself." Nodding, he raised his coffee cup, but his lips recoiled from the heat of it, puckered, and blew into the steam before they began to sip with gingerly impatience.

"Well," I said, "okay, but I'd check with Kramm before you start counting on anything."

"Check?" He put his cup down with a clatter. "What's to check? Listen, Mr. Kramm wants a column, right? You think he cares if I get a byline or not? Or the money, either—you think if I write a good column he's gonna quibble over payin' me for it? Ya crazy. *Finney's* the one, don'tcha see? *He* don't wanna gimme a break because he's worried about losing his *own* column. Get it? So all right. I check with nobody until I got that column written." He prodded his chest with a stiff thumb. "On my own time. Then I take it to Mr. Kramm and we talk business. You leave it to me." He settled down comfortably, elbows on the table, both hands cradling the cup just short of drinking position while he blew into the steam.

"Well," I said. "I hope you're right. Be nice if it does work out that way."

"Ah, it may not," he conceded, pulling his mouth into a grimace of speculation and tilting his head to one side. "You know. It's a gamble." But he was only saying that out of politeness, to minimize my envy. He could afford to express doubt because he felt none, and I could tell he was already planning the way he'd tell his wife about it.

The next morning Finney came around to each of our desks with instructions that we were to give Sobel any gossip or chatter items we might turn up; the column was scheduled to begin in the next issue. Later I saw him in conference with Sobel, briefing him on how the column was to be written, and I noticed that Finney did all the talking: Sobel just sat there making thin, contemptuous jets of cigarette smoke.

We had just put an issue to press, so the deadline for the column was two weeks away. Not many items turned up at first—it was hard enough getting news out of the unions we covered, let alone "chatter." Whenever someone did hand him a note, Sobel would frown over it, add a scribble of his own and drop it in a desk drawer; once or twice I saw him drop one in the wastebasket. I only remember one of the several pieces I gave him: the business agent of a steamfitters' local I covered had yelled at me through a closed door that he couldn't be bothered that day because his wife had just had twins. But Sobel didn't want it. "So, the guy's got twins," he said. "So what?"

"Suit yourself," I said. "You getting much other stuff?"

He shrugged. "Some. I'm not worried. I'll tellya one thing, though—I'm not using a lotta this crap. This chatter. Who the hell's gonna read it? You can't have a whole column fulla crap like that. Gotta be something to hold it together. Am I right?"

Another time (the column was all he talked about now) he chuckled affectionately and said, "My wife says I'm just as bad now as when I was working on my books. Write, write, write. She don't care, though," he added. "She's really getting excited about this thing. She's telling everybody—the neighbors, everybody. Her brother come over Sunday, starts asking me how the job's going—you know, in a wise-guy kinda way? I just kept quiet, but my wife pipes up: 'Leon's doing a column for the paper now'—and she tells him all about it. Boy, you oughta seen his face."

Every morning he brought in the work he had done the night before, a wad of handwritten papers, and used his lunch hour to type it out and revise it while he chewed a sandwich at his desk. And he was the last one to go home every night; we'd leave him there hammering his typewriter in a trance of concentration. Finney kept bothering him—"How you coming on that feature, Sobel?"—but he always parried the question with squinted eyes and a truculent lift of the chin. "Whaddya worried about? You'll get it." And he would wink at me.

On the morning of the deadline he came to work with a little patch of toilet paper on his cheek; he had cut himself shaving in his nervousness, but otherwise he looked as confident as ever. There were no calls to make that morning—on deadline days we all stayed in to work on copy and proofs—so the first thing he did was to spread out the finished manuscript for a final reading. His absorption was so complete that he didn't look up until Finney was standing at his elbow. "You wanna gimme that feature, Sobel?"

Sobel grabbed up the papers and shielded them with an arrogant forearm. He looked steadily at Finney and said, with a firmness that he must have been rehearsing for two weeks: "I'm showing this to Mr. Kramm. Not you."

Finney's whole face began to twitch in a fit of nerves. "Nah, nah, Mr. Kramm don't need to see it," he said. "Anyway, he's not in yet. C'mon, lemme have it."

"You're wasting your time, Finney," Sobel said. "I'm waiting for Mr. Kramm."

Muttering, avoiding Sobel's triumphant eyes, Finney went back to his own desk, where he was reading proof on BROAD-WAY BEAT.

My own job that morning was at the layout table, pasting up the dummy for the first section. I was standing there, working with the unwieldly page forms and the paste-clogged scissors, when Sobel sidled up behind me, looking anxious. "You wanna read it, McCabe?" he asked. "Before I turn it in?" And he handed me the manuscript.

The first thing that hit me was that he had clipped a photograph to the top of page 1, a small portrait of himself in his cloth hat. The next thing was his title:

SOBEL SPEAKING
BY LEON SOBEL

I can't remember the exact words of the opening paragraph, but it went something like this:

> This is the "debut" of a new department in *The Labor Leader* and, moreover, it is also "something new" for your correspondent, who has never handled a column before. However, he is far from being a novice with the written word, on the contrary

he is an "ink-stained veteran" of many battles on the field of ideas, to be exact nine books have emanated from his pen.

Naturally in those tomes his task was somewhat different than that which it will be in this column, and yet he hopes that this column will also strive as they did to penetrate the basic human mystery, in other words, to tell the truth.

When I looked up I saw he had picked open the razor cut on his cheek and it was bleeding freely. "Well," I said, "for one thing, I wouldn't give it to him with your picture that way—I mean, don't you think it might be better to let him read it first, and then—"

"Okay," he said, blotting at his face with a wadded gray handkerchief. "Okay, I'll take the picture off. G'ahead, read the rest."

But there wasn't time to read the rest. Kramm had come in, Finney had spoken to him, and now he was standing in the door of his office, champing crossly on a dead cigar. "You wanted to see me, Sobel?" he called.

"Just a second," Sobel said. He straightened the pages of SOBEL SPEAKING and detached the photograph, which he jammed into his hip pocket as he started for the door. Halfway there he remembered to take off his hat, and threw it unsuccessfully at the hat stand. Then he disappeared behind the partition, and we all settled down to listen.

It wasn't long before Kramm's reaction came through. "No, Sobel. No, no, no! What is this? What are you tryna put over on me here?"

Outside, Finney winced comically and clapped the side of his head, giggling, and O'Leary had to glare at him until he stopped.

We heard Sobel's voice, a blurred sentence or two of protest, and then Kramm came through again: " 'Basic human mystery'— this is gossip? This is chatter? You can't follow instructions? Wait a minute—Finney! Finney!"

Finney loped to the door, delighted to be of service, and we heard him making clear, righteous replies to Kramm's interrogation: Yes, he had told Sobel what kind of a column was wanted; yes, he had specified that there was to be no byline; yes, Sobel had been provided with ample gossip material. All we heard from Sobel was something indistinct, said in a very tight, flat voice. Kramm made a guttural reply, and even though we couldn't make out the words we knew it was all over. Then they came out, Finney wearing the foolish smile you sometimes see in the crowds that gape at street accidents, Sobel as expressionless as death.

He picked his hat off the floor and his coat off the stand, put them on, and came over to me. "So long, McCabe," he said. "Take it easy."

Shaking hands with him, I felt my face jump into Finney's idiot smile, and I asked a stupid question. "You leaving?"

He nodded. Then he shook hands with O'Leary—"So long, kid"—and hesitated, uncertain whether to shake hands with the rest of the staff. He settled for a little wave of the forefinger, and walked out to the street.

Finney lost no time in giving us all the inside story in an eager whisper: "The guy's *crazy*! He says to Kramm, 'You take this column or I quit'—just like that. Kramm just looks at him and says, 'Quit? Get outa here, you're fired.' I mean, what *else* could he say?"

Turning away, I saw that the snapshot of Sobel's wife and sons still lay taped to his desk. I stripped it off and took it out to the sidewalk. "Hey, Sobel!" I yelled. He was a block away, very small, walking toward the subway. I started to run after him, nearly breaking my neck on the frozen slush. "Hey *Sobel*!" But he didn't hear me.

Back at the office I found his address in the Bronx telephone directory, put the picture in an envelope and dropped it in the mail, and I wish that were the end of the story.

But that afternoon I called up the editor of a hardware trade journal I had worked on before the war, who said he had no va-

cancies on his staff but might soon, and would be willing to interview Sobel if he wanted to drop in. It was a foolish idea: the
wages there were even lower than on the *Leader,* and besides, it
was a place for very young men whose fathers wanted them to
learn the hardware business—Sobel would probably have been
ruled out the minute he opened his mouth. But it seemed better than nothing, and as soon as I was out of the office that
night I went to a phone booth and looked up Sobel's name
again.

A woman's voice answered, but it wasn't the high, faint voice
I'd expected. It was low and melodious—that was the first of my
several surprises.

"Mrs. Sobel?" I asked, absurdly smiling into the mouthpiece.
"Is Leon there?"

She started to say, "Just a minute," but changed it to "Who's
calling, please? I'd rather not disturb him right now."

I told her my name and tried to explain about the hardware
deal.

"I don't understand," she said. "What kind of a paper is it, exactly?"

"Well, it's a trade journal," I said. "It doesn't amount to much,
I guess, but it's—*you* know, a pretty good little thing, of its kind."

"I see," she said. "And you want him to go in and apply for a
job? Is that it?"

"Well I mean, if he *wants* to, is all," I said. I was beginning to
sweat. It was impossible to reconcile the wan face in Sobel's
snapshot with this serene, almost beautiful voice. "I just thought
he might like to give it a try, is all."

"Well," she said, "just a minute, I'll ask him." She put down the
phone, and I heard them talking in the background. Their words
were muffled at first but then I heard Sobel say, "Ah, I'll talk to
him—I'll just say thanks for calling." And I heard her answer, with
infinite tenderness, "No, honey, why should you? He doesn't de-
serve it."

"McCabe's all right," he said.

"No he's not," she told him, "or he'd have the decency to leave you alone. Let me do it. Please. I'll get rid of him."

When she came back to the phone she said, "No, my husband says he wouldn't be interested in a job of that kind." Then she thanked me politely, said goodbye, and left me to climb guilty and sweating out of the phone booth.